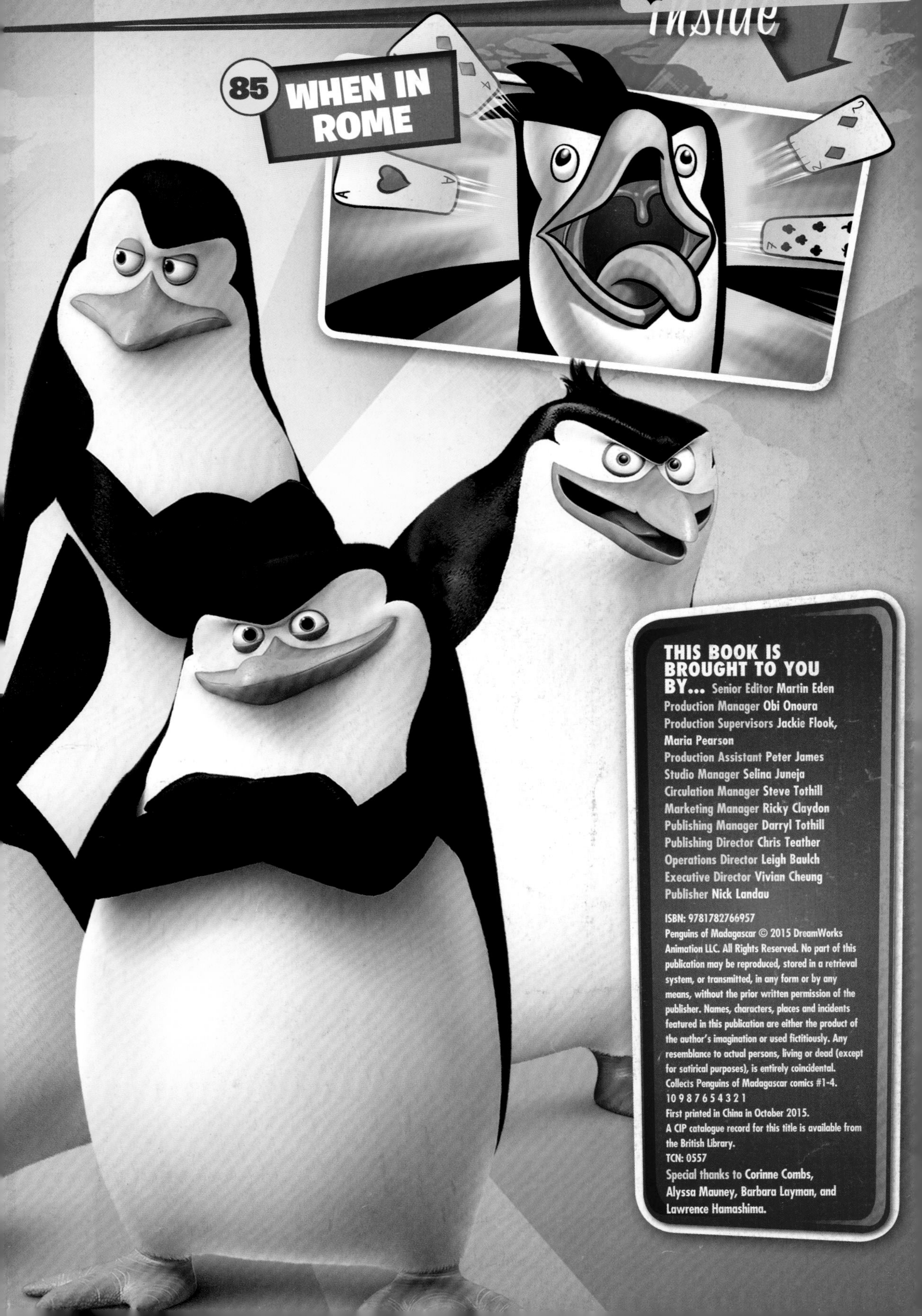
Inside
85
WHEN IN ROME

THIS BOOK IS BROUGHT TO YOU BY... Senior Editor Martin Eden
Production Manager Obi Onoura
Production Supervisors Jackie Flook, Maria Pearson
Production Assistant Peter James
Studio Manager Selina Juneja
Circulation Manager Steve Tothill
Marketing Manager Ricky Claydon
Publishing Manager Darryl Tothill
Publishing Director Chris Teather
Operations Director Leigh Baulch
Executive Director Vivian Cheung
Publisher Nick Landau

ISBN: 9781782766957

Collects Penguins of Madagascar comics #1-4.
10 9 8 7 6 5 4 3 2 1
First printed in China in October 2015.
A CIP catalogue record for this title is available from the British Library.
TCN: 0557
Special thanks to Corinne Combs, Alyssa Mauney, Barbara Layman, and Lawrence Hamashima.

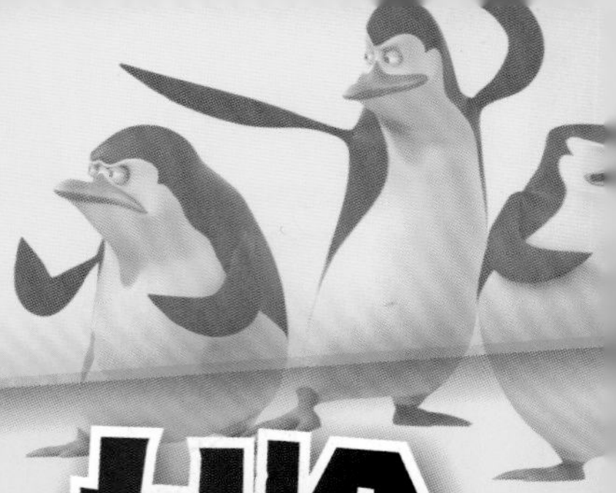

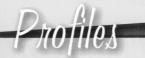

Meet the

Just what makes Skipper and the other penguins tick? Find out more about your favorite flippered characters in our tell-all guide!

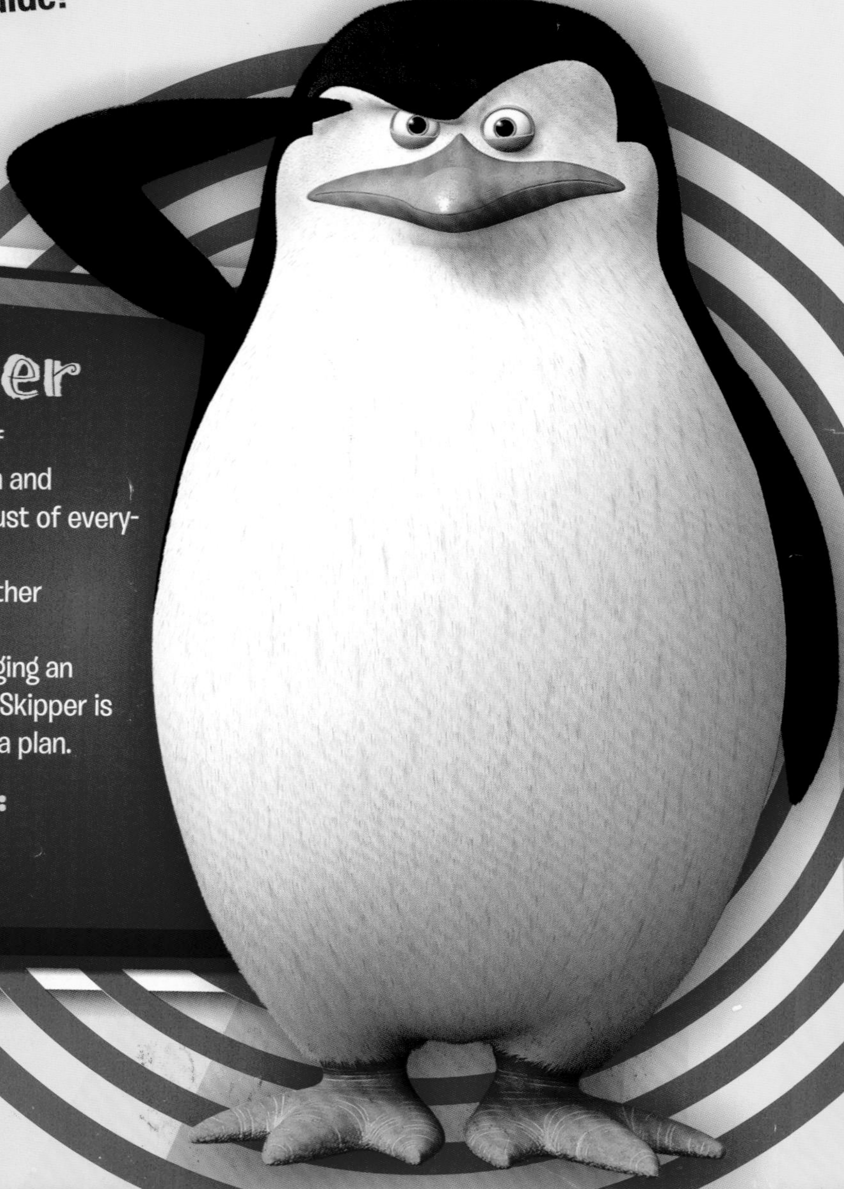

Skipper

He's the leader of the penguin team and he has got the trust of every-one around him (just about). Whether he's tangling with octopi or challenging an undercover wolf, Skipper is the penguin with a plan.

Most likely to: Motivate you

DreamWorks

PENGUINS of MADAGASCAR

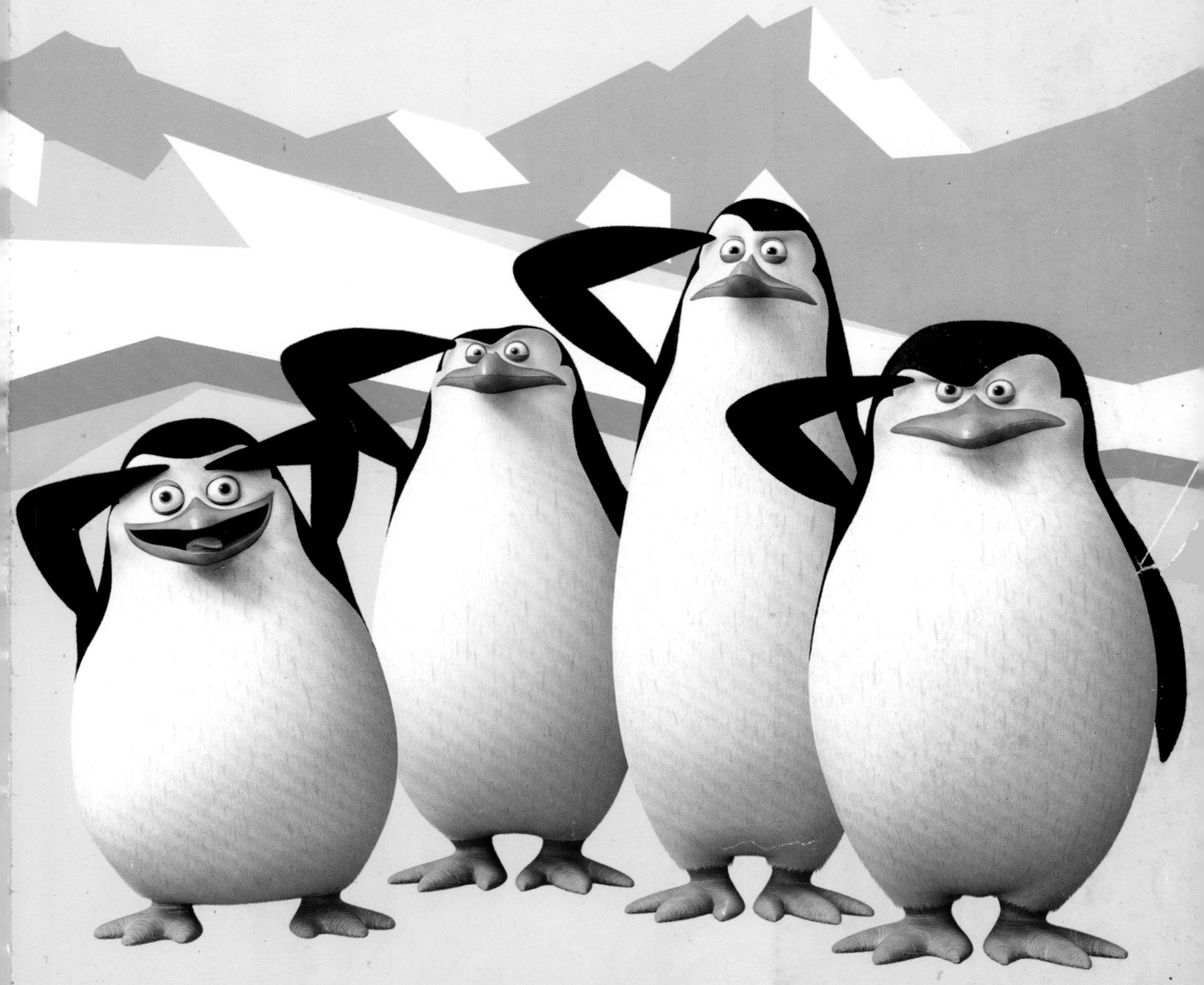

THE GREAT DRAIN ROBBERY

Inside 5 Comic Strips

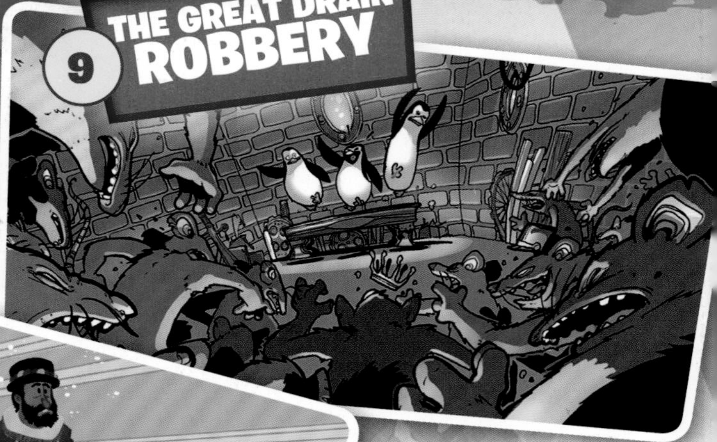

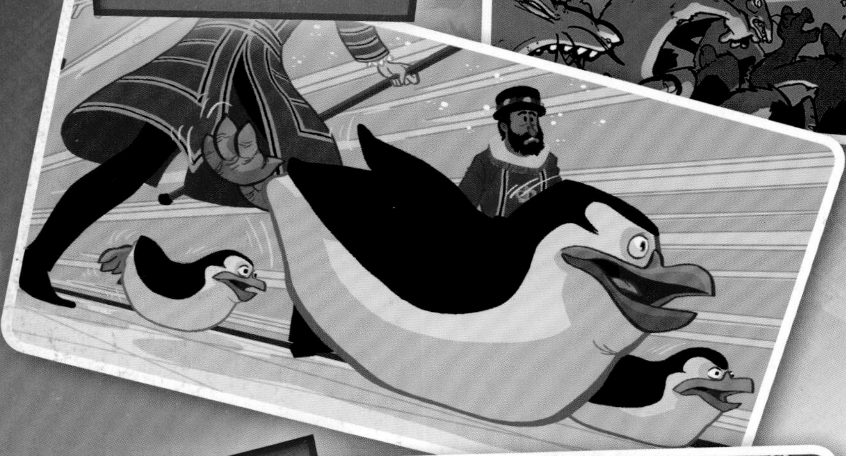

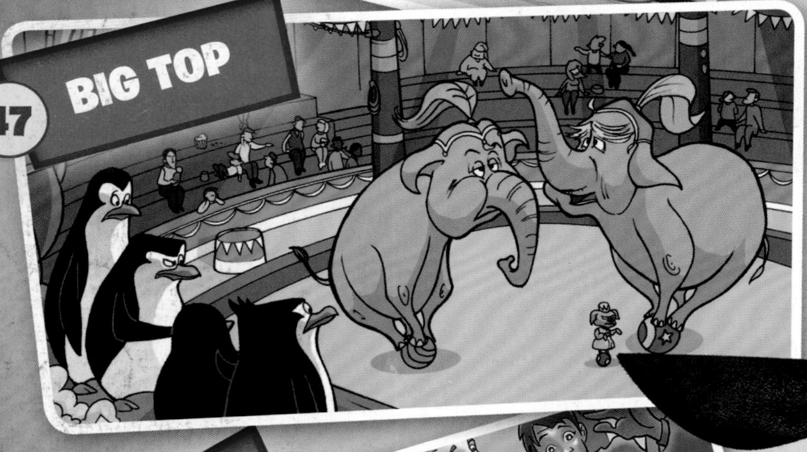

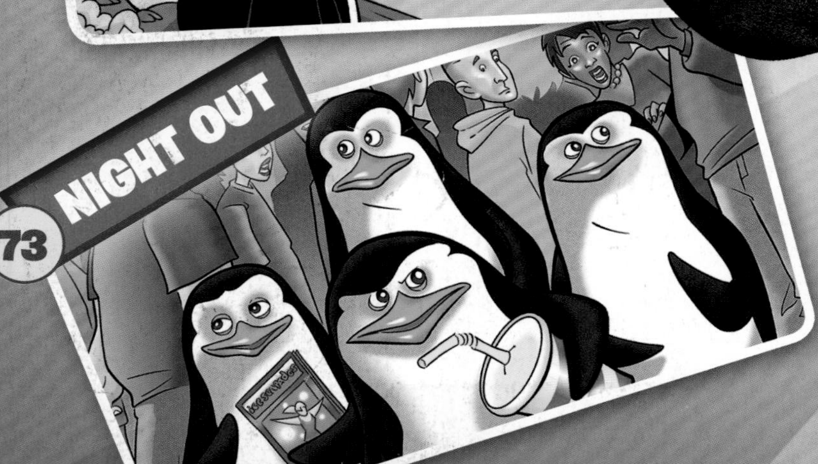

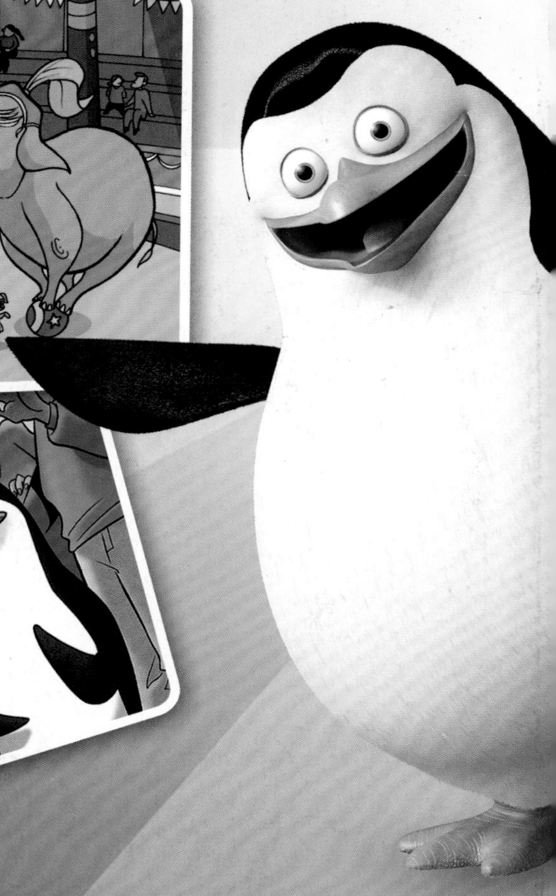

GANG!

Kowalski

The options guy and Skipper's right-hand man. When the team needs to make a move or change course, Kowalski will calculate a way to make it happen!

Most likely to: Escape from any situation!

Meet the

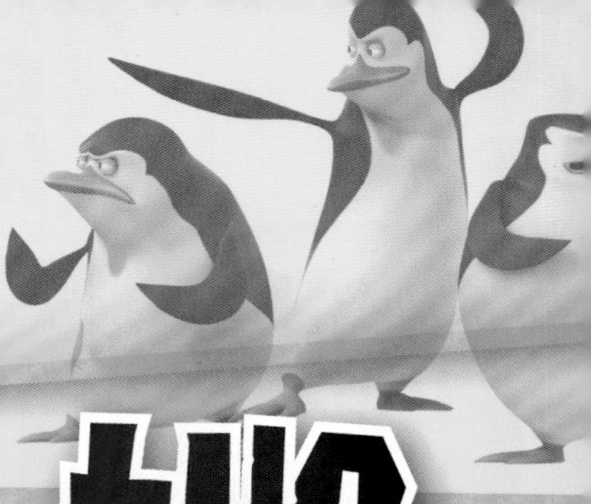

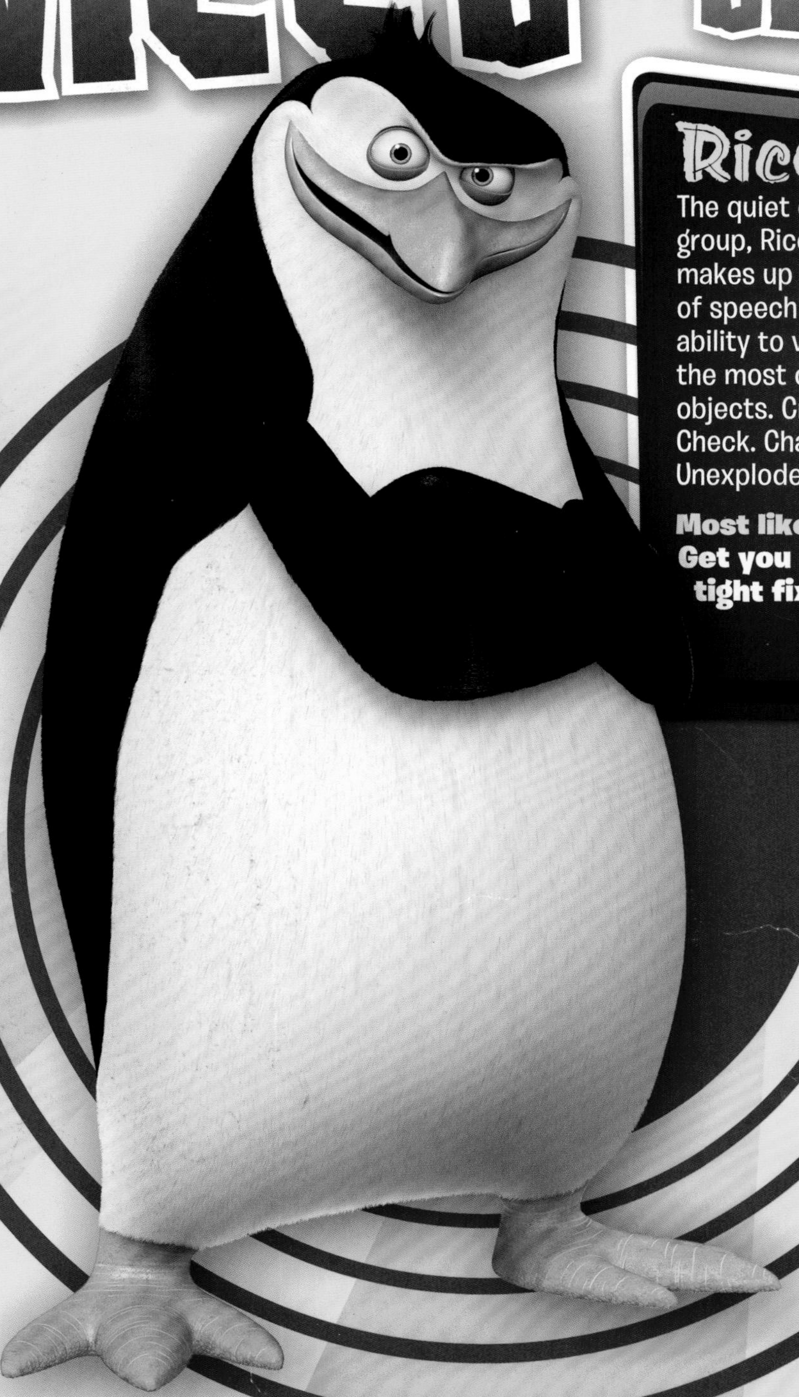

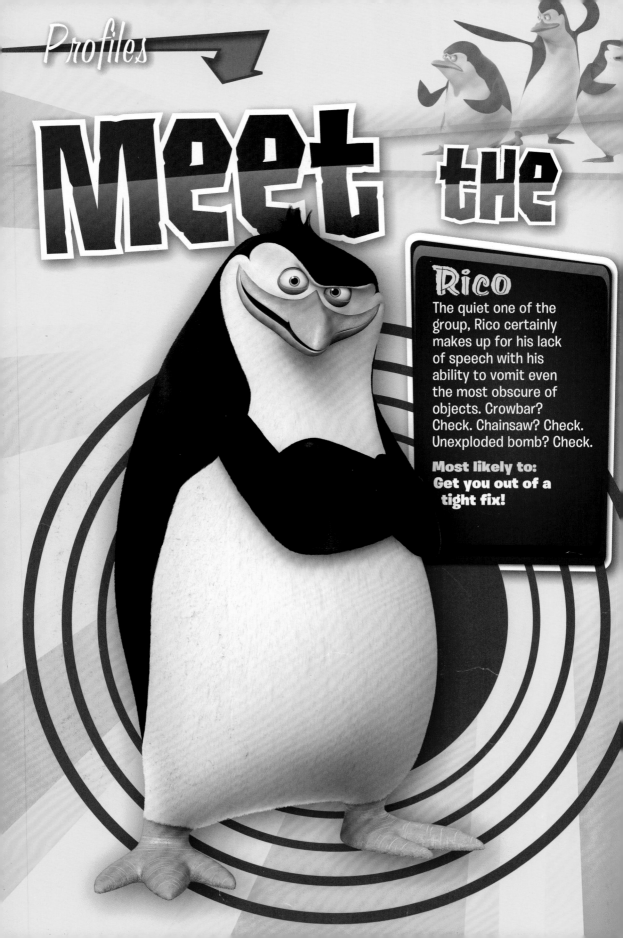

Rico

The quiet one of the group, Rico certainly makes up for his lack of speech with his ability to vomit even the most obscure of objects. Crowbar? Check. Chainsaw? Check. Unexploded bomb? Check.

Most likely to:
Get you out of a tight fix!

GANG!

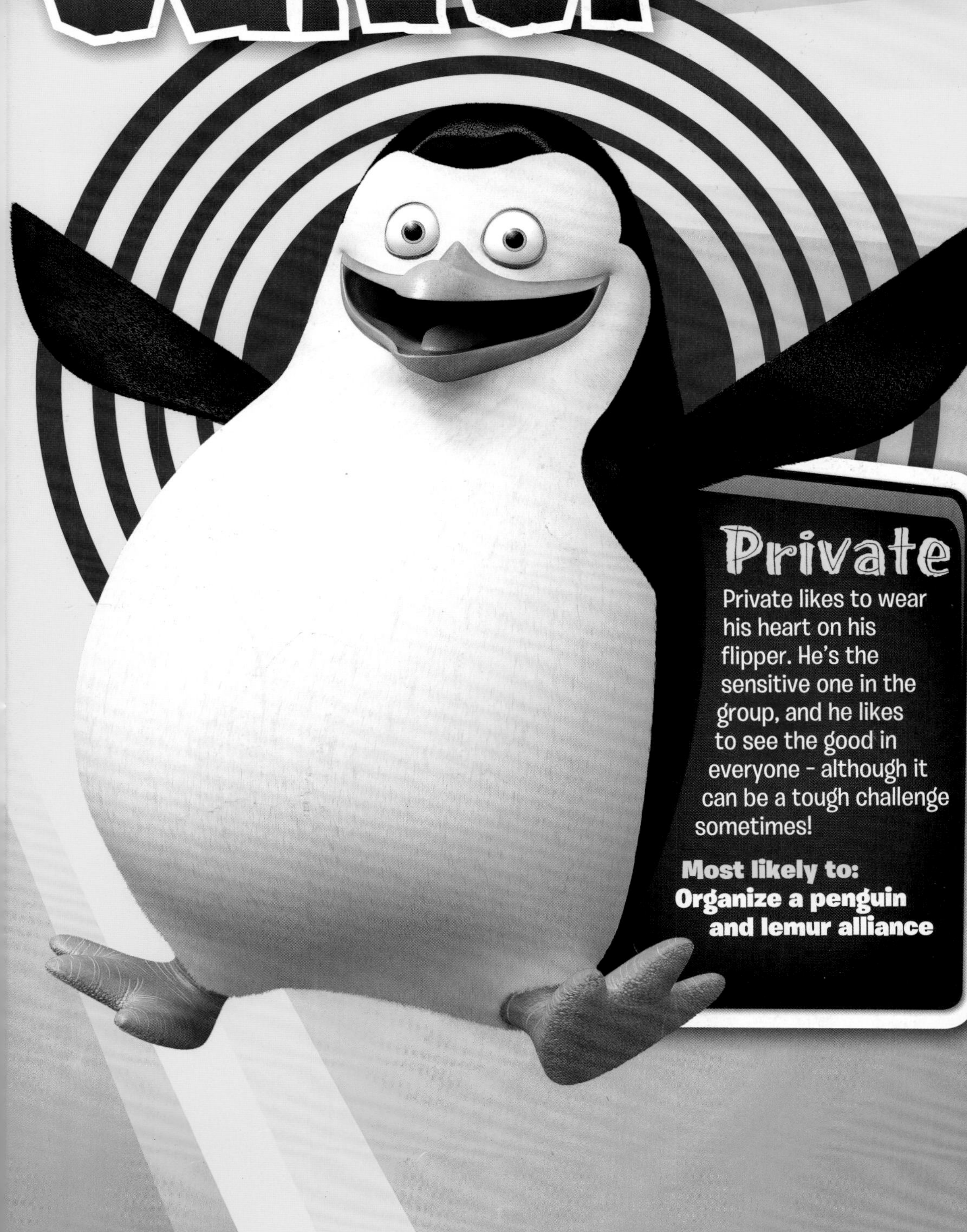

Private

Private likes to wear his heart on his flipper. He's the sensitive one in the group, and he likes to see the good in everyone - although it can be a tough challenge sometimes!

Most likely to:
Organize a penguin and lemur alliance

THE GREAT DRAIN ROBBERY

SCRIPT
Jai Nitz

ART
Lawrence Etherington

LETTERING
Jimmy Betancourt/
Comicraft

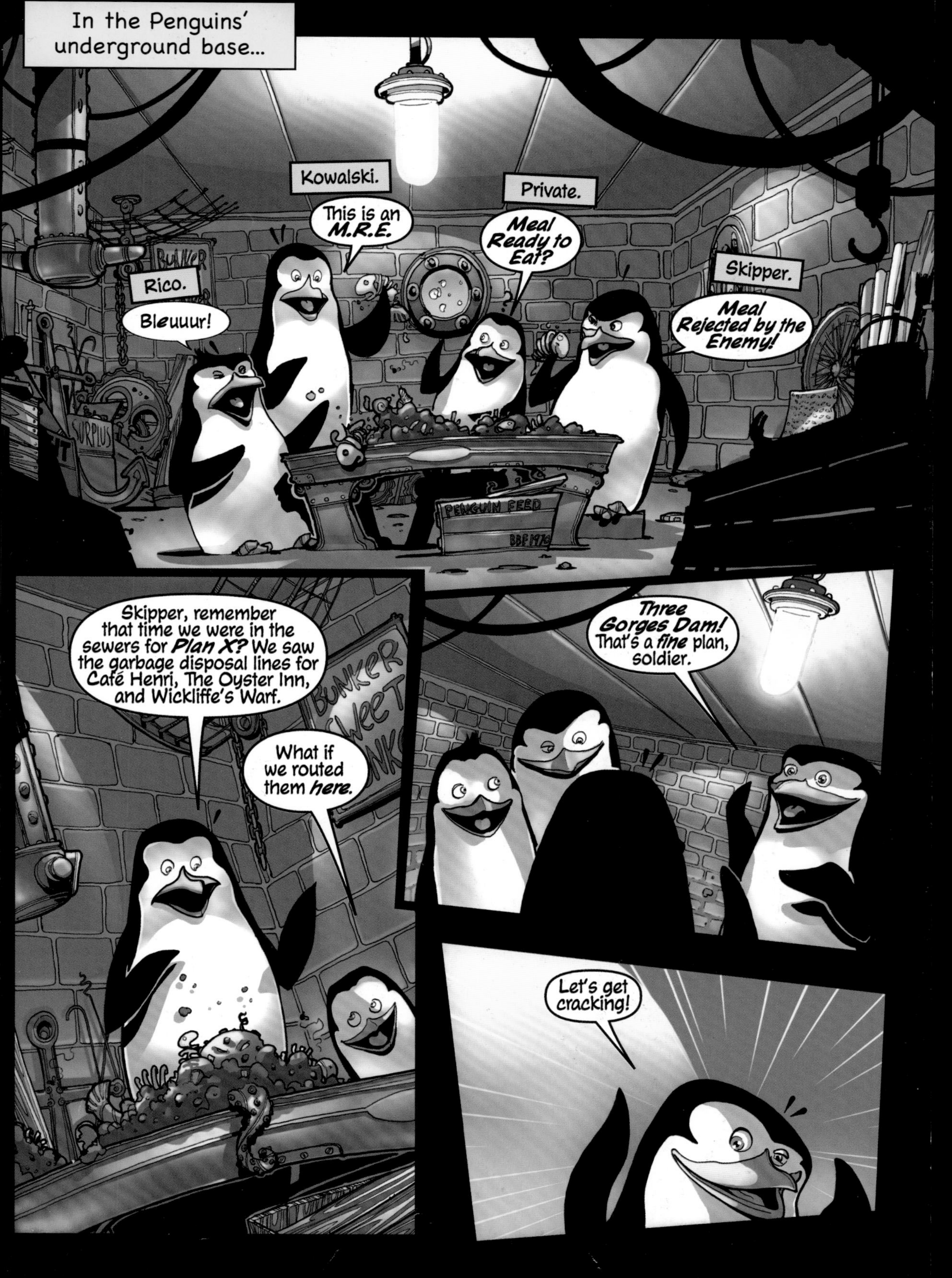
In the Penguins' underground base...
Kowalski.
This is an M.R.E.
Private.
Meal Ready to Eat?
Rico.
Bleuuur!
Skipper.
Meal Rejected by the Enemy!
PENGUIN FEED
SURPLUS
Skipper, remember that time we were in the sewers for Plan X? We saw the garbage disposal lines for Café Henri, The Oyster Inn, and Wickliffe's Warf.
What if we routed them here.
Three Gorges Dam! That's a fine plan, soldier.
Let's get cracking!

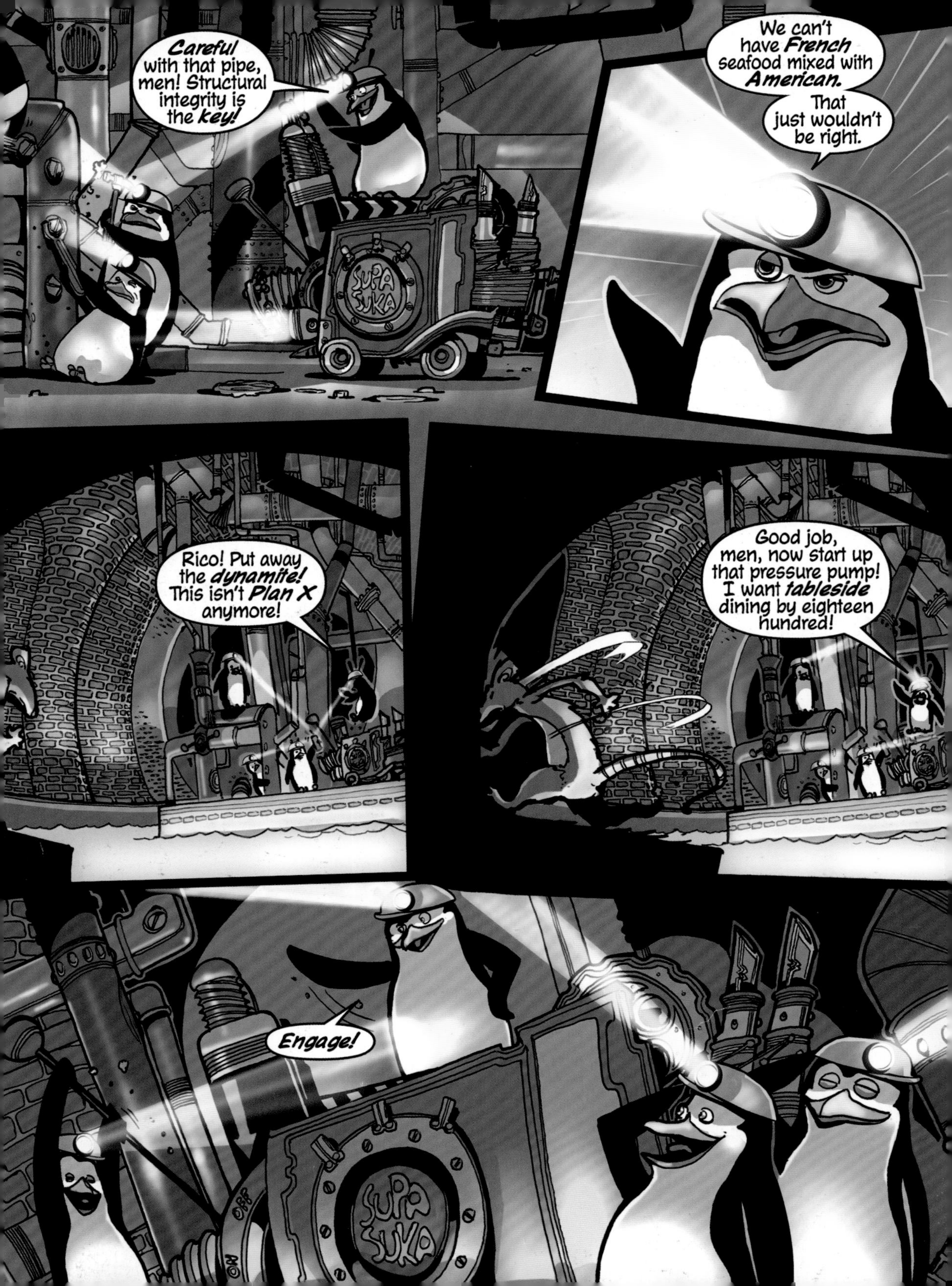
Careful with that pipe, men! Structural integrity is the key!
SUPA SUKA
We can't have French seafood mixed with American.
That just wouldn't be right.
Rico! Put away the dynamite! This isn't Plan X anymore!
Good job, men, now start up that pressure pump! I want tableside dining by eighteen hundred!
Engage!
SUPA SUKA

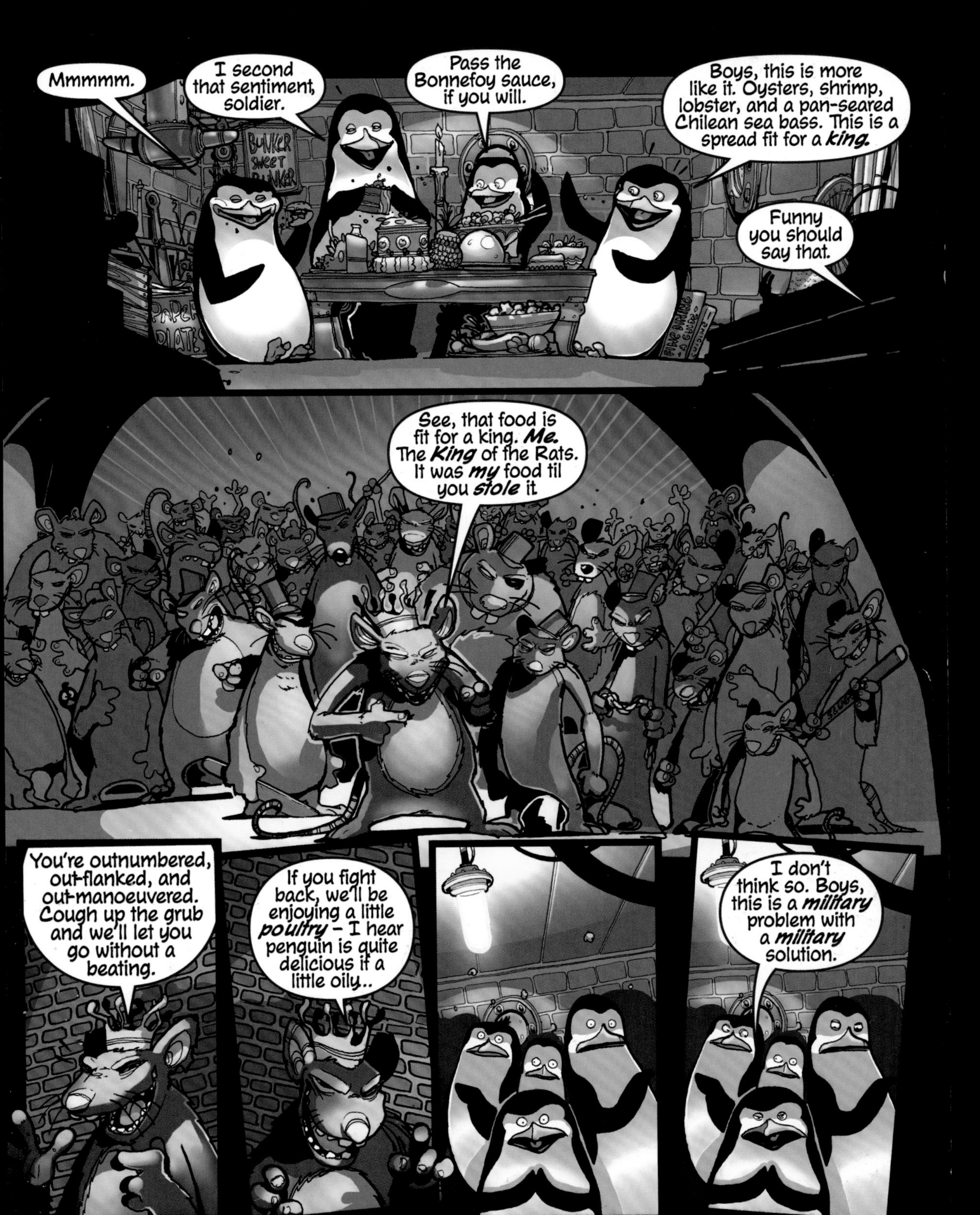
Mmmmm.
I second that sentiment, soldier.
Pass the Bonnefoy sauce, if you will.
Boys, this is more like it. Oysters, shrimp, lobster, and a pan-seared Chilean sea bass. This is a spread fit for a *king.*
BUNKER SWEET BUNKER
PAPER PLATES
Funny you should say that.
See, that food is fit for a king. *Me.* The *King* of the Rats. It was *my* food til you *stole* it.
You're outnumbered, out-flanked, and out-manoeuvered. Cough up the grub and we'll let you go without a beating.
If you fight back, we'll be enjoying a little *poultry* – I hear penguin is quite delicious if a little oily..
I don't think so. Boys, this is a *military* problem with a *military* solution.

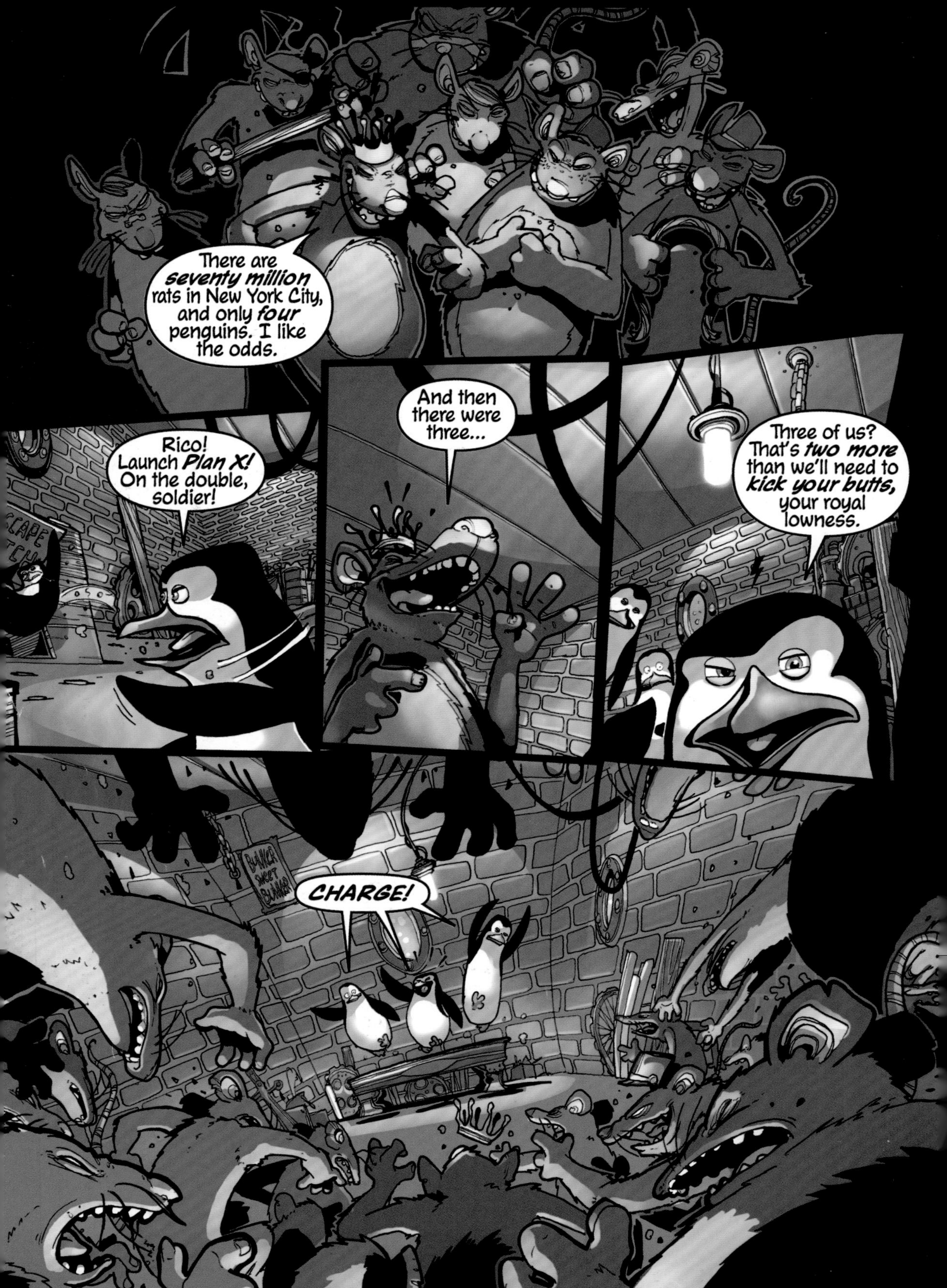
There are *seventy million* rats in New York City, and only *four* penguins. I like the odds.
Rico! Launch *Plan X!* On the double, soldier!
And then there were three...
Three of us? That's *two more* than we'll need to *kick your butts,* your royal lowness.
CHARGE!

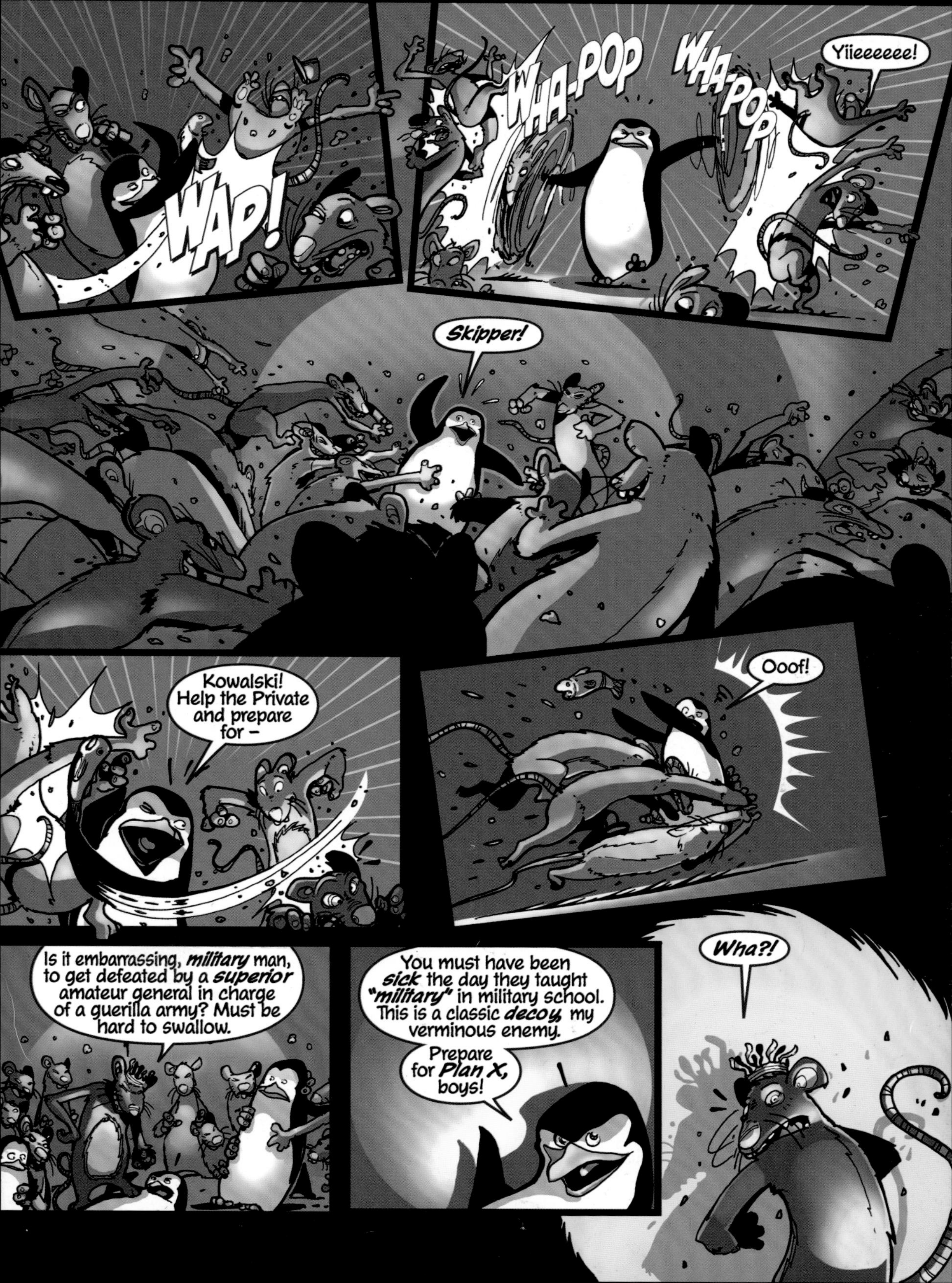
WAP!
WHA-POP
WHA-POP
Yiieeeeee!
Skipper!
Kowalski! Help the Private and prepare for –
Ooof!
Is it embarrassing, *military* man, to get defeated by a *superior* amateur general in charge of a guerilla army? Must be hard to swallow.
You must have been *sick* the day they taught *"military"* in military school. This is a classic *decoy,* my verminous enemy.
Prepare for *Plan X,* boys!
Wha?!

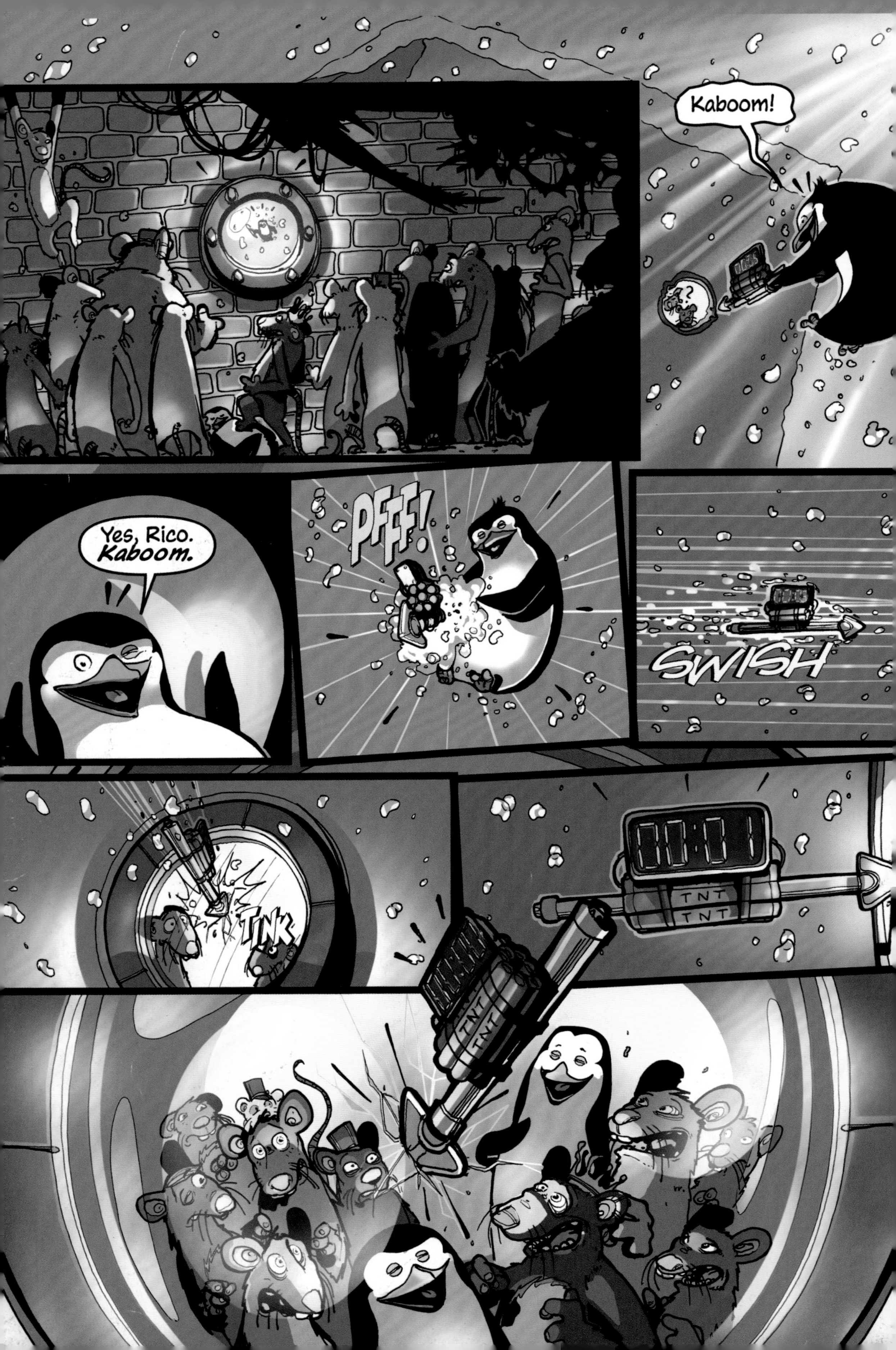
Kaboom!
Yes, Rico.
Kaboom.
PFFF!
SWISH
TINK
TNT
TNT

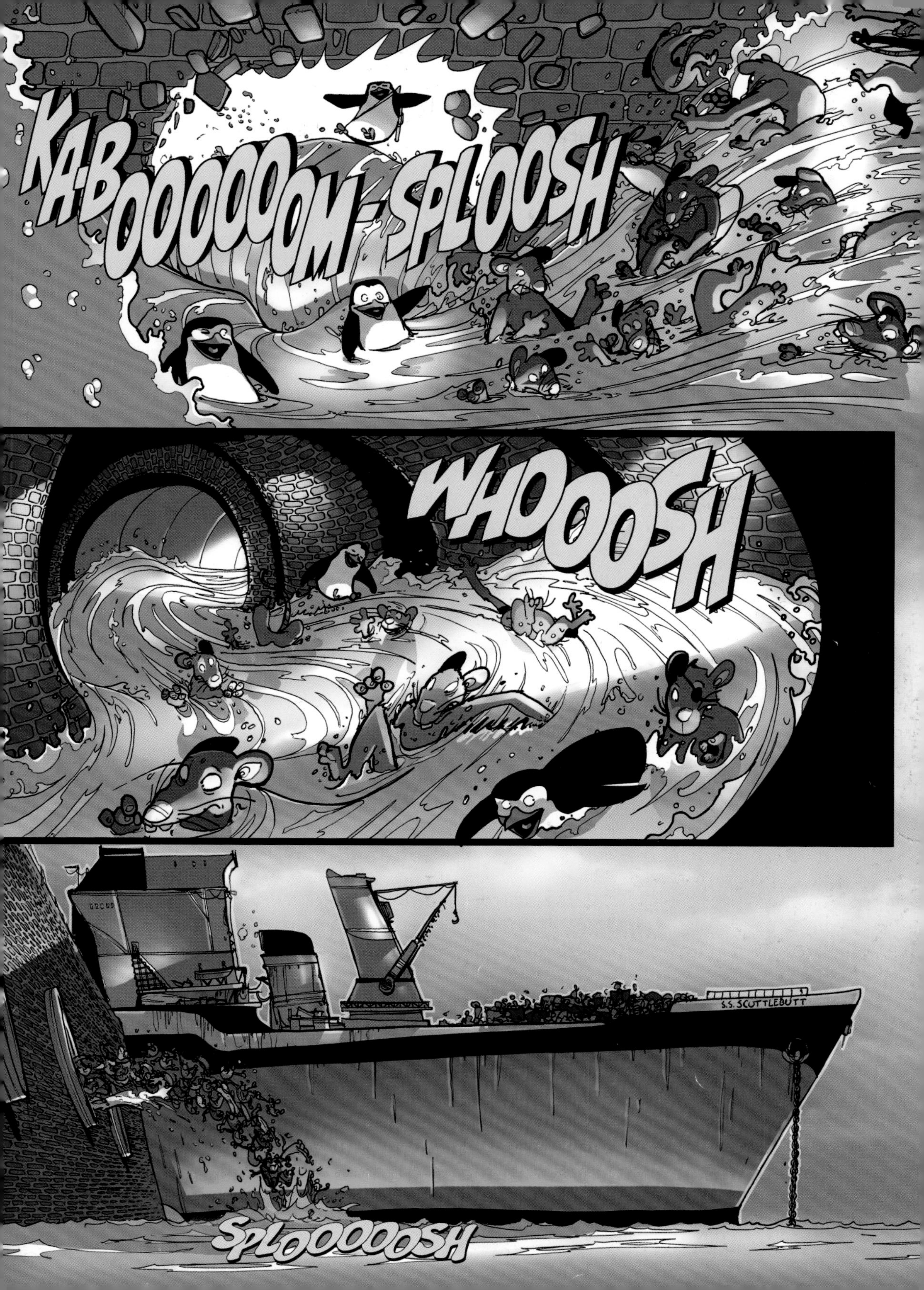
KA-BOOOOOOOM! SPLOOSH
WHOOOSH
S.S. SCUTTLEBUTT
SPLOOOOOSH

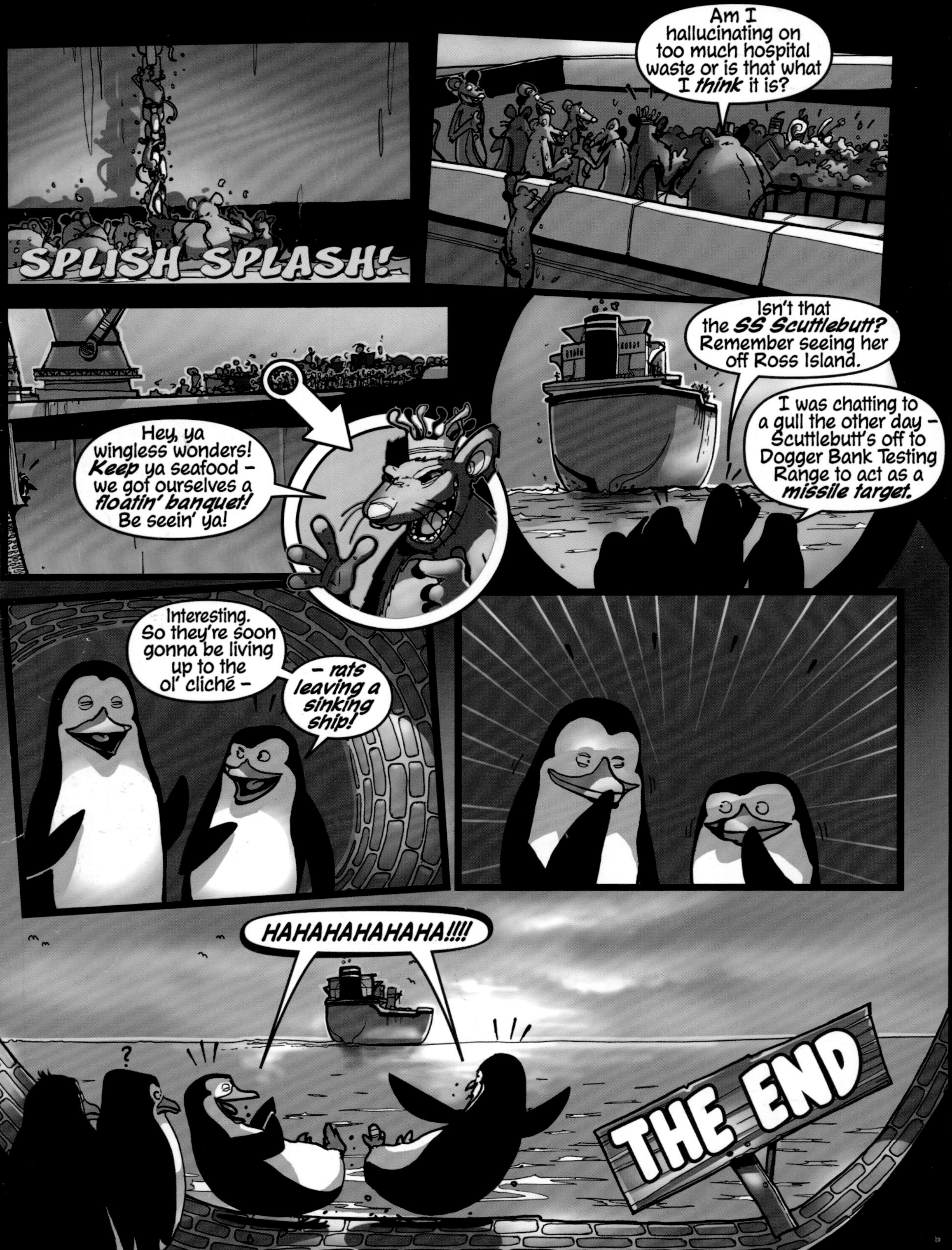
SPLISH SPLASH!
Am I hallucinating on too much hospital waste or is that what I *think* it is?
Isn't that the *SS Scuttlebutt?* Remember seeing her off Ross Island.
I was chatting to a gull the other day – Scuttlebutt's off to Dogger Bank Testing Range to act as a *missile target.*
Hey, ya wingless wonders! *Keep* ya seafood – we got ourselves a *floatin' banquet!* Be seein' ya!
Interesting. So they're soon gonna be living up to the ol' cliché –
– rats leaving a sinking ship!
HAHAHAHAHAHA!!!!
?
THE END

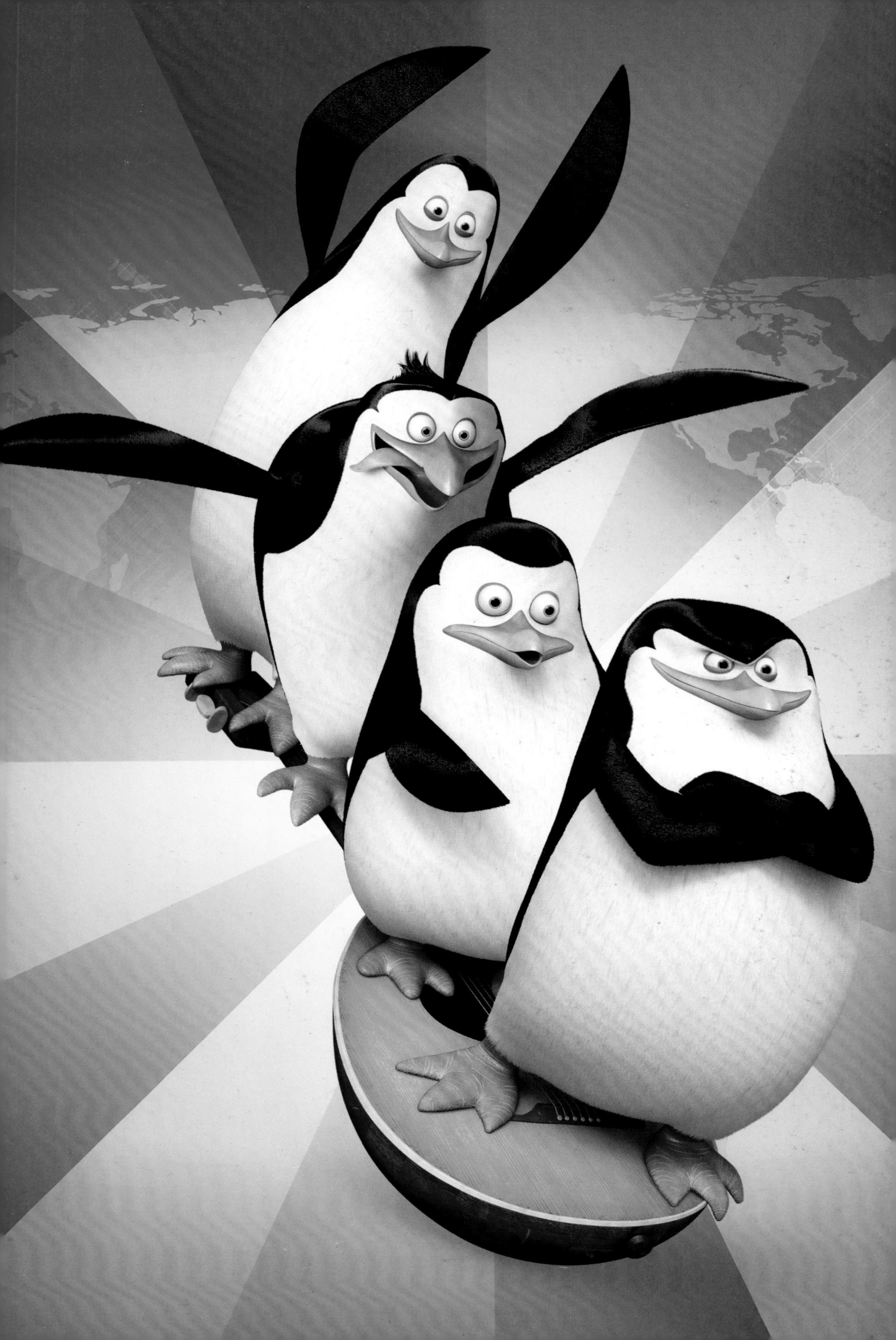

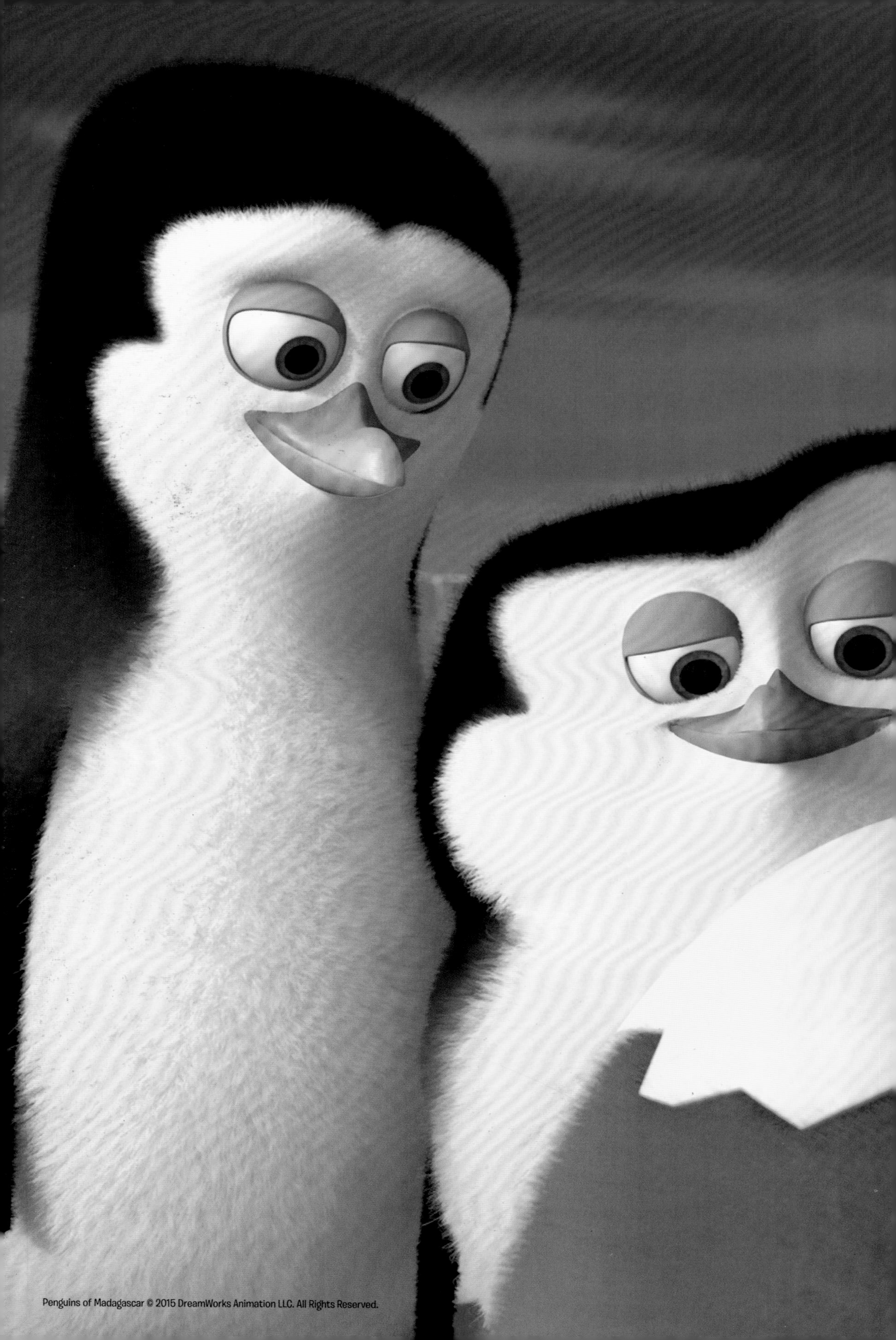

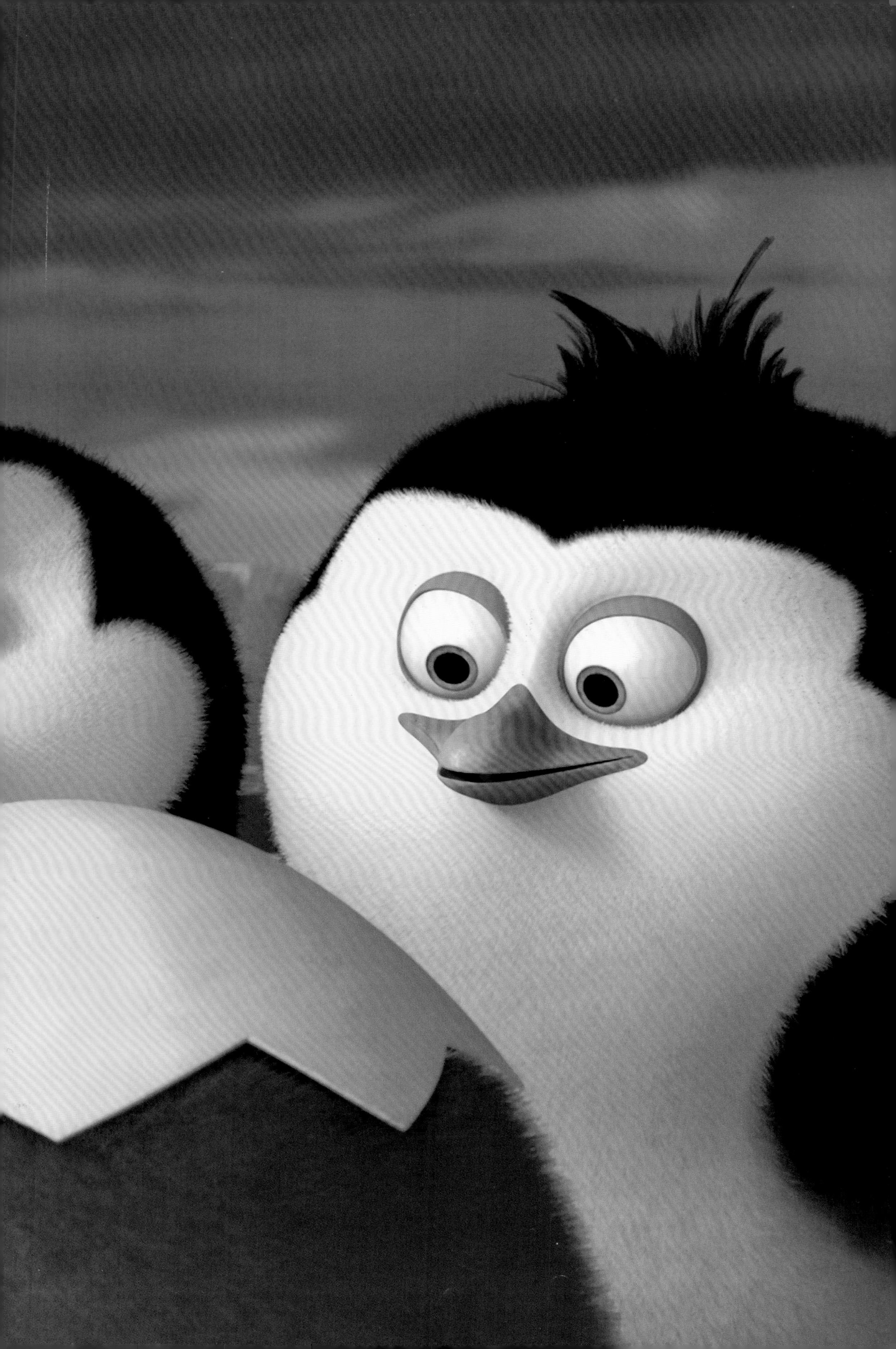

OPERATION: HEIST

SCRIPT
Cavan Scott

ART
Lucas Ferreyra

LETTERING
Jim Campbell

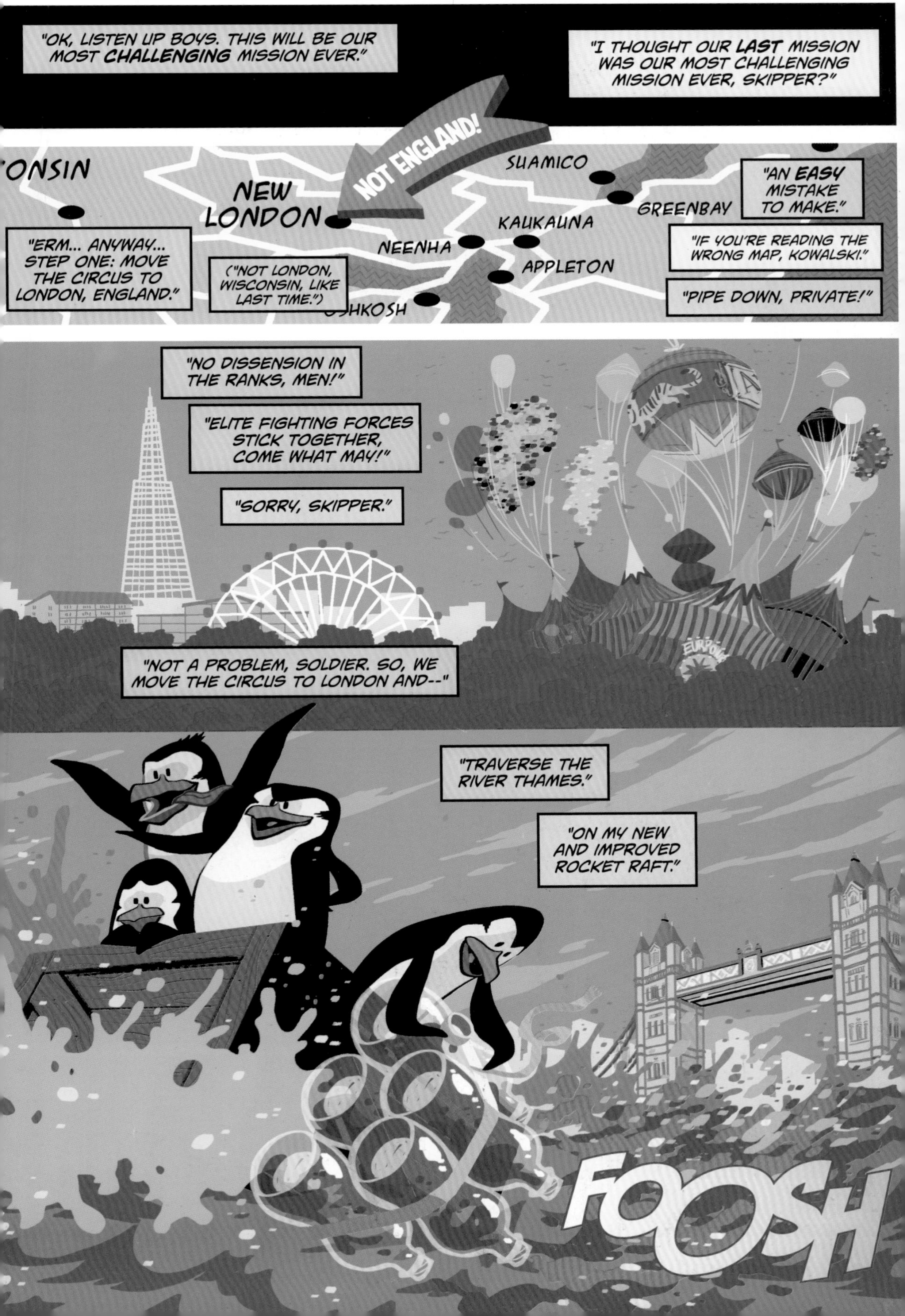
"OK, LISTEN UP BOYS. THIS WILL BE OUR MOST CHALLENGING MISSION EVER."
"I THOUGHT OUR LAST MISSION WAS OUR MOST CHALLENGING MISSION EVER, SKIPPER?"
NOT ENGLAND!
SUAMICO
NEW LONDON
GREENBAY
KAUKAUNA
NEENHA
APPLETON
"ERM... ANYWAY... STEP ONE: MOVE THE CIRCUS TO LONDON, ENGLAND."
("NOT LONDON, WISCONSIN, LIKE LAST TIME.")
"AN EASY MISTAKE TO MAKE."
"IF YOU'RE READING THE WRONG MAP, KOWALSKI."
"PIPE DOWN, PRIVATE!"
"NO DISSENSION IN THE RANKS, MEN!"
"ELITE FIGHTING FORCES STICK TOGETHER, COME WHAT MAY!"
"SORRY, SKIPPER."
"NOT A PROBLEM, SOLDIER. SO, WE MOVE THE CIRCUS TO LONDON AND--"
"TRAVERSE THE RIVER THAMES."
"ON MY NEW AND IMPROVED ROCKET RAFT."
FOOSH

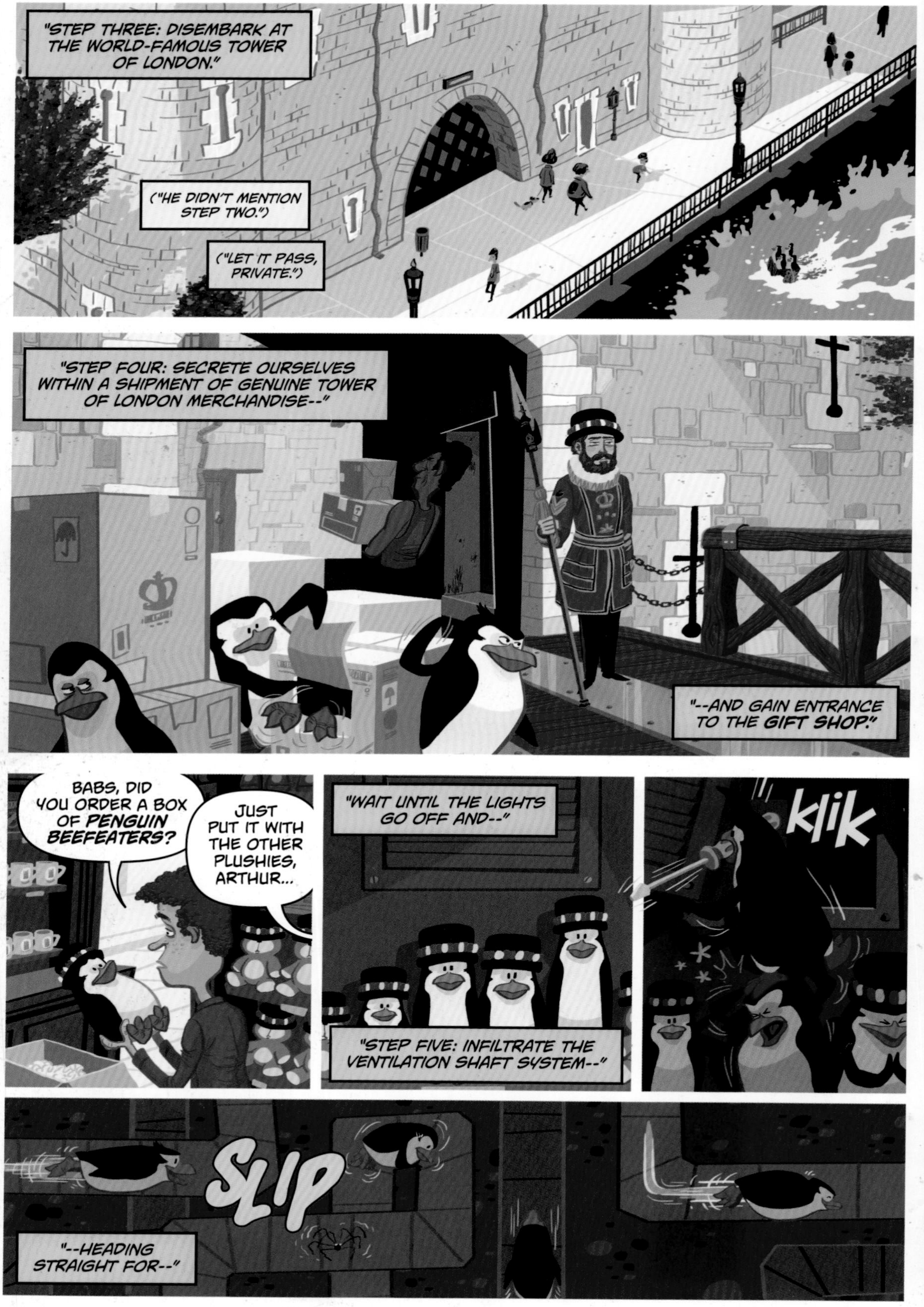
"STEP THREE: DISEMBARK AT THE WORLD-FAMOUS TOWER OF LONDON."
("HE DIDN'T MENTION STEP TWO.")
("LET IT PASS, PRIVATE.")
"STEP FOUR: SECRETE OURSELVES WITHIN A SHIPMENT OF GENUINE TOWER OF LONDON MERCHANDISE--"
"--AND GAIN ENTRANCE TO THE GIFT SHOP."
BABS, DID YOU ORDER A BOX OF PENGUIN BEEFEATERS?
JUST PUT IT WITH THE OTHER PLUSHIES, ARTHUR...
"WAIT UNTIL THE LIGHTS GO OFF AND--"
"STEP FIVE: INFILTRATE THE VENTILATION SHAFT SYSTEM--"
KLIK
SLIP
"--HEADING STRAIGHT FOR--"

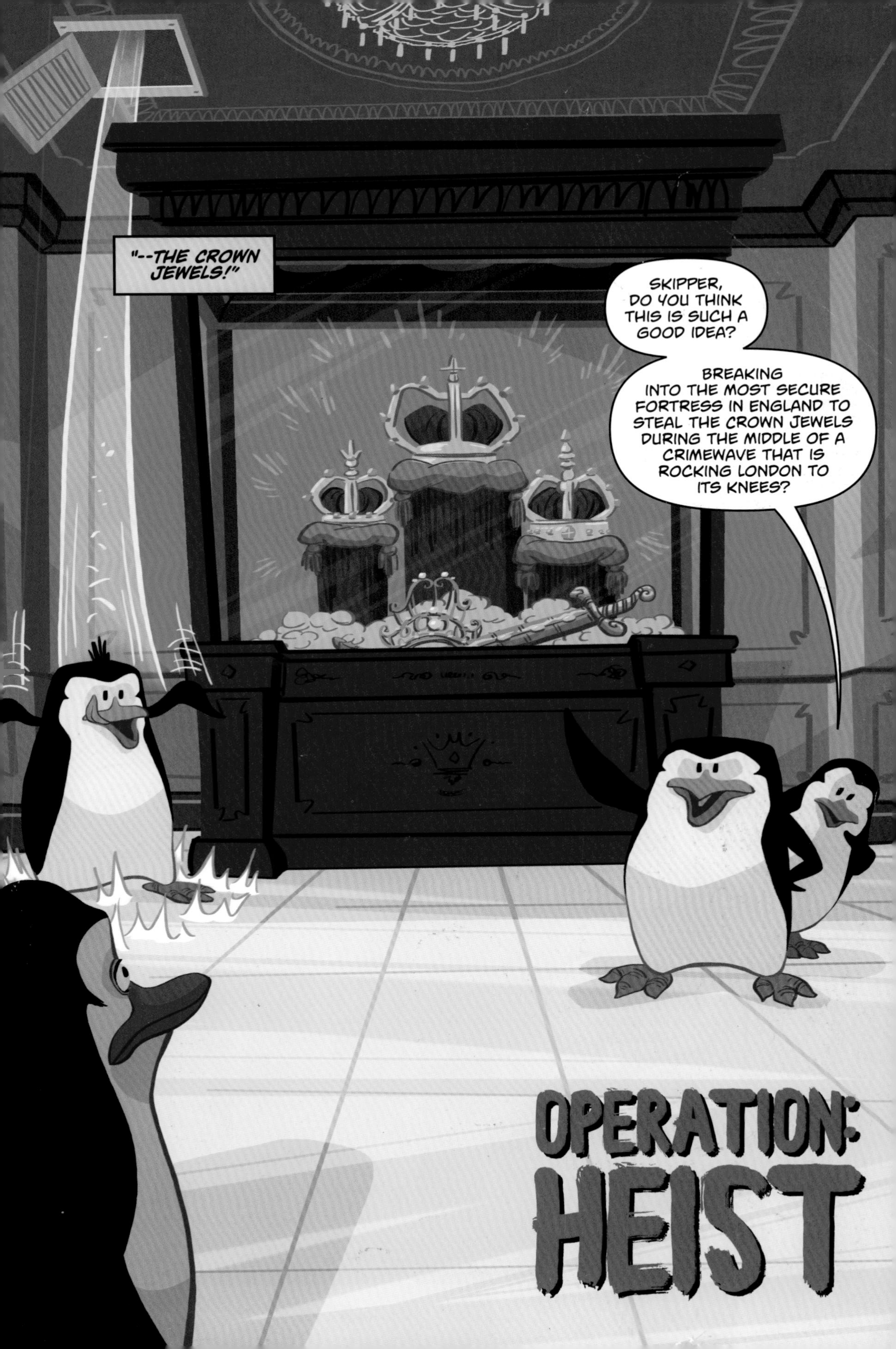
"--THE CROWN JEWELS!"
SKIPPER, DO YOU THINK THIS IS SUCH A GOOD IDEA?
BREAKING INTO THE MOST SECURE FORTRESS IN ENGLAND TO STEAL THE CROWN JEWELS DURING THE MIDDLE OF A CRIMEWAVE THAT IS ROCKING LONDON TO ITS KNEES?
OPERATION: HEIST

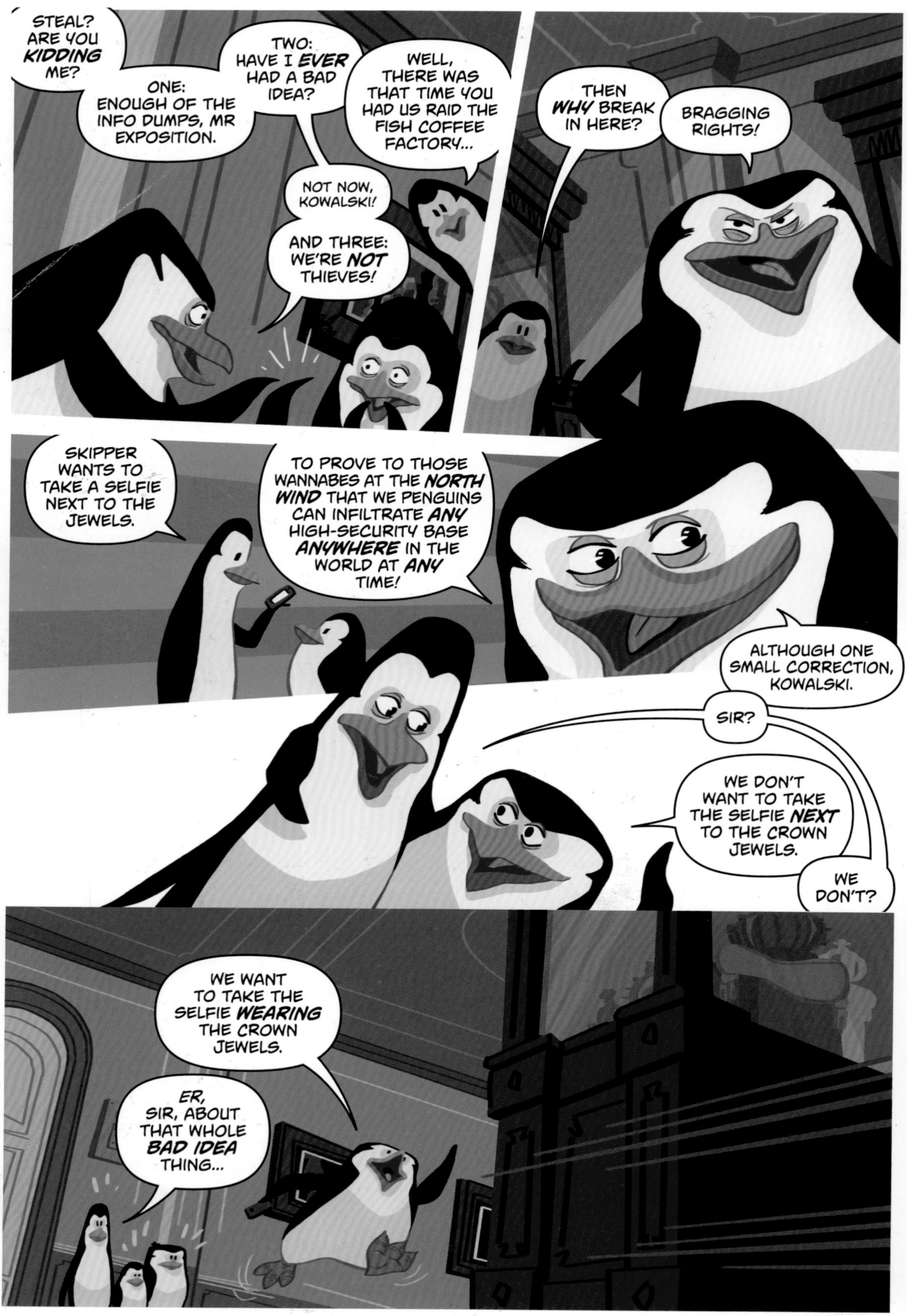
STEAL? ARE YOU KIDDING ME?
ONE: ENOUGH OF THE INFO DUMPS, MR EXPOSITION.
TWO: HAVE I EVER HAD A BAD IDEA?
WELL, THERE WAS THAT TIME YOU HAD US RAID THE FISH COFFEE FACTORY...
NOT NOW, KOWALSKI!
AND THREE: WE'RE NOT THIEVES!
THEN WHY BREAK IN HERE?
BRAGGING RIGHTS!
SKIPPER WANTS TO TAKE A SELFIE NEXT TO THE JEWELS.
TO PROVE TO THOSE WANNABES AT THE NORTH WIND THAT WE PENGUINS CAN INFILTRATE ANY HIGH-SECURITY BASE ANYWHERE IN THE WORLD AT ANY TIME!
ALTHOUGH ONE SMALL CORRECTION, KOWALSKI.
SIR?
WE DON'T WANT TO TAKE THE SELFIE NEXT TO THE CROWN JEWELS.
WE DON'T?
WE WANT TO TAKE THE SELFIE WEARING THE CROWN JEWELS.
ER, SIR, ABOUT THAT WHOLE BAD IDEA THING...

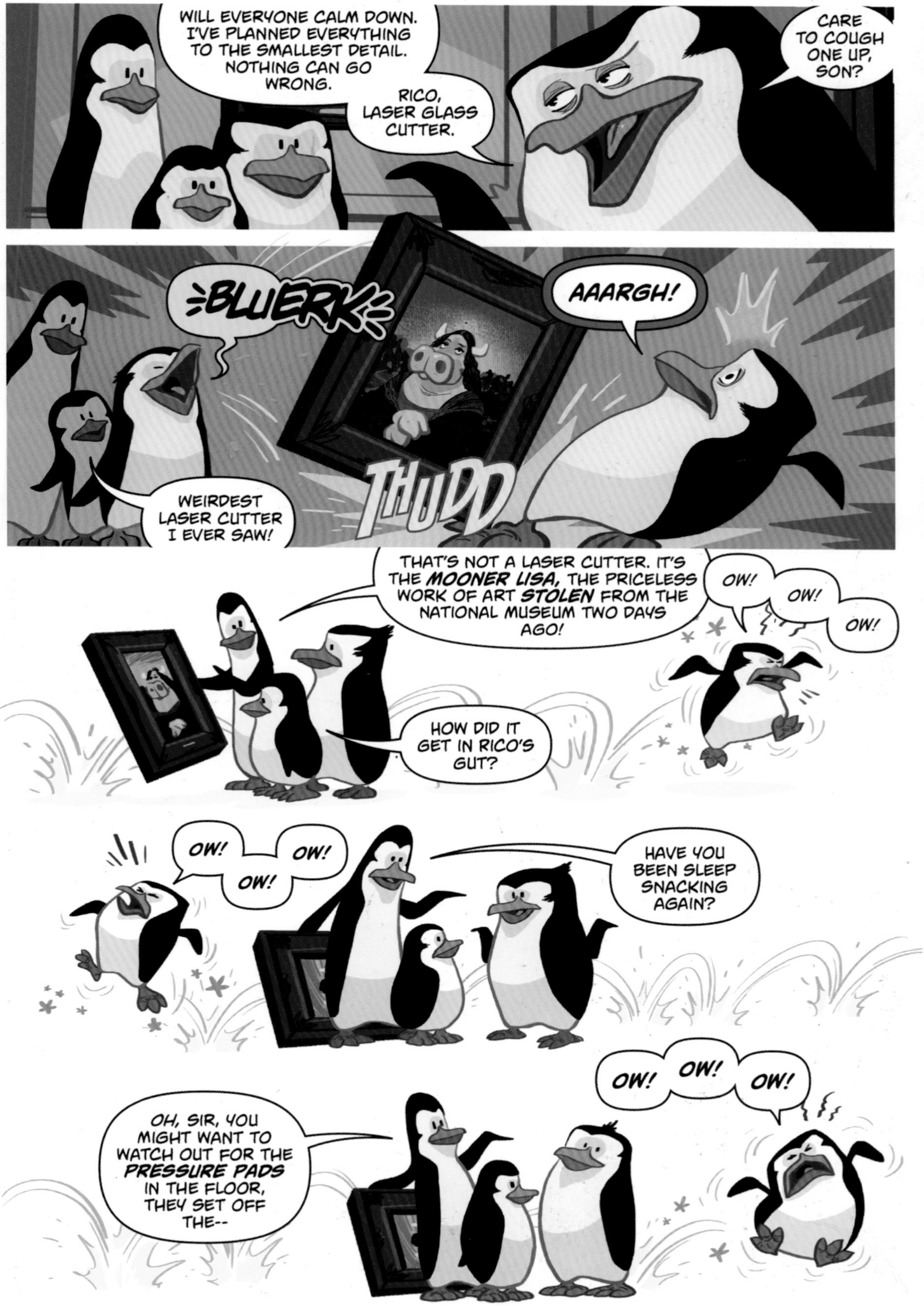

WILL EVERYONE CALM DOWN. I'VE PLANNED EVERYTHING TO THE SMALLEST DETAIL. NOTHING CAN GO WRONG.
RICO, LASER GLASS CUTTER.
CARE TO COUGH ONE UP, SON?
BLUERK
AAARGH!
THUDD
WEIRDEST LASER CUTTER I EVER SAW!
THAT'S NOT A LASER CUTTER. IT'S THE MOONER LISA, THE PRICELESS WORK OF ART STOLEN FROM THE NATIONAL MUSEUM TWO DAYS AGO!
OW!
OW!
OW!
HOW DID IT GET IN RICO'S GUT?
OW!
OW!
OW!
HAVE YOU BEEN SLEEP SNACKING AGAIN?
OH, SIR, YOU MIGHT WANT TO WATCH OUT FOR THE PRESSURE PADS IN THE FLOOR, THEY SET OFF THE--
OW!
OW!
OW!

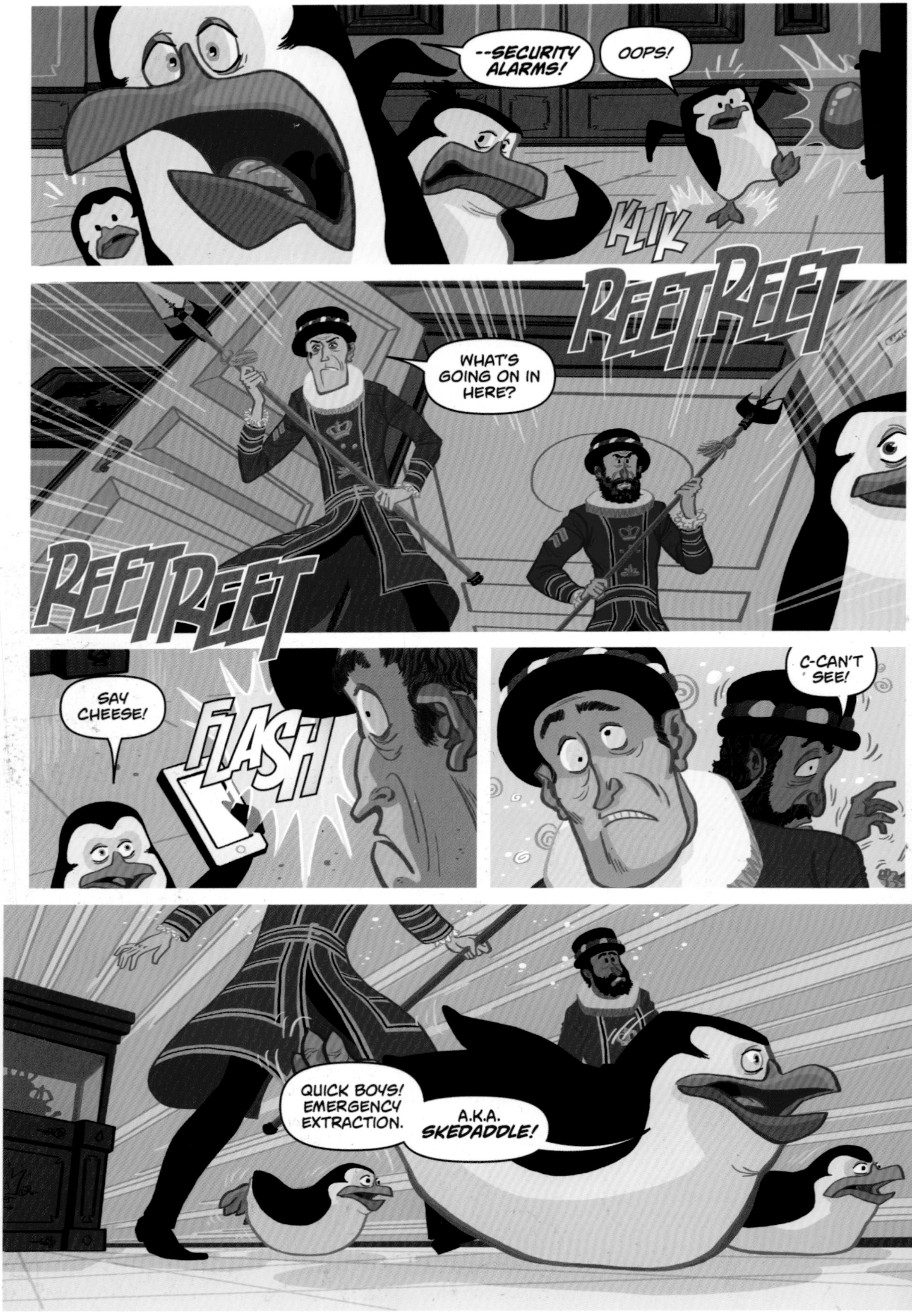
--SECURITY ALARMS!
OOPS!
KLIK
REETREET
WHAT'S GOING ON IN HERE?
REETREET
SAY CHEESE!
FLASH
C-CAN'T SEE!
QUICK BOYS! EMERGENCY EXTRACTION.
A.K.A. SKEDADDLE!

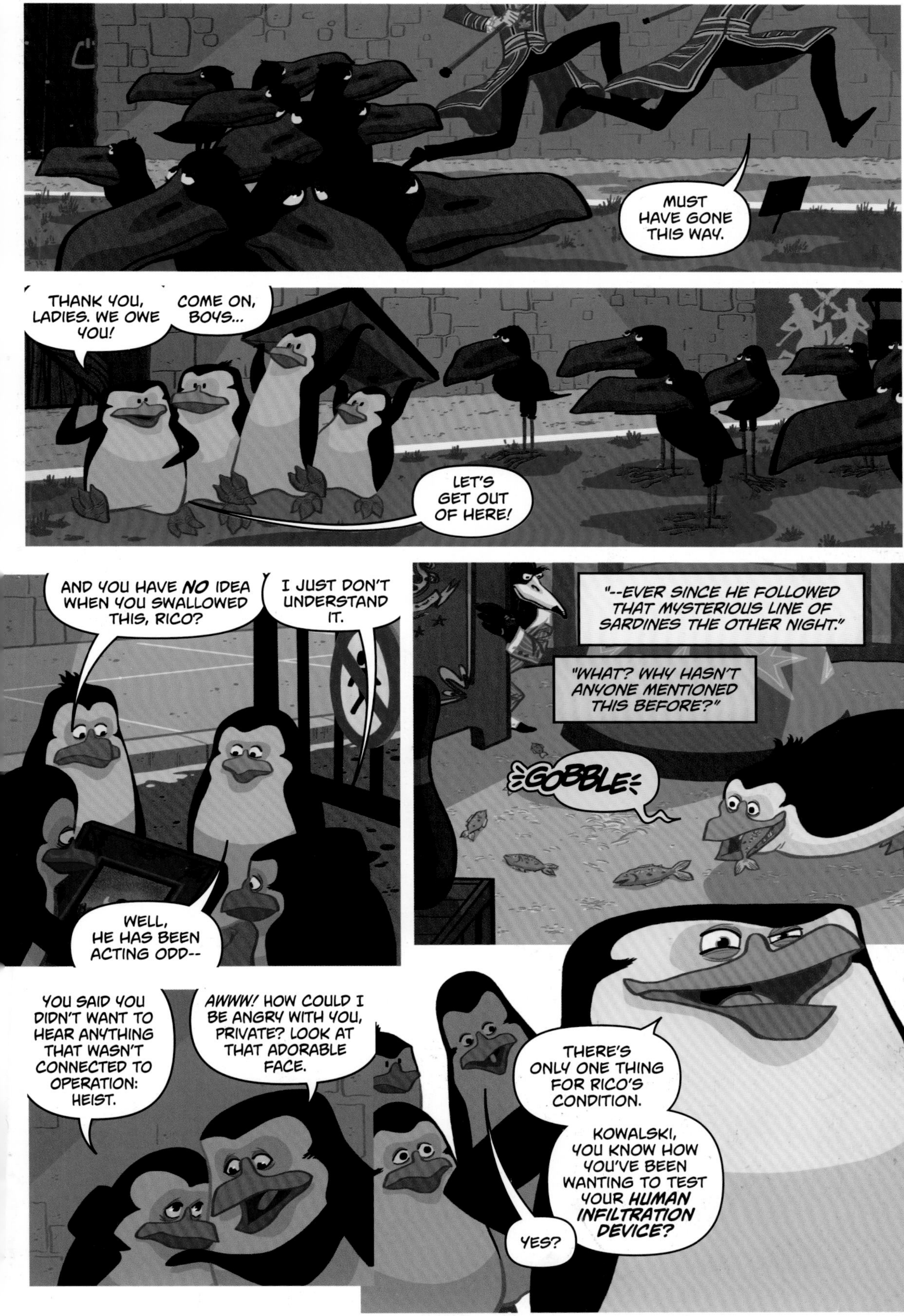

MUST HAVE GONE THIS WAY.
THANK YOU, LADIES. WE OWE YOU!
COME ON, BOYS...
LET'S GET OUT OF HERE!
AND YOU HAVE NO IDEA WHEN YOU SWALLOWED THIS, RICO?
I JUST DON'T UNDERSTAND IT.
WELL, HE HAS BEEN ACTING ODD--
"--EVER SINCE HE FOLLOWED THAT MYSTERIOUS LINE OF SARDINES THE OTHER NIGHT."
"WHAT? WHY HASN'T ANYONE MENTIONED THIS BEFORE?"
GOBBLE
YOU SAID YOU DIDN'T WANT TO HEAR ANYTHING THAT WASN'T CONNECTED TO OPERATION: HEIST.
AWWW! HOW COULD I BE ANGRY WITH YOU, PRIVATE? LOOK AT THAT ADORABLE FACE.
THERE'S ONLY ONE THING FOR RICO'S CONDITION.
KOWALSKI, YOU KNOW HOW YOU'VE BEEN WANTING TO TEST YOUR HUMAN INFILTRATION DEVICE?
YES?

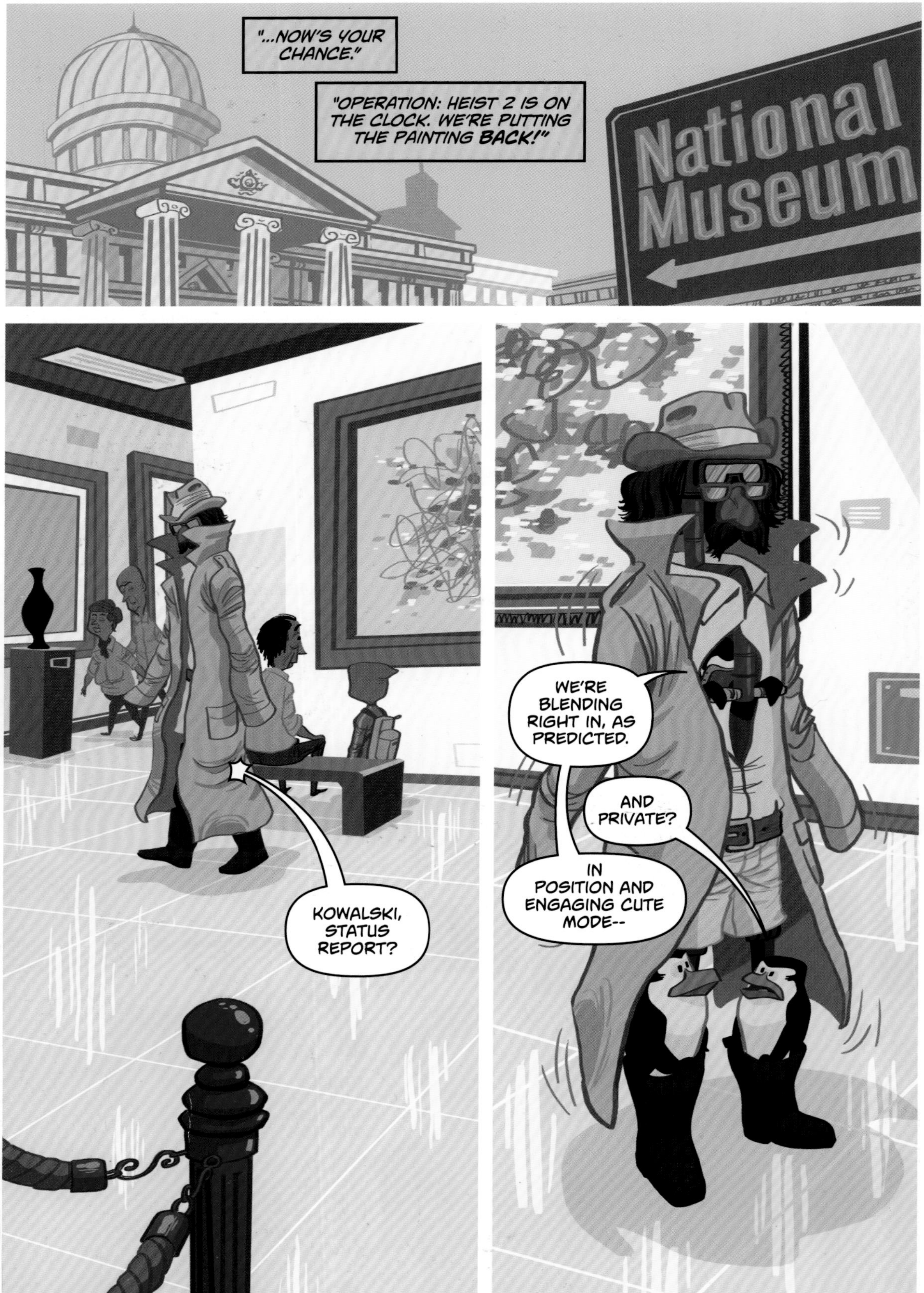
"...NOW'S YOUR CHANCE."
"OPERATION: HEIST 2 IS ON THE CLOCK. WE'RE PUTTING THE PAINTING BACK!"
National Museum
KOWALSKI, STATUS REPORT?
WE'RE BLENDING RIGHT IN, AS PREDICTED.
AND PRIVATE?
IN POSITION AND ENGAGING CUTE MODE--

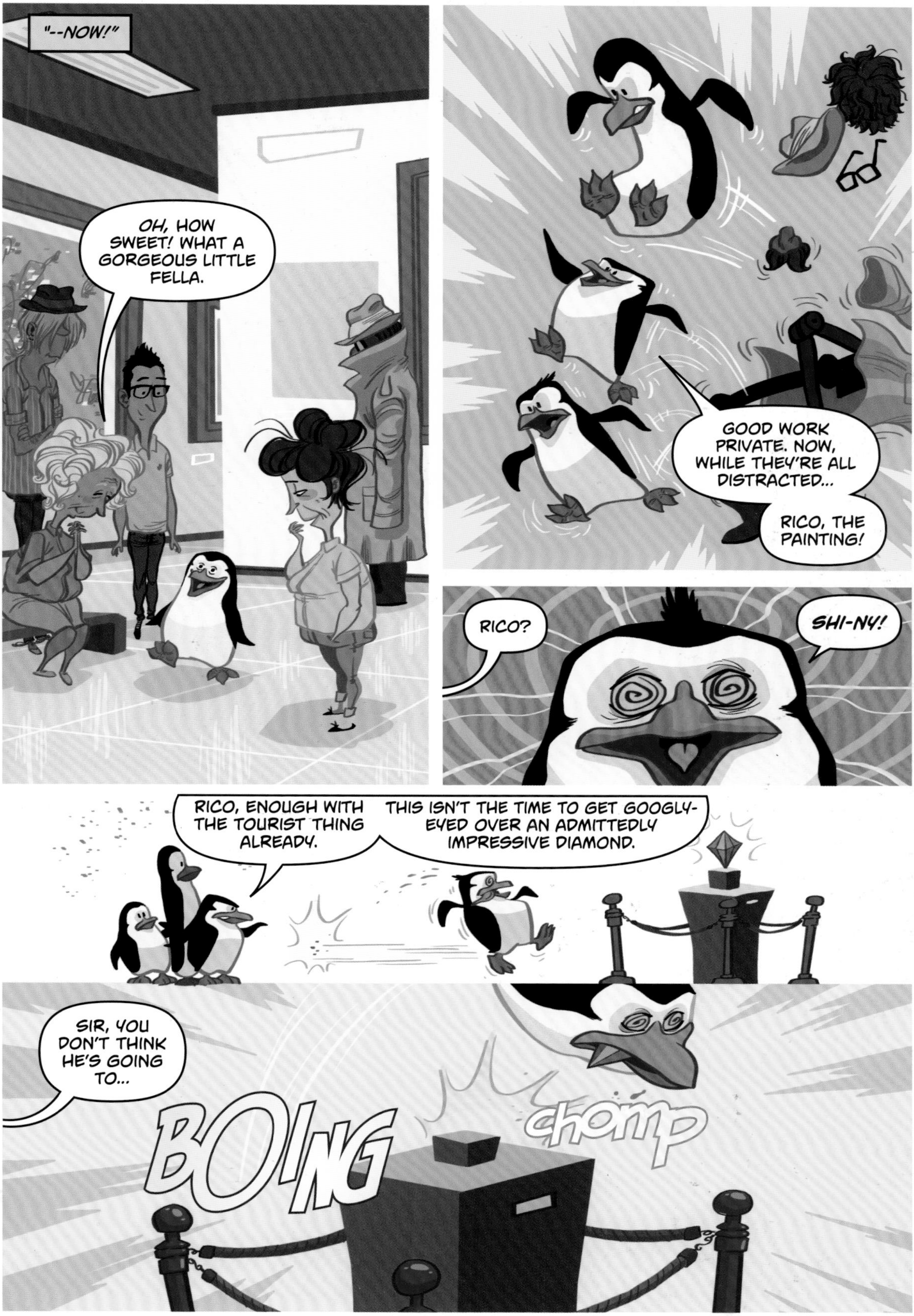
"--NOW!"
OH, HOW SWEET! WHAT A GORGEOUS LITTLE FELLA.
GOOD WORK PRIVATE. NOW, WHILE THEY'RE ALL DISTRACTED...
RICO, THE PAINTING!
RICO?
SHI-NY!
RICO, ENOUGH WITH THE TOURIST THING ALREADY.
THIS ISN'T THE TIME TO GET GOOGLY-EYED OVER AN ADMITTEDLY IMPRESSIVE DIAMOND.
SIR, YOU DON'T THINK HE'S GOING TO...
BOING
chomp

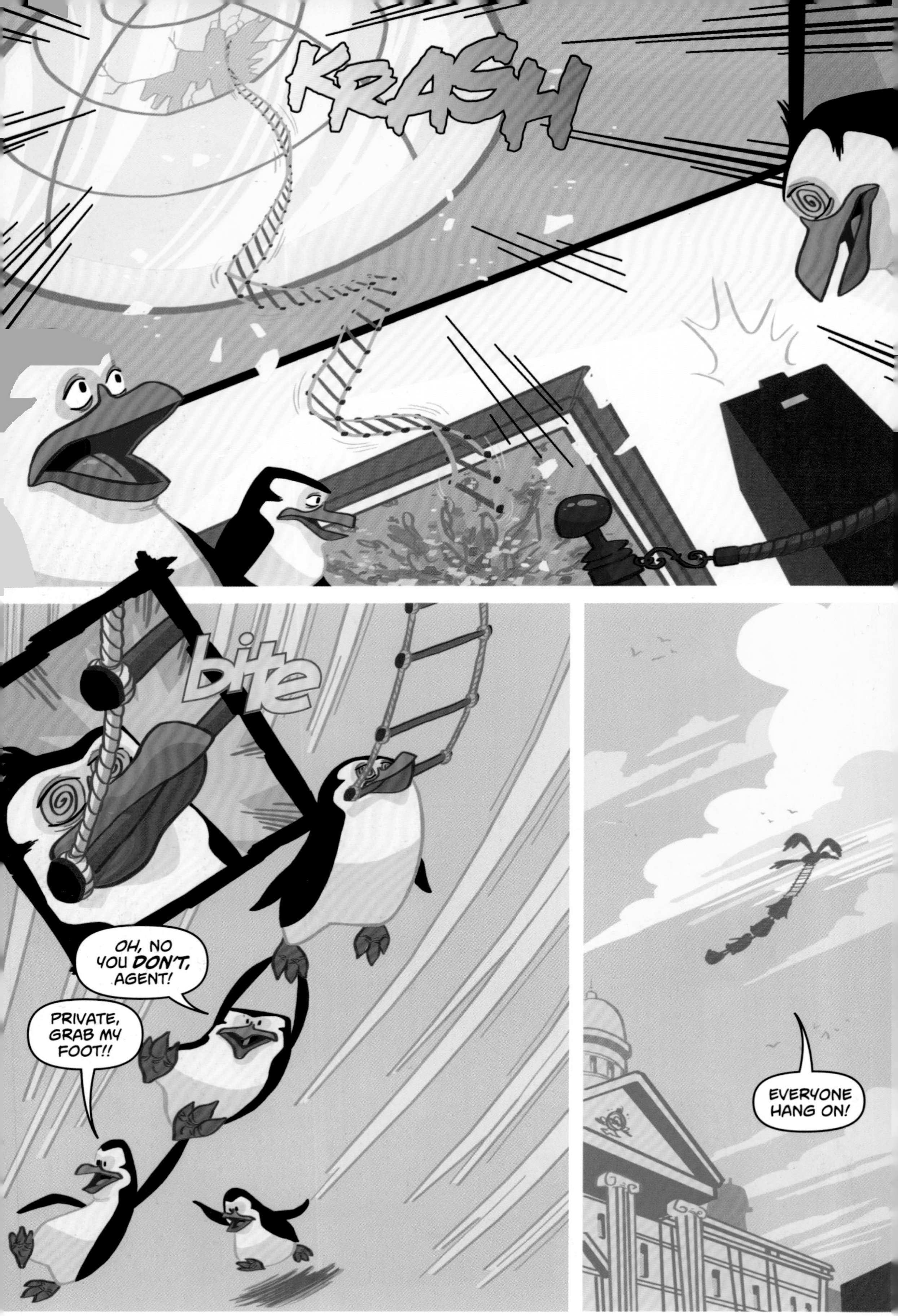
KRASH
bite
OH, NO YOU DON'T, AGENT!
PRIVATE, GRAB MY FOOT!!
EVERYONE HANG ON!

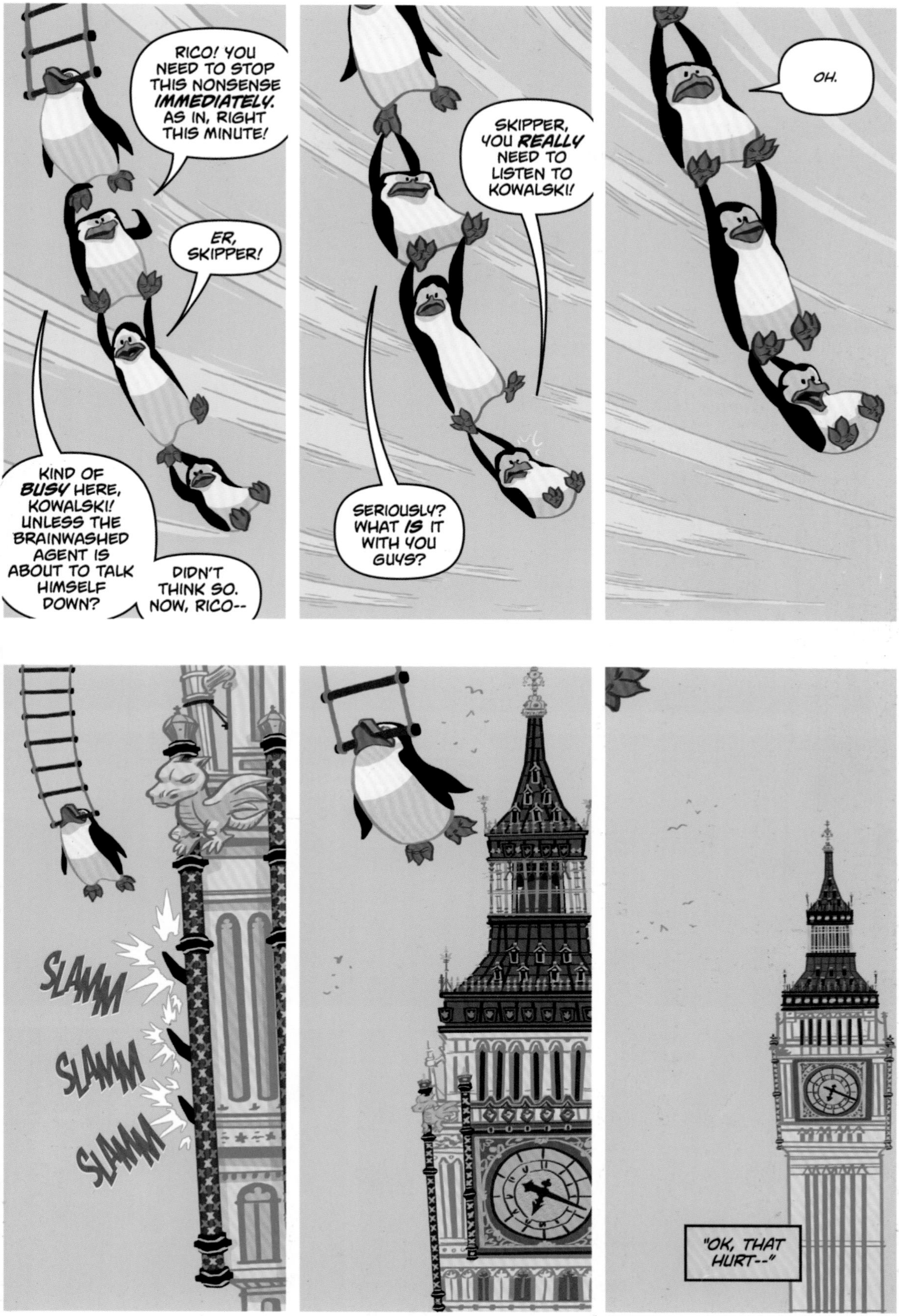
RICO! YOU NEED TO STOP THIS NONSENSE IMMEDIATELY. AS IN, RIGHT THIS MINUTE!
ER, SKIPPER!
KIND OF BUSY HERE, KOWALSKI! UNLESS THE BRAINWASHED AGENT IS ABOUT TO TALK HIMSELF DOWN?
DIDN'T THINK SO. NOW, RICO--
SKIPPER, YOU REALLY NEED TO LISTEN TO KOWALSKI!
SERIOUSLY? WHAT IS IT WITH YOU GUYS?
OH.
SLAMM
SLAMM
SLAMM
"OK, THAT HURT--"

"--BUT WE HAVE A ROGUE AGENT...

AND WE NEED TO BRING HIM HOME.

KOWALSKI? INTELLIGENCE.

HOPEFULLY INTACT AFTER THAT RATHER NASTY KNOCK ON THE HEAD. MAYBE A LITTLE *CONCUSSION* AT WORST.

OH, THAT'S NOT WHAT YOU MEAN, IS IT?

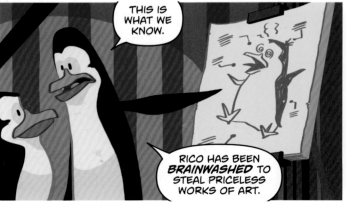

THIS IS WHAT WE KNOW.

RICO HAS BEEN *BRAINWASHED* TO STEAL PRICELESS WORKS OF ART.

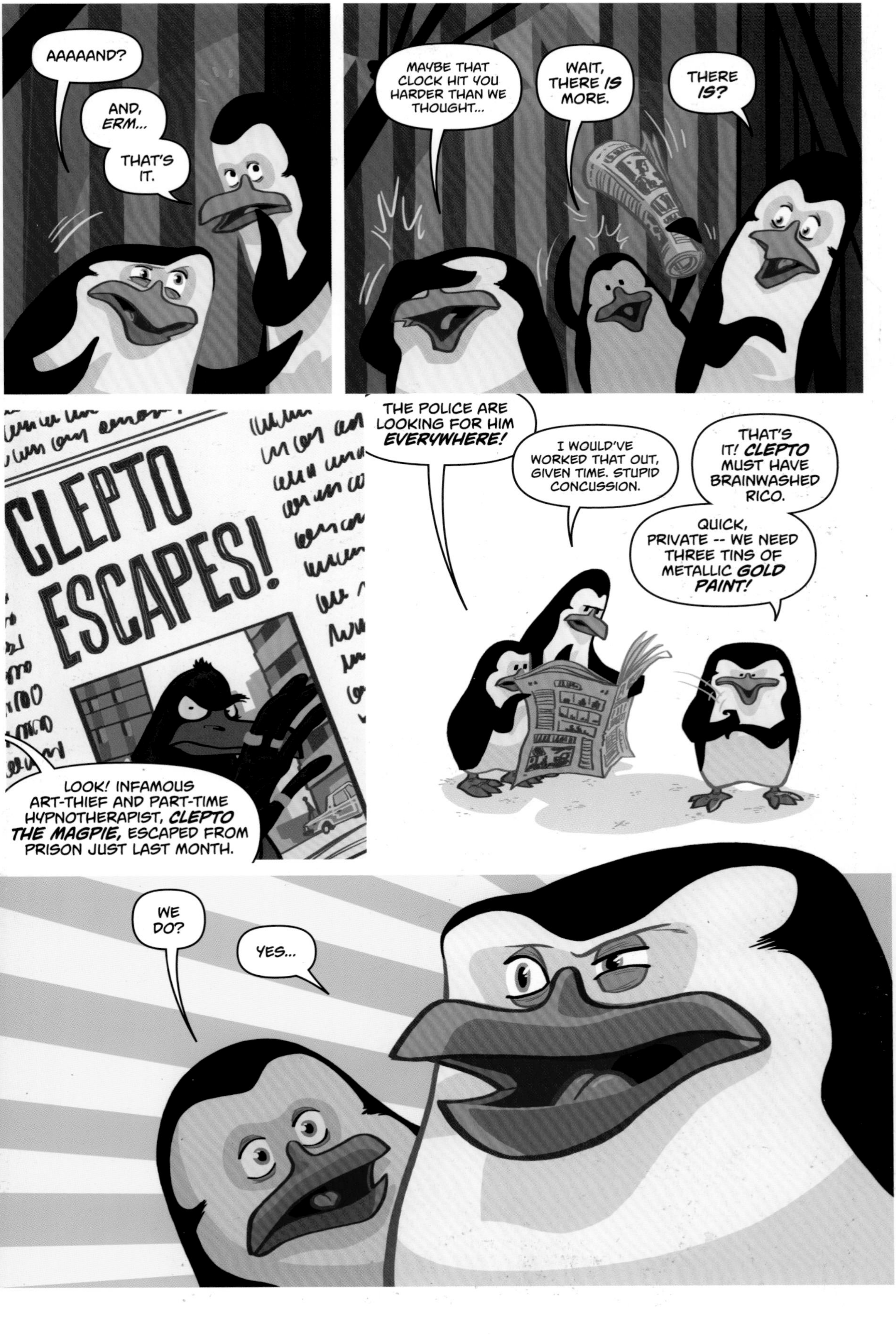
AAAAAND?
AND, ERM...
THAT'S IT.
MAYBE THAT CLOCK HIT YOU HARDER THAN WE THOUGHT...
WAIT, THERE *IS* MORE.
THERE *IS?*
CLEPTO ESCAPES!
LOOK! INFAMOUS ART-THIEF AND PART-TIME HYPNOTHERAPIST, *CLEPTO THE MAGPIE,* ESCAPED FROM PRISON JUST LAST MONTH.
THE POLICE ARE LOOKING FOR HIM *EVERYWHERE!*
I WOULD'VE WORKED THAT OUT, GIVEN TIME. STUPID CONCUSSION.
THAT'S IT! *CLEPTO* MUST HAVE BRAINWASHED RICO.
QUICK, PRIVATE -- WE NEED THREE TINS OF METALLIC *GOLD PAINT!*
WE DO?
YES...

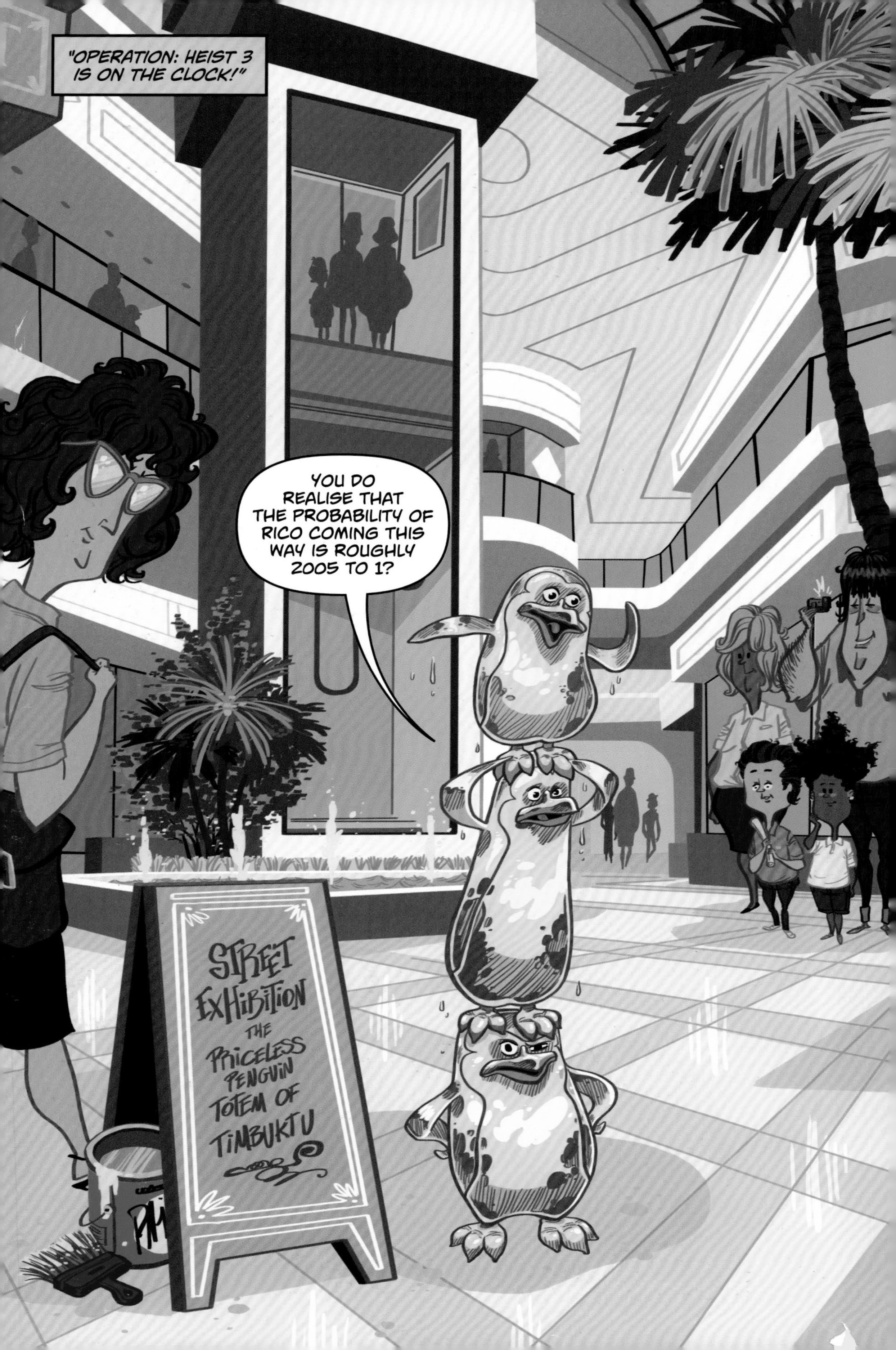
"OPERATION: HEIST 3 IS ON THE CLOCK!"
YOU DO REALISE THAT THE PROBABILITY OF RICO COMING THIS WAY IS ROUGHLY 2005 TO 1?
STREET EXHIBITION THE PRICELESS PENGUIN TOTEM OF TIMBUKTU

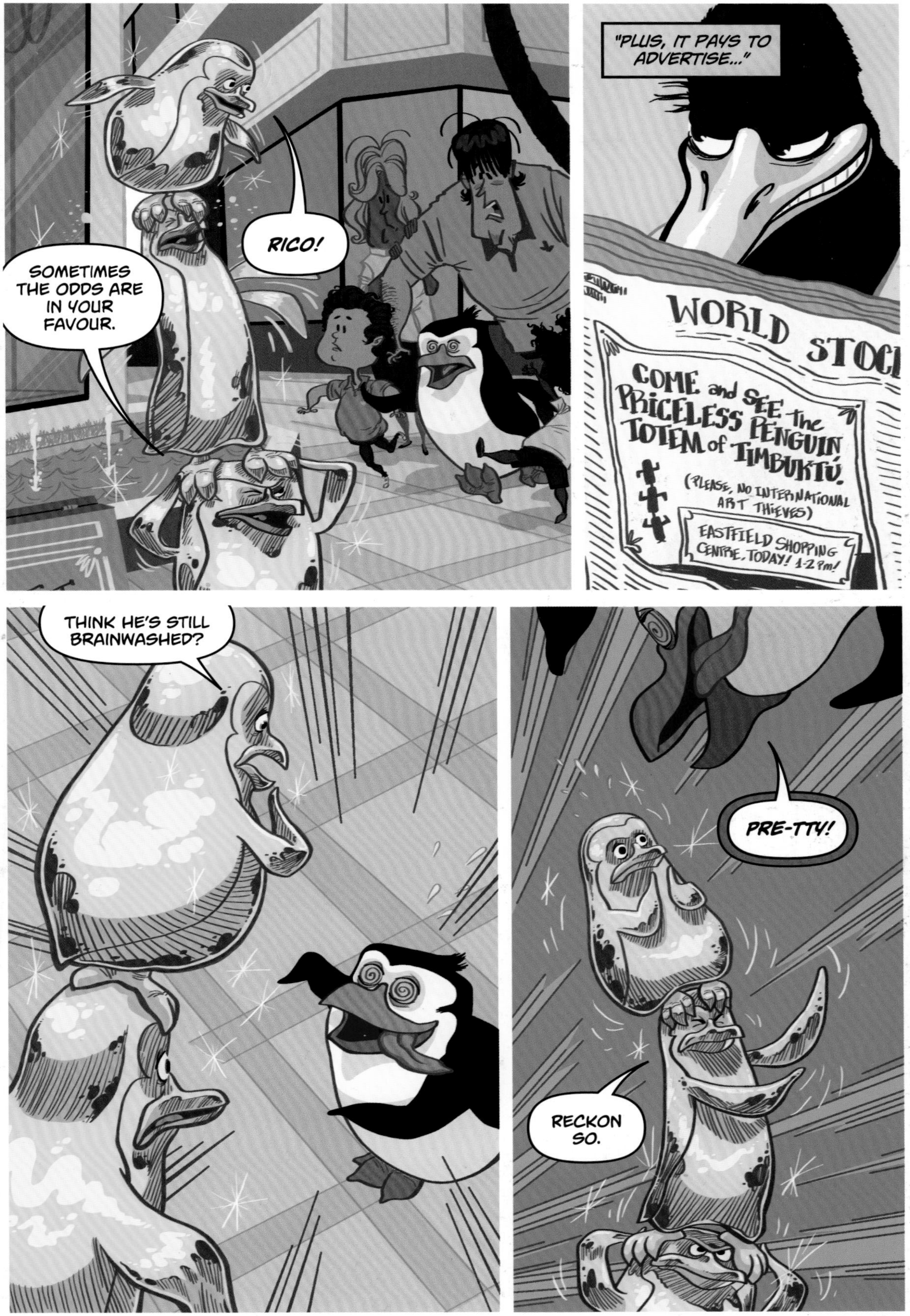
RICO!
SOMETIMES THE ODDS ARE IN YOUR FAVOUR.
"PLUS, IT PAYS TO ADVERTISE..."
WORLD STOC
COME and SEE the PRICELESS PENGUIN TOTEM of TIMBUKTÚ
(PLEASE, NO INTERNATIONAL ART THIEVES)
EASTFIELD SHOPPING CENTRE, TODAY! 1-2 PM!
THINK HE'S STILL BRAINWASHED?
PRE-TTY!
RECKON SO.

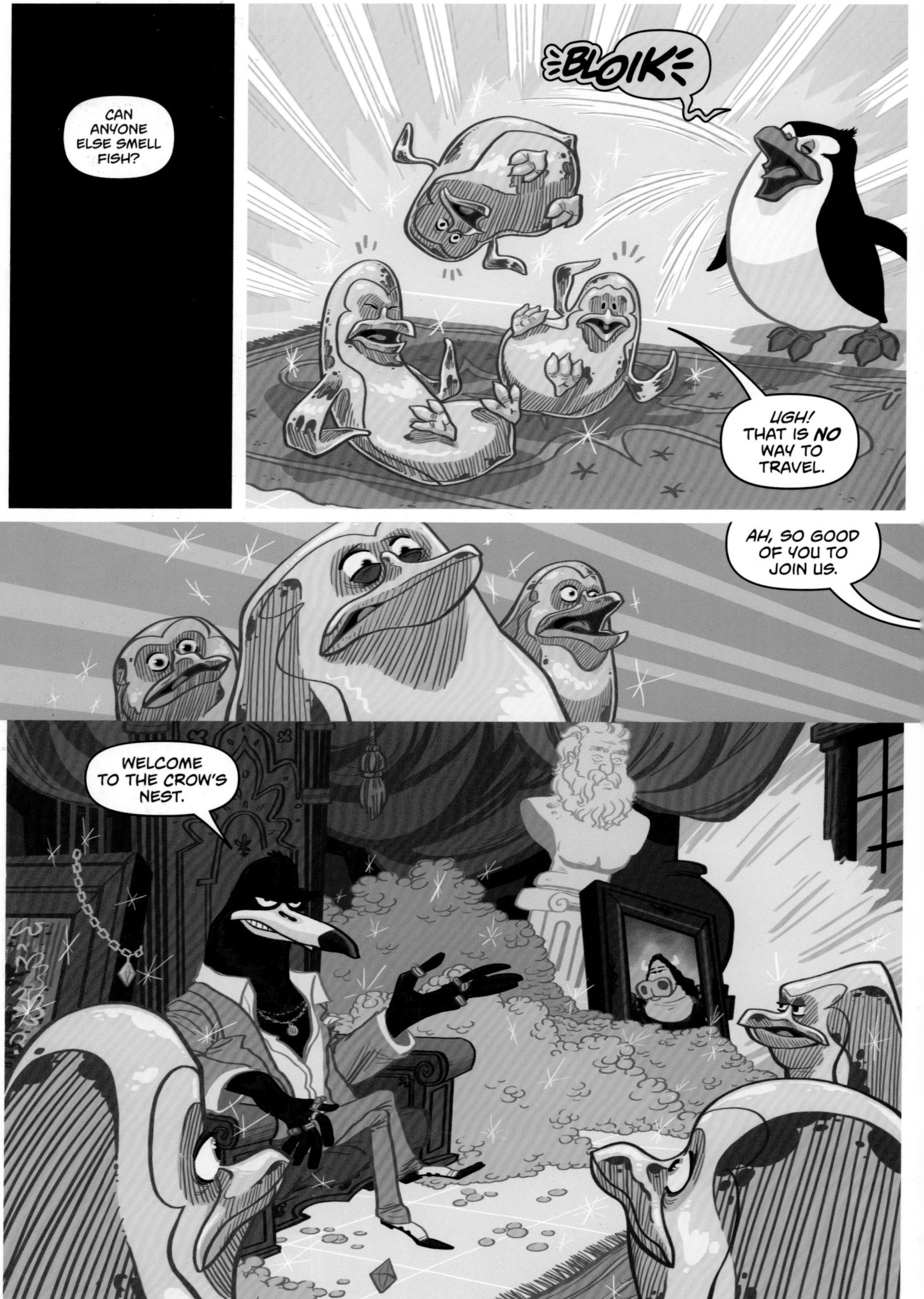
CAN ANYONE ELSE SMELL FISH?
BLOIK
UGH! THAT IS NO WAY TO TRAVEL.
AH, SO GOOD OF YOU TO JOIN US.
WELCOME TO THE CROW'S NEST.

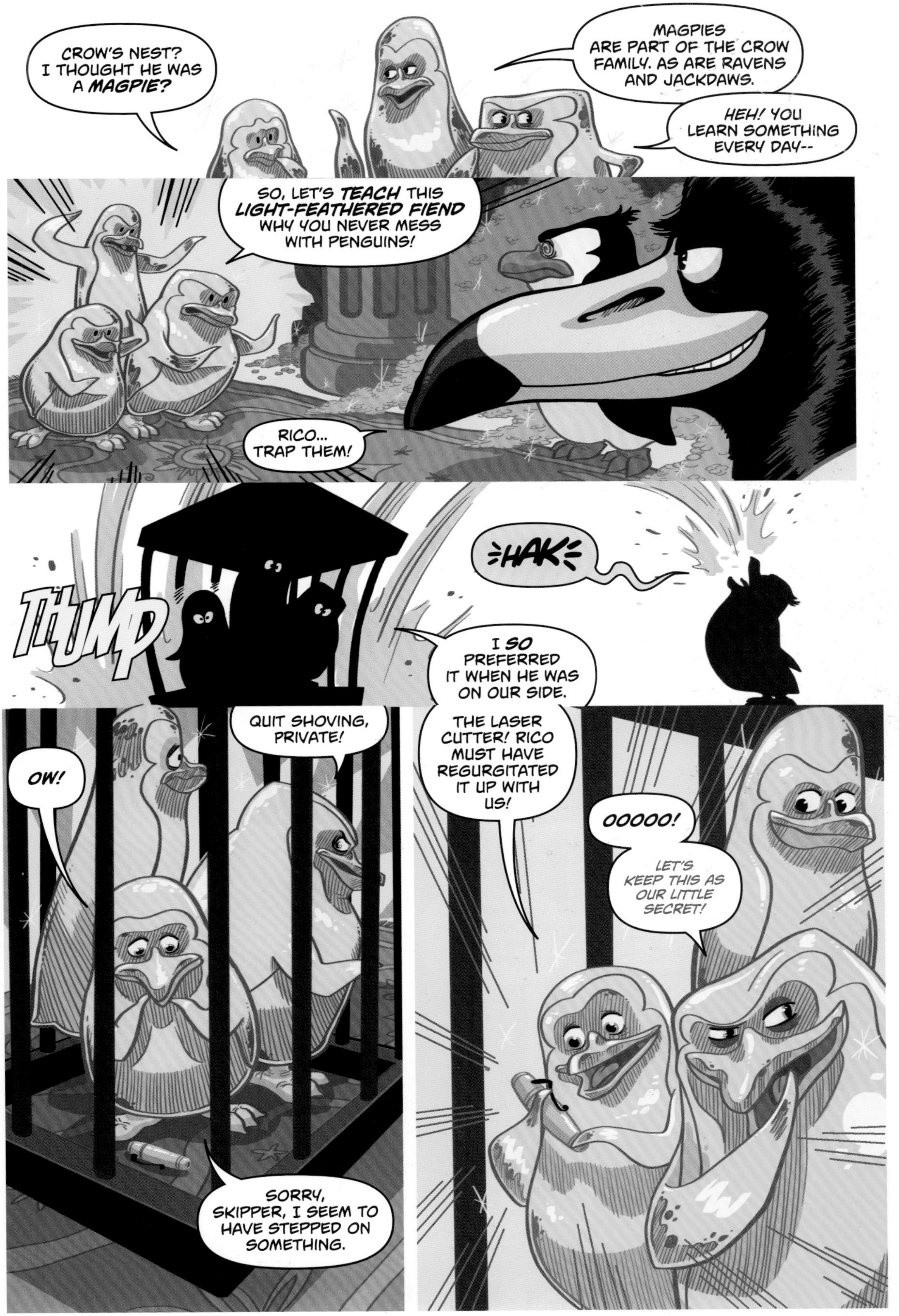
CROW'S NEST? I THOUGHT HE WAS A MAGPIE?
MAGPIES ARE PART OF THE CROW FAMILY. AS ARE RAVENS AND JACKDAWS.
HEH! YOU LEARN SOMETHING EVERY DAY--
SO, LET'S TEACH THIS LIGHT-FEATHERED FIEND WHY YOU NEVER MESS WITH PENGUINS!
RICO... TRAP THEM!
THUMP
HAK
I SO PREFERRED IT WHEN HE WAS ON OUR SIDE.
OW!
QUIT SHOVING, PRIVATE!
SORRY, SKIPPER, I SEEM TO HAVE STEPPED ON SOMETHING.
THE LASER CUTTER! RICO MUST HAVE REGURGITATED IT UP WITH US!
OOOOO!
LET'S KEEP THIS AS OUR LITTLE SECRET!

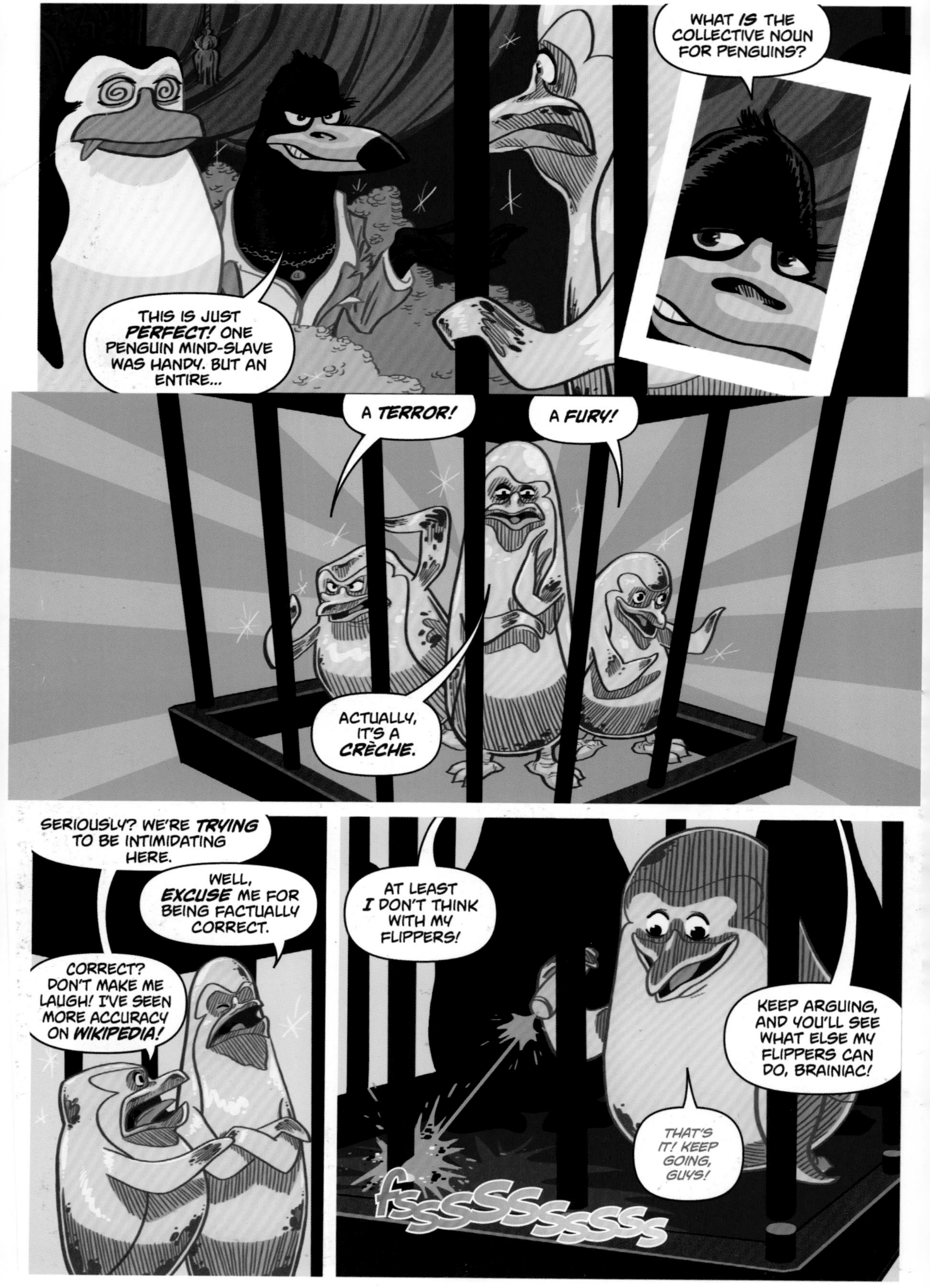
THIS IS JUST PERFECT! ONE PENGUIN MIND-SLAVE WAS HANDY. BUT AN ENTIRE...
WHAT IS THE COLLECTIVE NOUN FOR PENGUINS?
A TERROR!
A FURY!
ACTUALLY, IT'S A CRÈCHE.
SERIOUSLY? WE'RE TRYING TO BE INTIMIDATING HERE.
WELL, EXCUSE ME FOR BEING FACTUALLY CORRECT.
CORRECT? DON'T MAKE ME LAUGH! I'VE SEEN MORE ACCURACY ON WIKIPEDIA!
AT LEAST I DON'T THINK WITH MY FLIPPERS!
KEEP ARGUING, AND YOU'LL SEE WHAT ELSE MY FLIPPERS CAN DO, BRAINIAC!
THAT'S IT! KEEP GOING, GUYS!
fsssSSSsssss

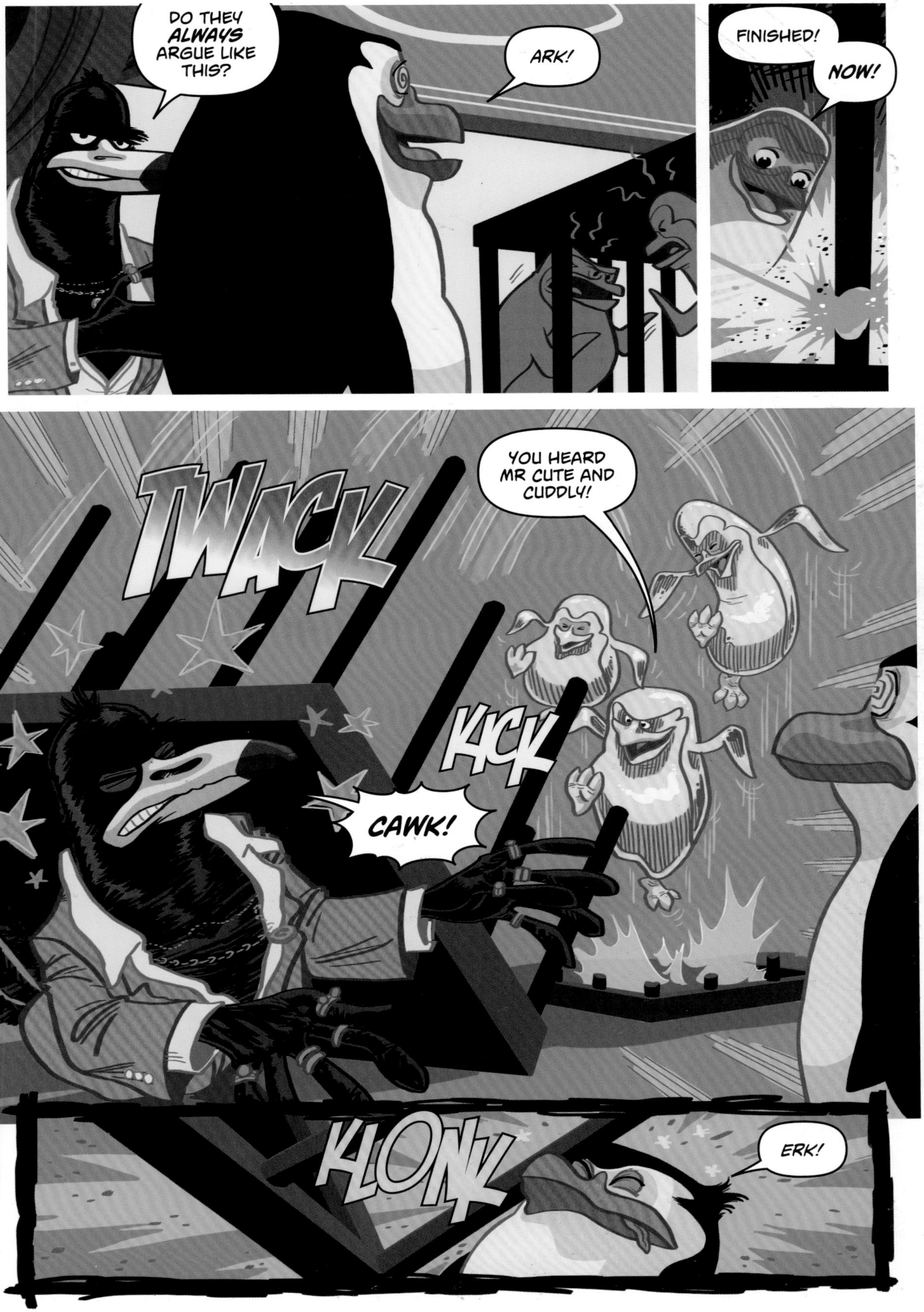
DO THEY ALWAYS ARGUE LIKE THIS?
ARK!
FINISHED!
NOW!
TWACK
YOU HEARD MR CUTE AND CUDDLY!
KICK
CAWK!
KLONK
ERK!

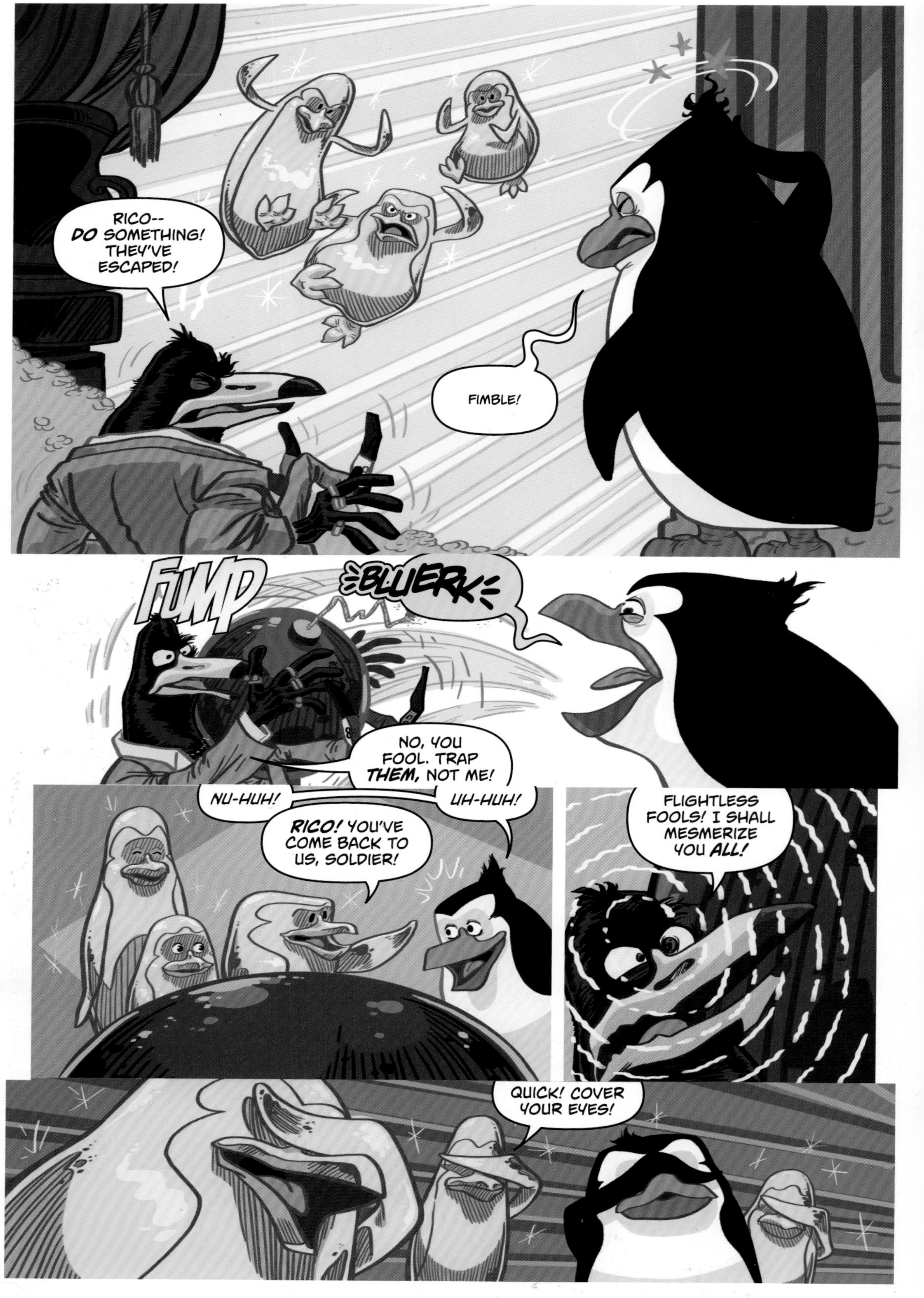
RICO-- DO SOMETHING! THEY'VE ESCAPED!
FIMBLE!
FUMP
BLUERK
NO, YOU FOOL. TRAP THEM, NOT ME!
NU-HUH!
UH-HUH!
RICO! YOU'VE COME BACK TO US, SOLDIER!
FLIGHTLESS FOOLS! I SHALL MESMERIZE YOU ALL!
QUICK! COVER YOUR EYES!

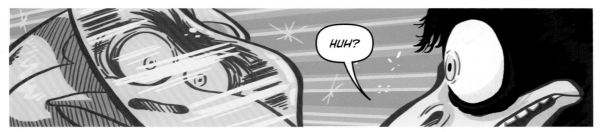

HUH?

PRE-TTY!

YES! HE HYPNOTIZED HIMSELF!

YOU MIGHT SAY THAT HE *REFLECTED BADLY* ON HIMSELF!

OR, MAYBE NOT...

NOW LISTEN, BIRDBRAIN. YOU'RE GOING TO *PERSONALLY* DELIVER ALL OF THESE TREASURES BACK TO WHERE THEY BELONG.

YEAH, AND THEN GIVE YOURSELF UP TO THE POLICE, RIGHT?

RII-IGHT...

MISSION ACCOMPLISHED! LET'S BLOW THIS JOINT!

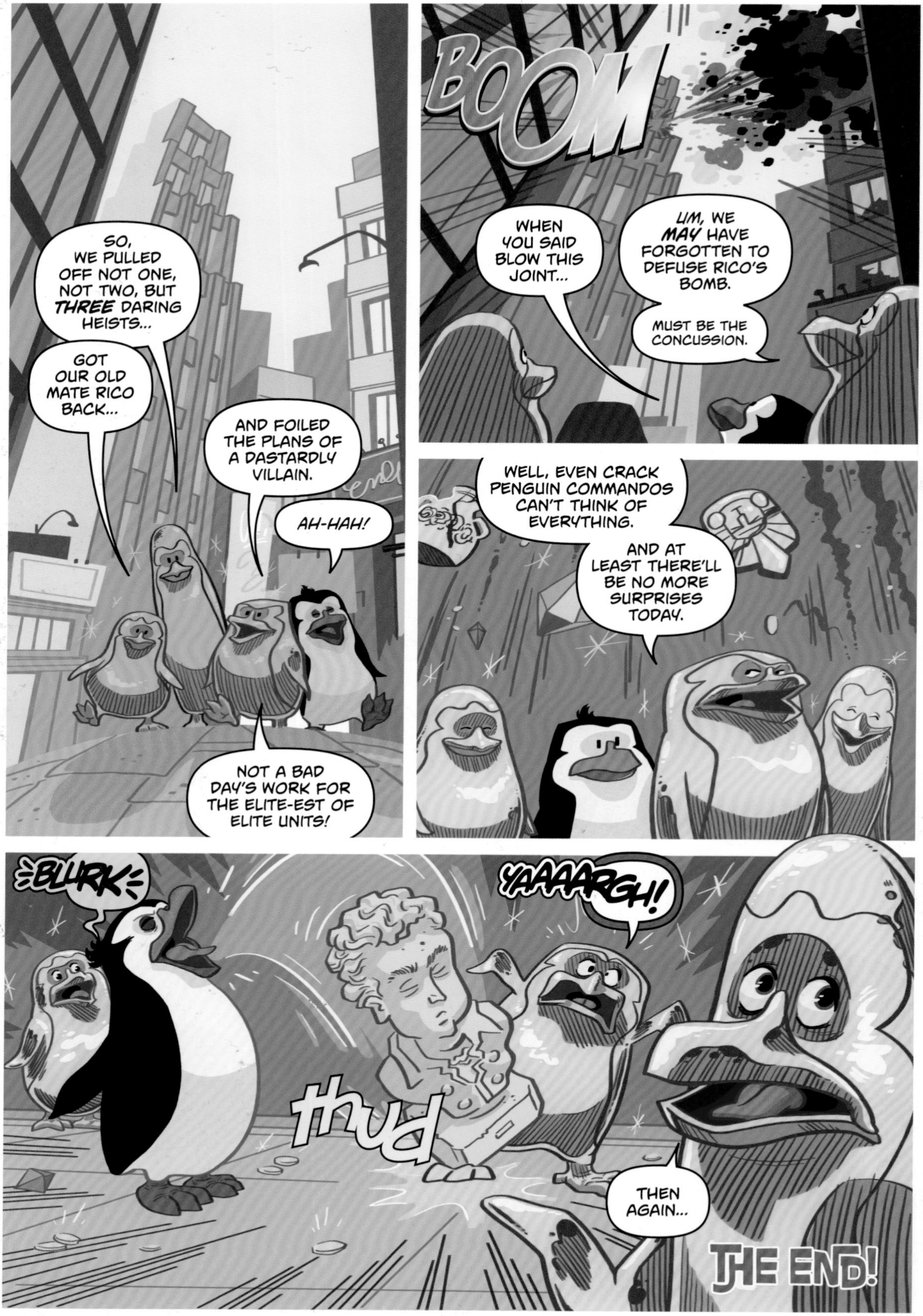
SO, WE PULLED OFF NOT ONE, NOT TWO, BUT THREE DARING HEISTS...
GOT OUR OLD MATE RICO BACK...
AND FOILED THE PLANS OF A DASTARDLY VILLAIN.
AH-HAH!
NOT A BAD DAY'S WORK FOR THE ELITE-EST OF ELITE UNITS!
BOOM
WHEN YOU SAID BLOW THIS JOINT...
UM, WE MAY HAVE FORGOTTEN TO DEFUSE RICO'S BOMB.
MUST BE THE CONCUSSION.
WELL, EVEN CRACK PENGUIN COMMANDOS CAN'T THINK OF EVERYTHING.
AND AT LEAST THERE'LL BE NO MORE SURPRISES TODAY.
BLURK
YAAAARGH!
thud
THEN AGAIN...
THE END!

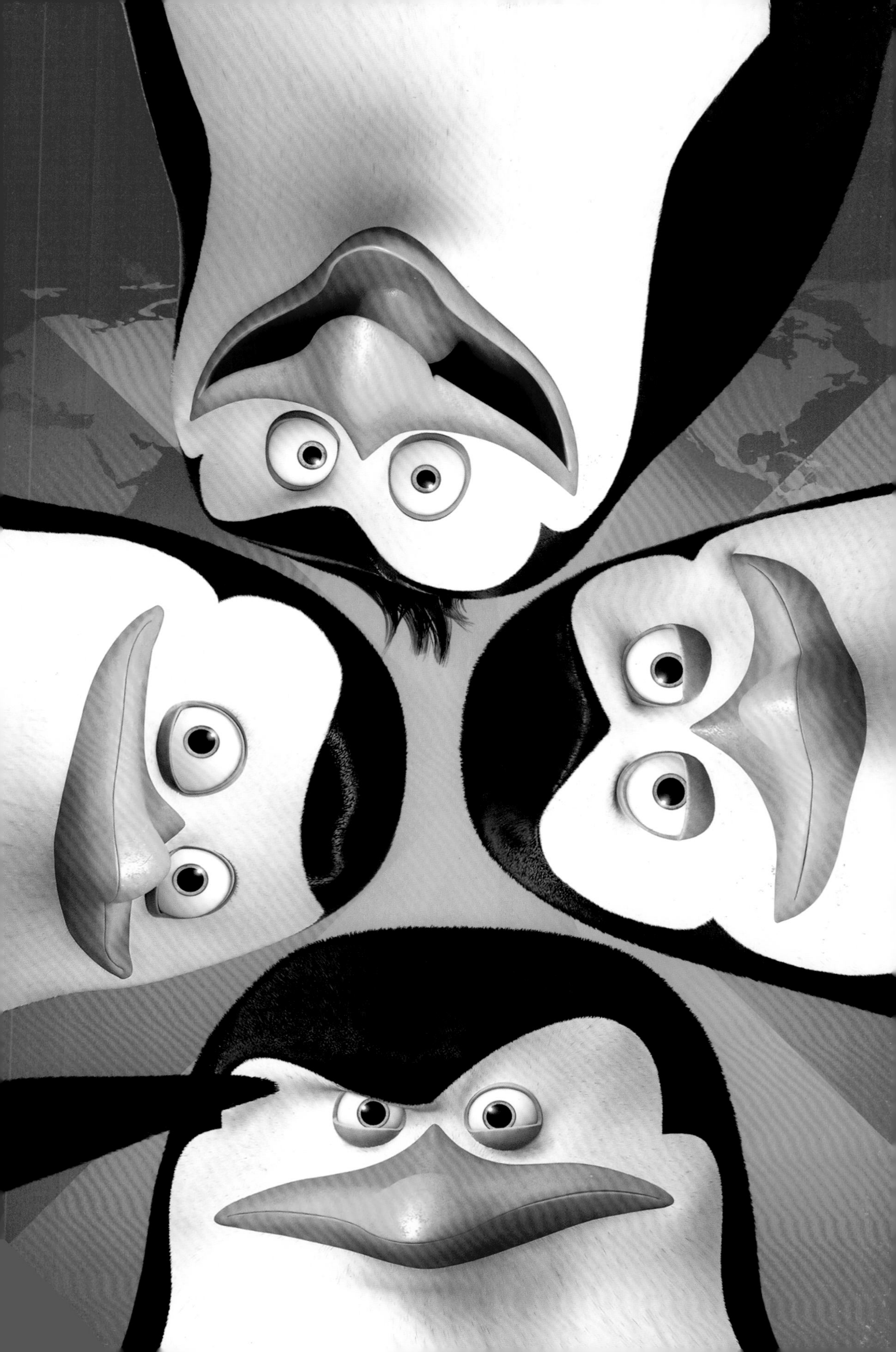

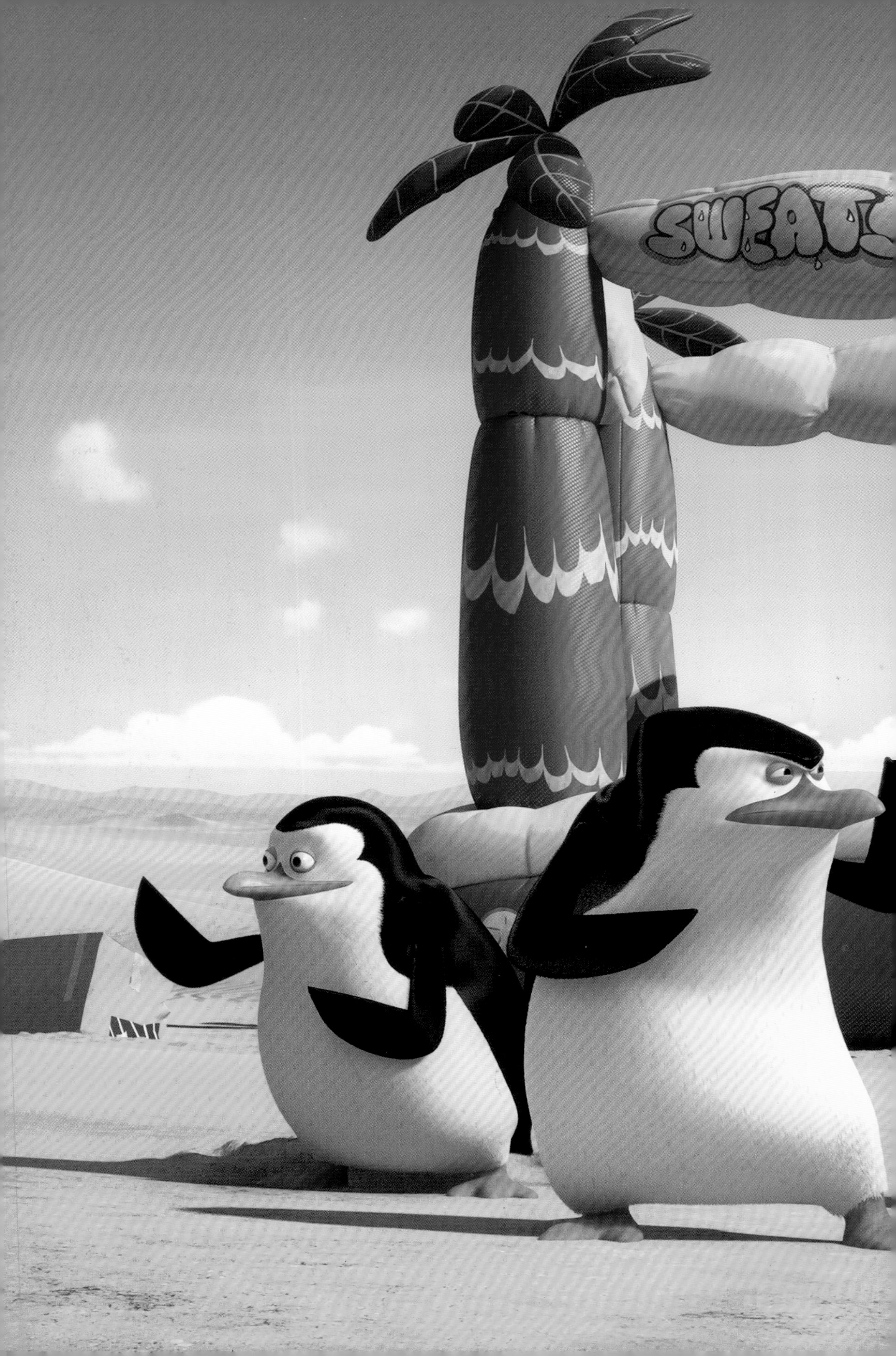

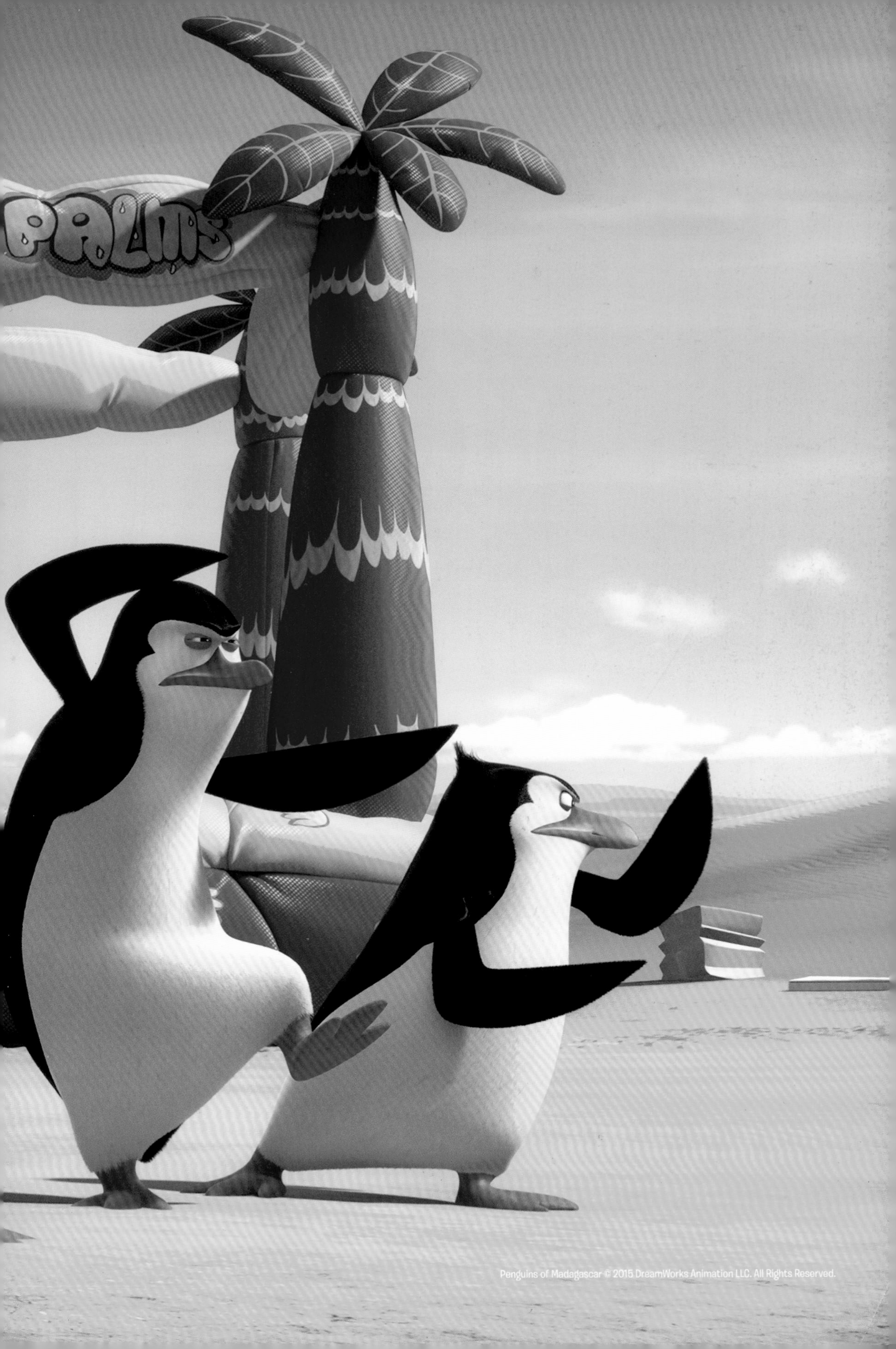
PALMS

BIG TOP

SCRIPT
Jim Alexander

ART
Egle Bartolini

COLORS
M.L. Sanapo

LETTERING
Jim Campbell

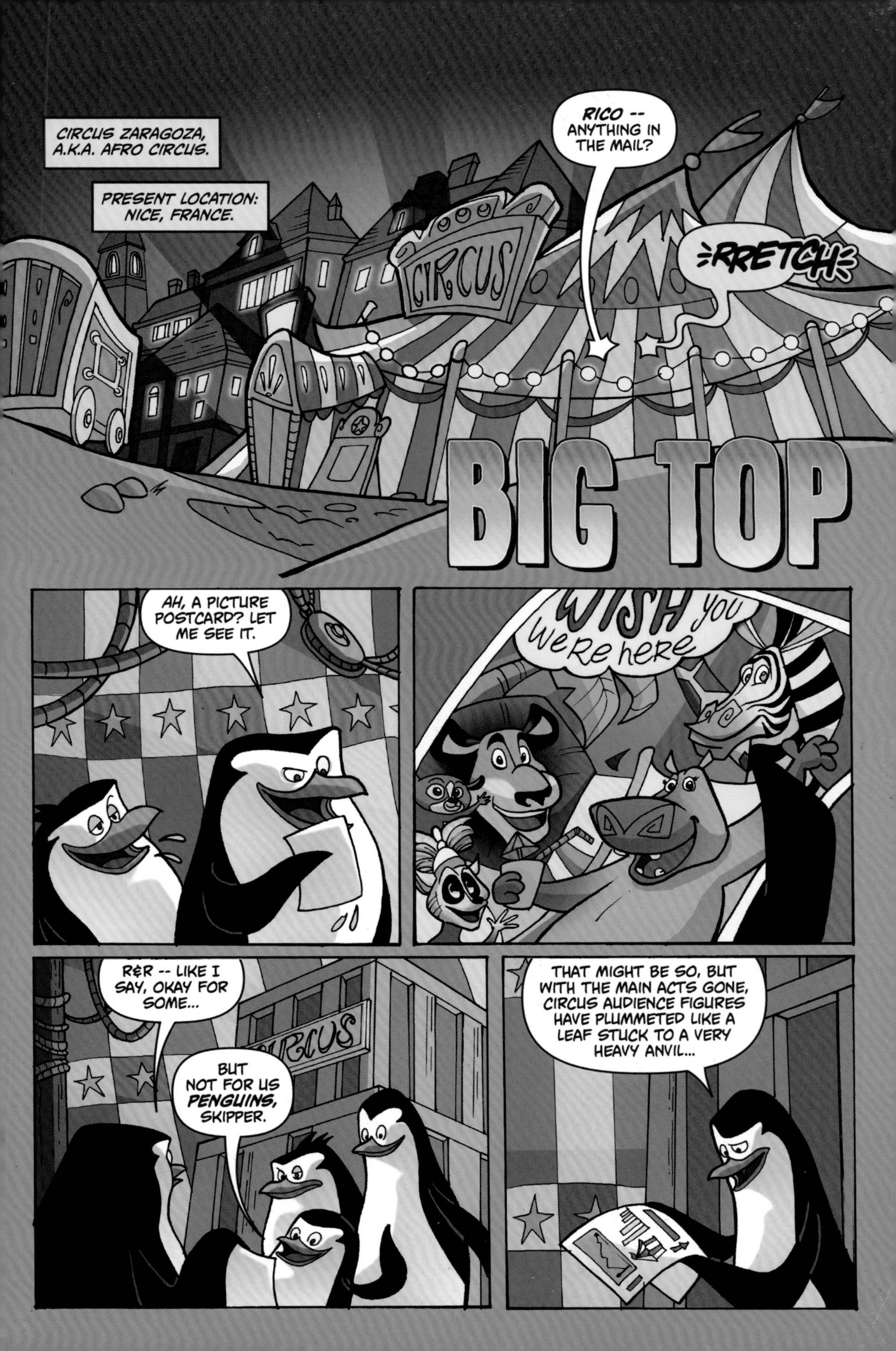
CIRCUS ZARAGOZA, A.K.A. AFRO CIRCUS.
PRESENT LOCATION: NICE, FRANCE.
RICO -- ANYTHING IN THE MAIL?
RRETCH
CIRCUS
BIG TOP
AH, A PICTURE POSTCARD? LET ME SEE IT.
WISH you were here
R&R -- LIKE I SAY, OKAY FOR SOME...
BUT NOT FOR US PENGUINS, SKIPPER.
THAT MIGHT BE SO, BUT WITH THE MAIN ACTS GONE, CIRCUS AUDIENCE FIGURES HAVE PLUMMETED LIKE A LEAF STUCK TO A VERY HEAVY ANVIL...

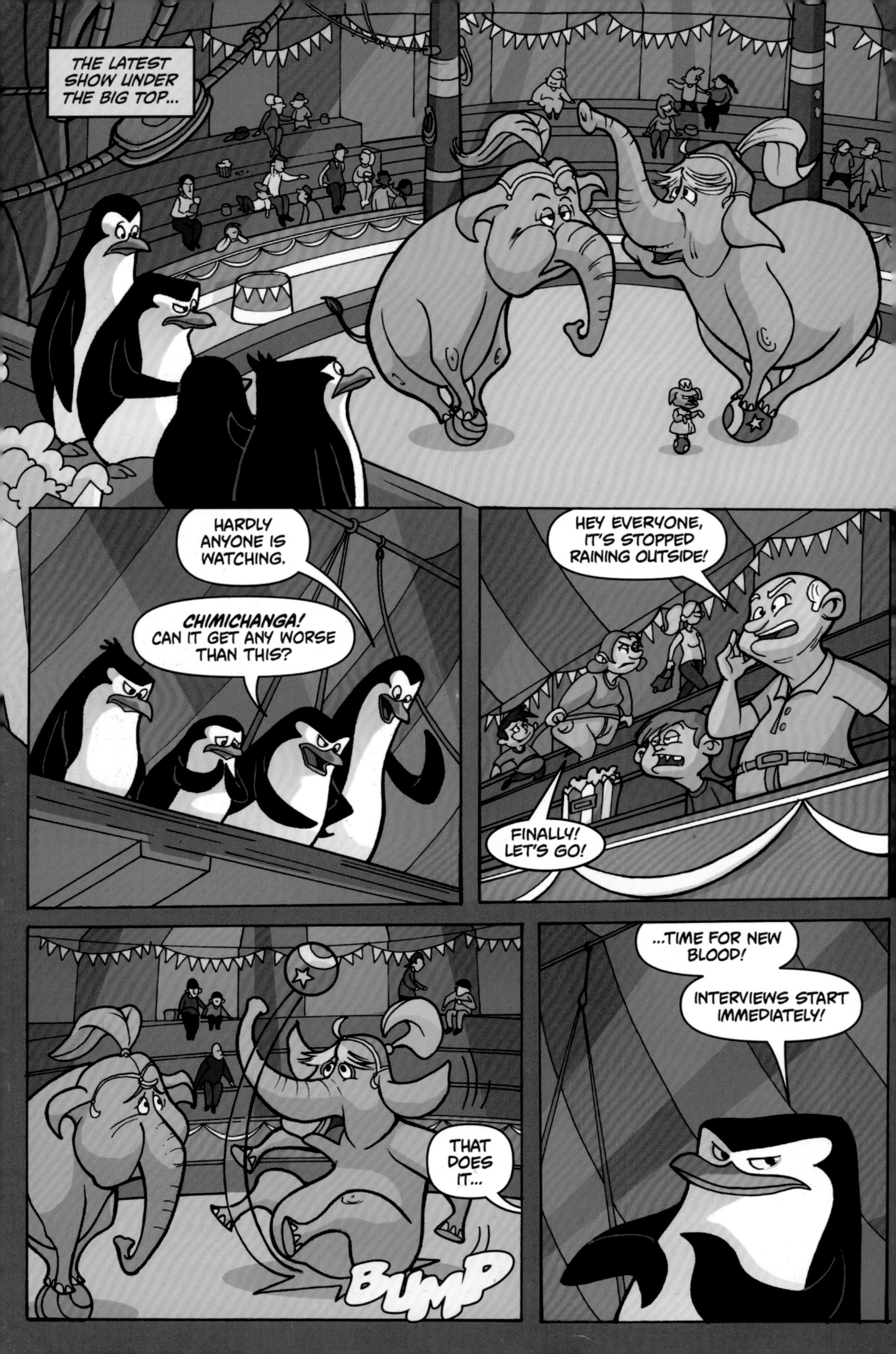
THE LATEST SHOW UNDER THE BIG TOP...
HARDLY ANYONE IS WATCHING.
CHIMICHANGA! CAN IT GET ANY WORSE THAN THIS?
HEY EVERYONE, IT'S STOPPED RAINING OUTSIDE!
FINALLY! LET'S GO!
THAT DOES IT...
BUMP
...TIME FOR NEW BLOOD!
INTERVIEWS START IMMEDIATELY!

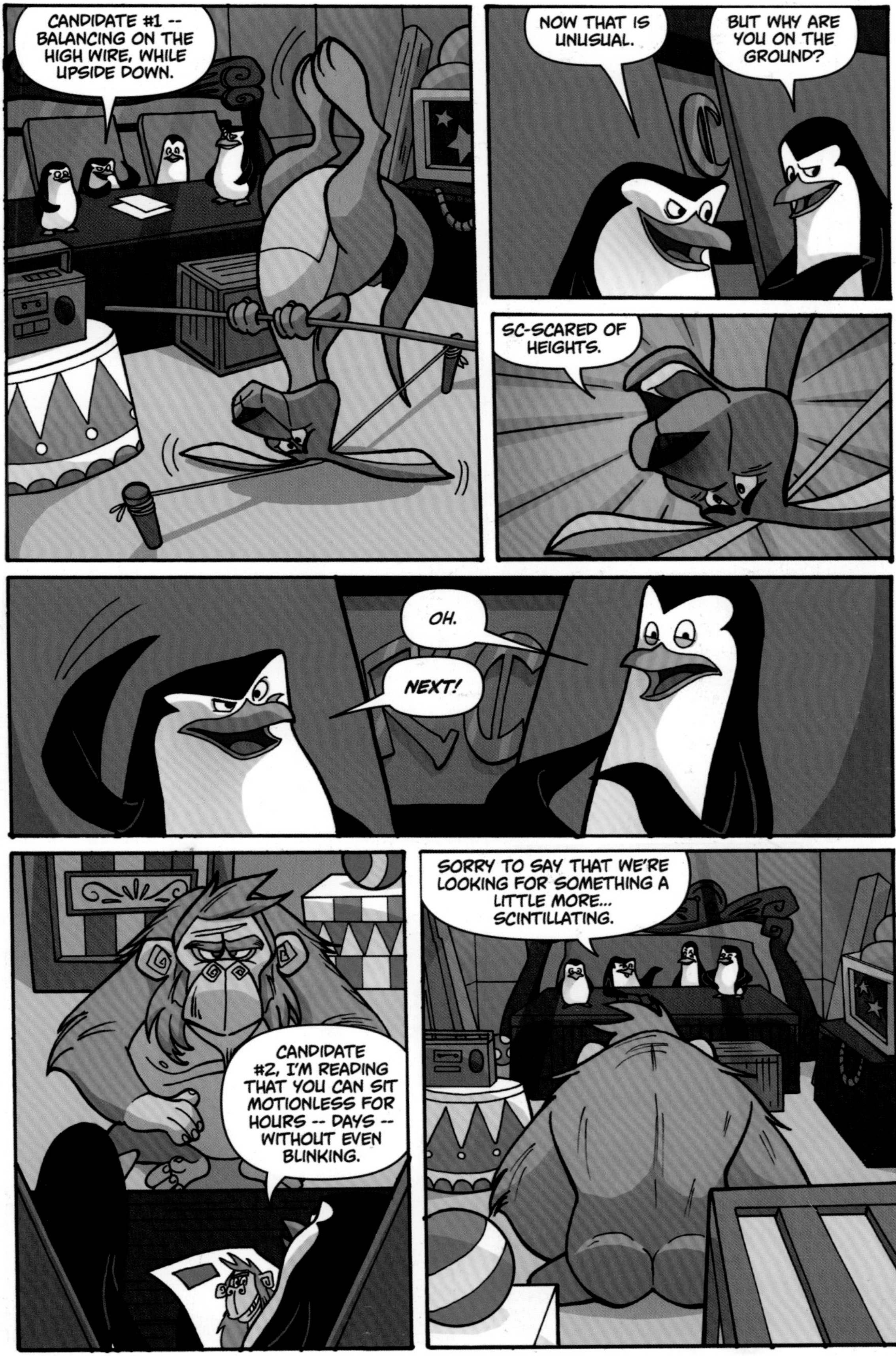
CANDIDATE #1 -- BALANCING ON THE HIGH WIRE, WHILE UPSIDE DOWN.
NOW THAT IS UNUSUAL.
BUT WHY ARE YOU ON THE GROUND?
SC-SCARED OF HEIGHTS.
OH.
NEXT!
CANDIDATE #2, I'M READING THAT YOU CAN SIT MOTIONLESS FOR HOURS -- DAYS -- WITHOUT EVEN BLINKING.
SORRY TO SAY THAT WE'RE LOOKING FOR SOMETHING A LITTLE MORE... SCINTILLATING.

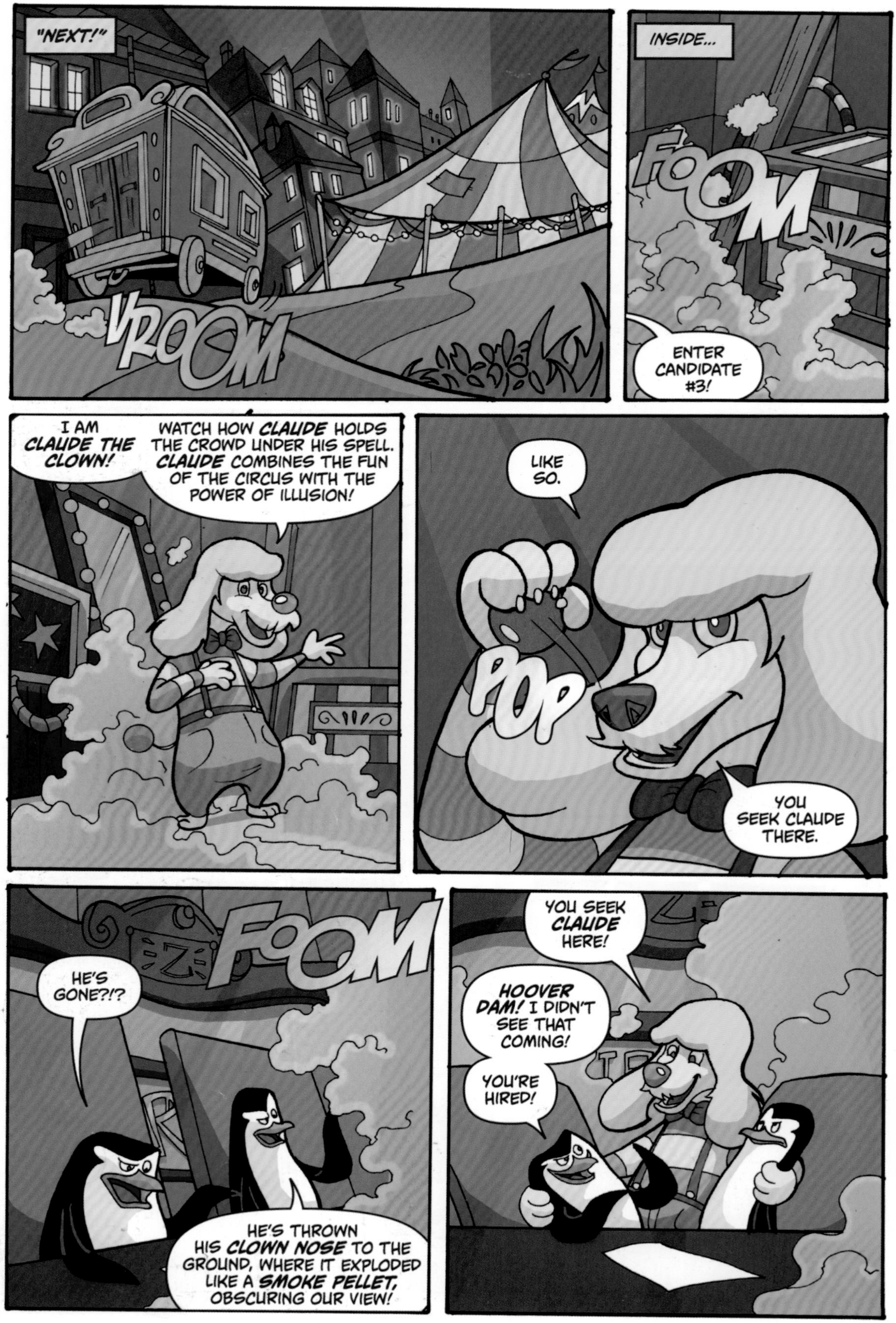
"NEXT!"
VROOM
INSIDE...
FOOM
ENTER CANDIDATE #3!
I AM CLAUDE THE CLOWN!
WATCH HOW CLAUDE HOLDS THE CROWD UNDER HIS SPELL. CLAUDE COMBINES THE FUN OF THE CIRCUS WITH THE POWER OF ILLUSION!
LIKE SO.
POP
YOU SEEK CLAUDE THERE.
FOOM
HE'S GONE?!?
HE'S THROWN HIS CLOWN NOSE TO THE GROUND, WHERE IT EXPLODED LIKE A SMOKE PELLET, OBSCURING OUR VIEW!
YOU SEEK CLAUDE HERE!
HOOVER DAM! I DIDN'T SEE THAT COMING!
YOU'RE HIRED!

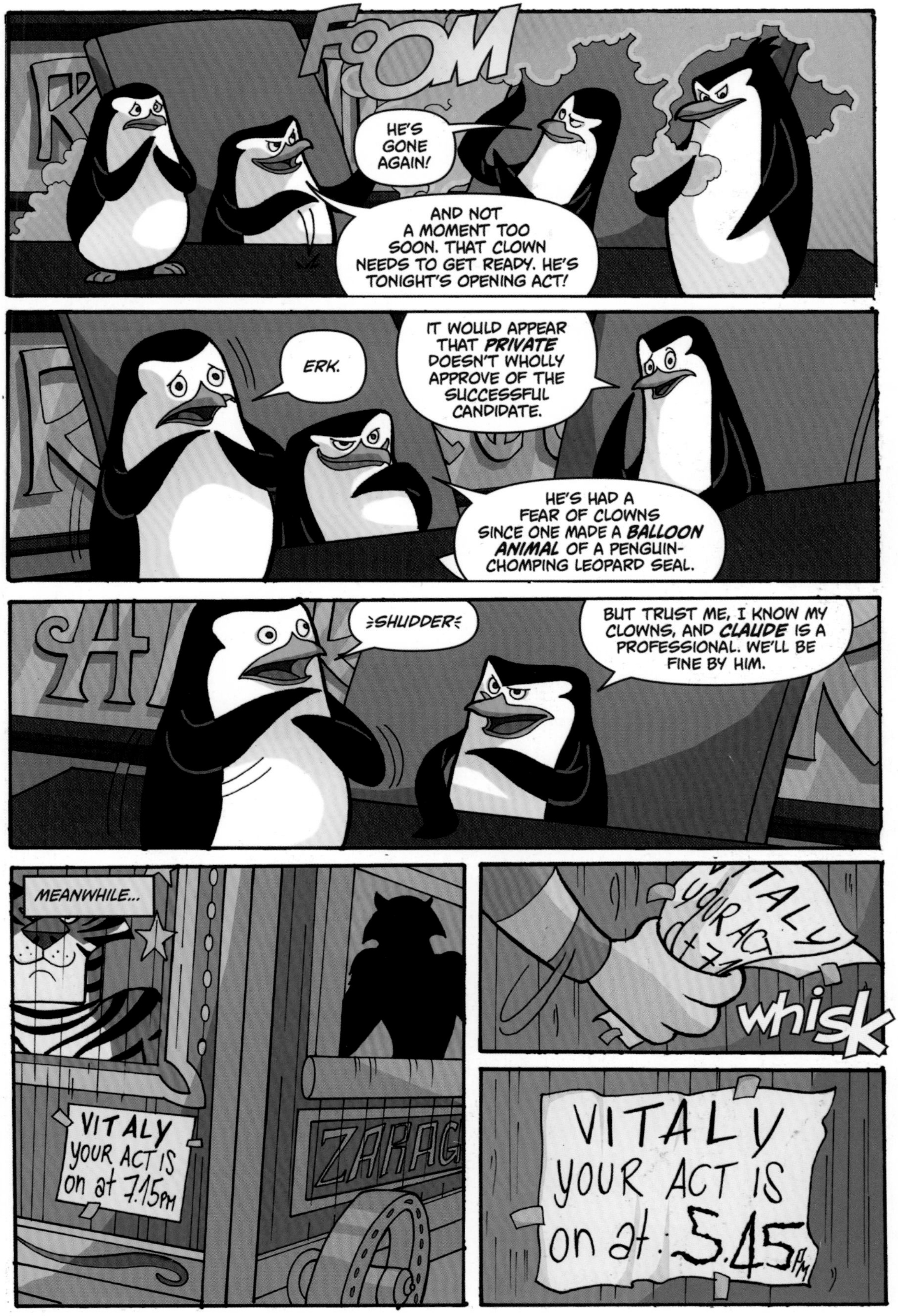
FOOM
HE'S GONE AGAIN!
AND NOT A MOMENT TOO SOON. THAT CLOWN NEEDS TO GET READY. HE'S TONIGHT'S OPENING ACT!
ERK.
IT WOULD APPEAR THAT *PRIVATE* DOESN'T WHOLLY APPROVE OF THE SUCCESSFUL CANDIDATE.
HE'S HAD A FEAR OF CLOWNS SINCE ONE MADE A *BALLOON ANIMAL* OF A PENGUIN-CHOMPING LEOPARD SEAL.
SHUDDER
BUT TRUST ME, I KNOW MY CLOWNS, AND *CLAUDE* IS A PROFESSIONAL. WE'LL BE FINE BY HIM.
MEANWHILE...
VITALY YOUR ACT IS on at 7.15PM
whisk
VITALY YOUR ACT IS on at 5.45PM

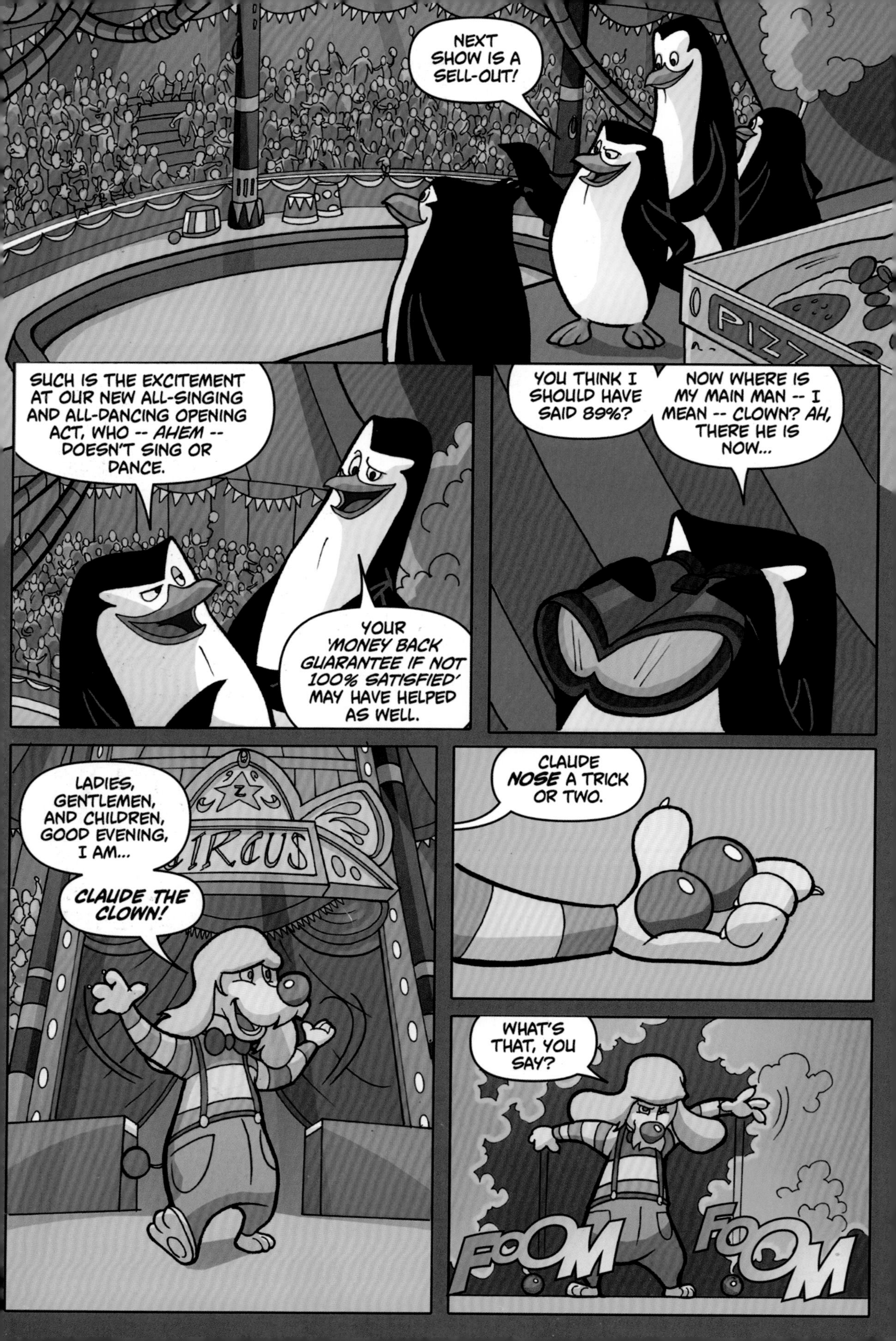
NEXT SHOW IS A SELL-OUT!
SUCH IS THE EXCITEMENT AT OUR NEW ALL-SINGING AND ALL-DANCING OPENING ACT, WHO -- *AHEM* -- DOESN'T SING OR DANCE.
YOUR *'MONEY BACK GUARANTEE IF NOT 100% SATISFIED'* MAY HAVE HELPED AS WELL.
YOU THINK I SHOULD HAVE SAID 89%?
NOW WHERE IS MY MAIN MAN -- I MEAN -- CLOWN? *AH,* THERE HE IS NOW...
LADIES, GENTLEMEN, AND CHILDREN, GOOD EVENING, I AM...
CLAUDE THE CLOWN!
CIRCUS
CLAUDE ***NOSE*** A TRICK OR TWO.
WHAT'S THAT, YOU SAY?
FOOM
FOOM

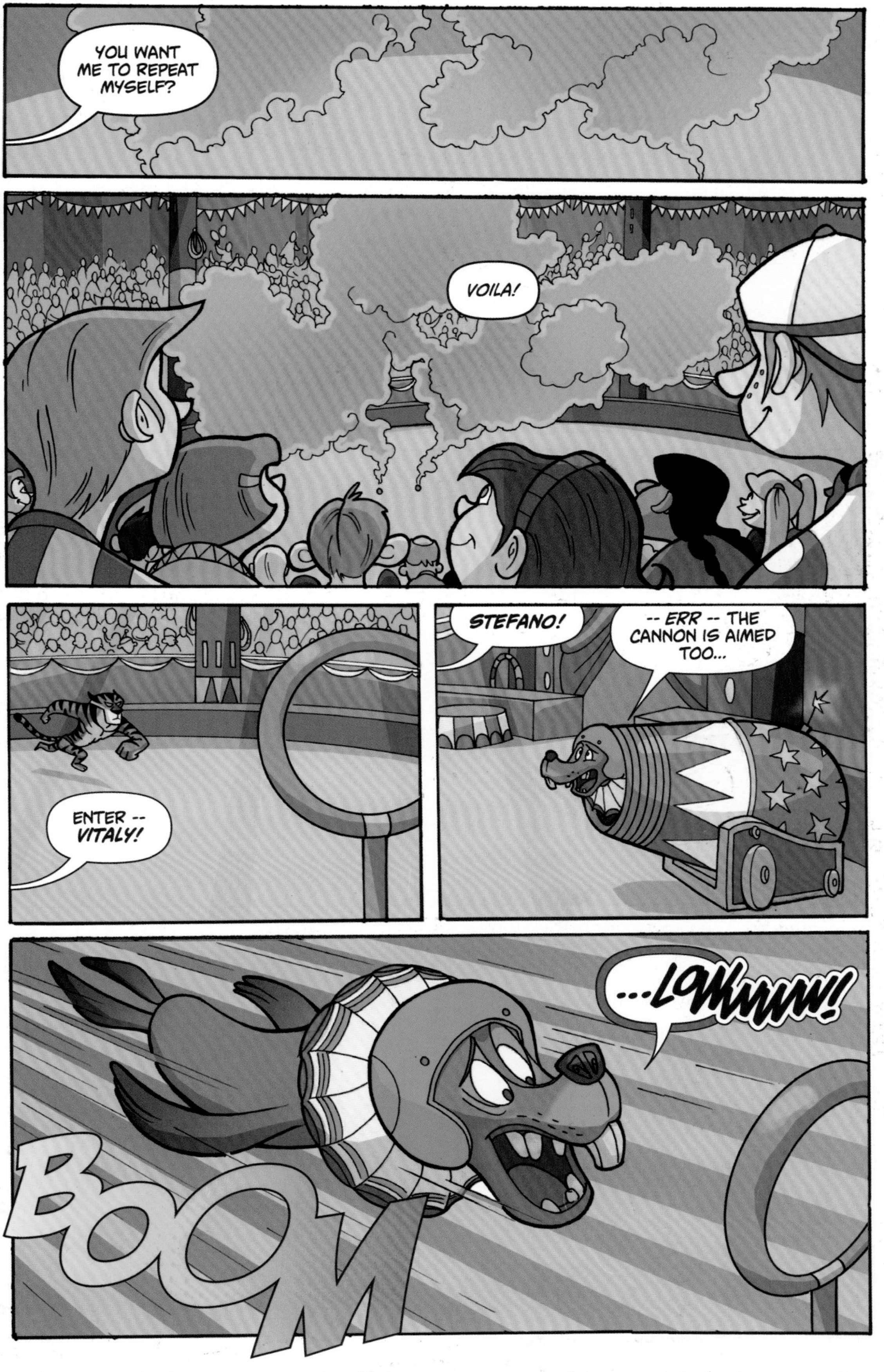
YOU WANT ME TO REPEAT MYSELF?
VOILA!
ENTER -- VITALY!
STEFANO!
-- ERR -- THE CANNON IS AIMED TOO...
...LOWWWW!
BOOM

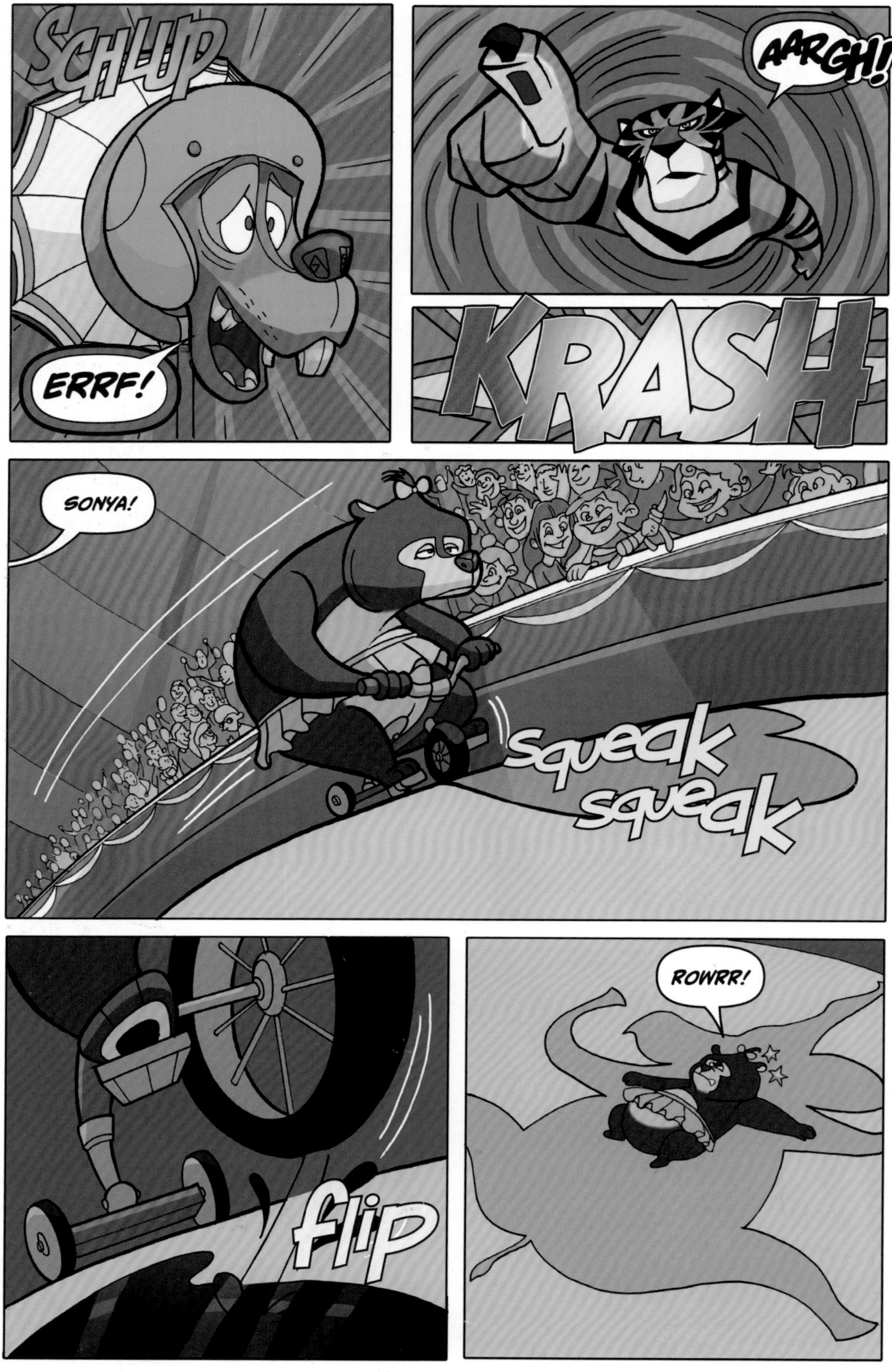
SCHLUP
ERRF!
AARGH!
KRASH
SONYA!
squeak
squeak
flip
ROWRR!

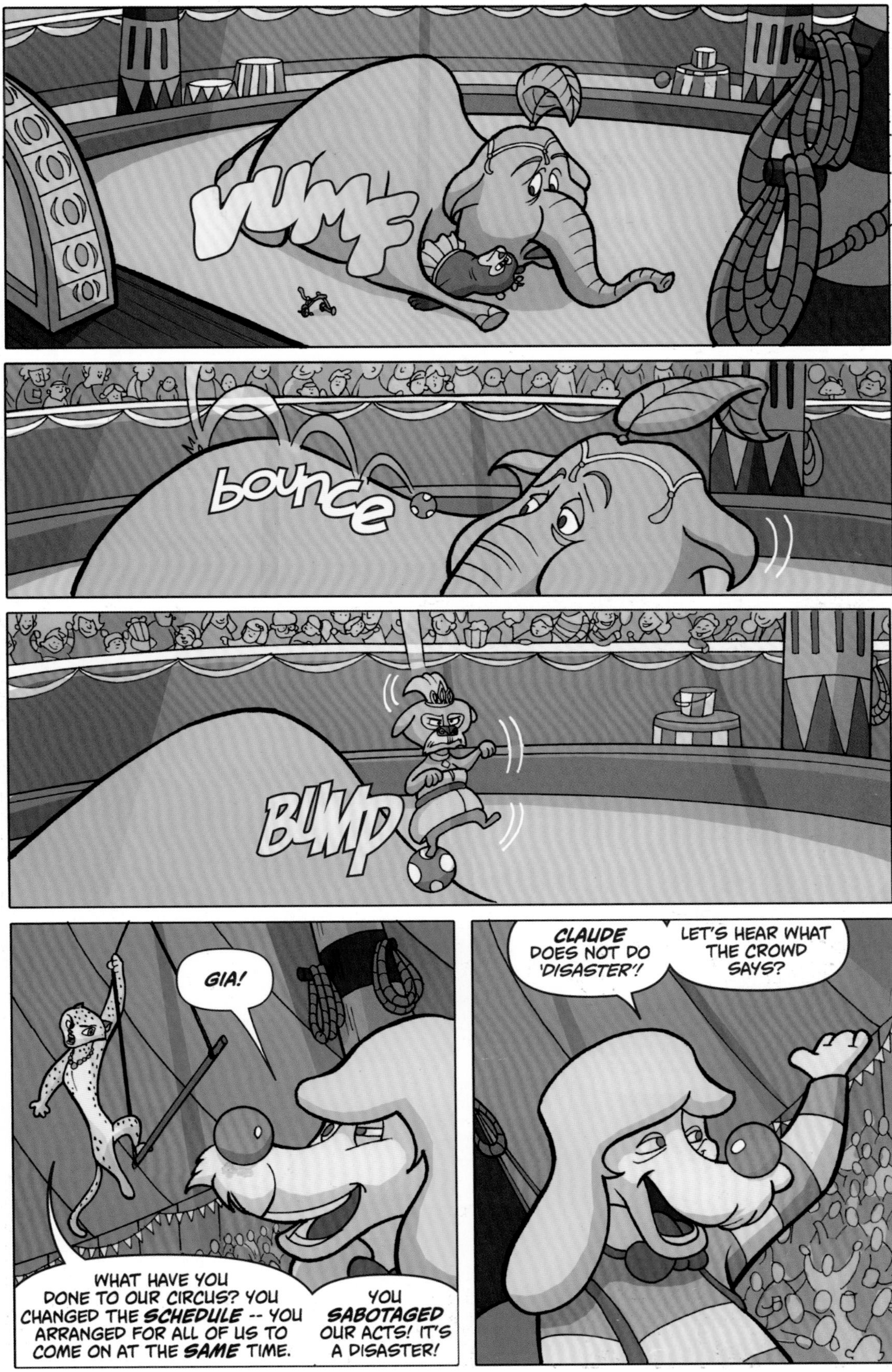
VUMF
bounce
BUMP
GIA!
WHAT HAVE YOU DONE TO OUR CIRCUS? YOU CHANGED THE **SCHEDULE** -- YOU ARRANGED FOR ALL OF US TO COME ON AT THE **SAME** TIME.
YOU **SABOTAGED** OUR ACTS! IT'S A DISASTER!
CLAUDE DOES NOT DO 'DISASTER'!
LET'S HEAR WHAT THE CROWD SAYS?

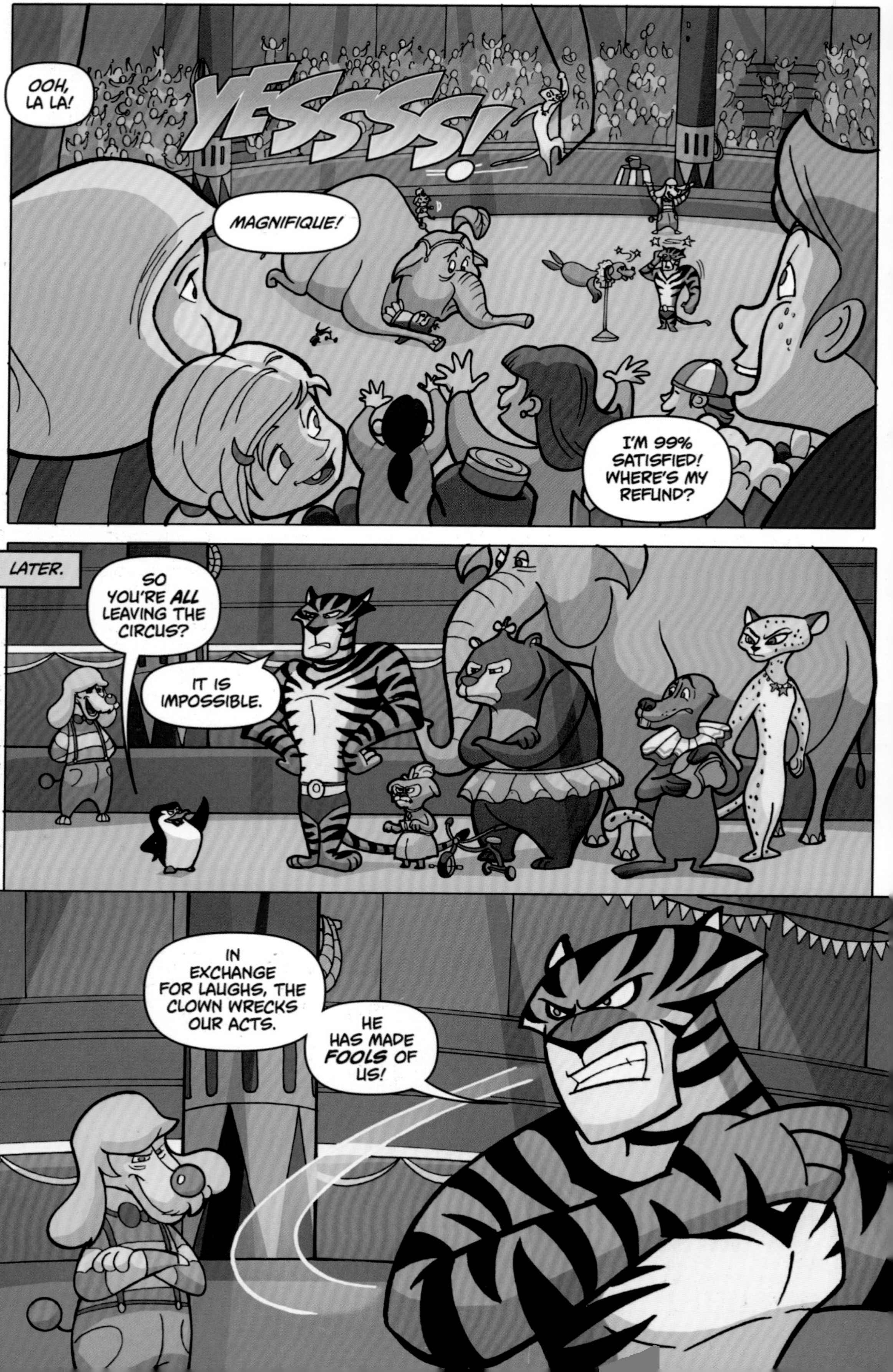
OOH, LA LA!
YESSSS!
MAGNIFIQUE!
I'M 99% SATISFIED! WHERE'S MY REFUND?
LATER.
SO YOU'RE ALL LEAVING THE CIRCUS?
IT IS IMPOSSIBLE.
IN EXCHANGE FOR LAUGHS, THE CLOWN WRECKS OUR ACTS.
HE HAS MADE FOOLS OF US!

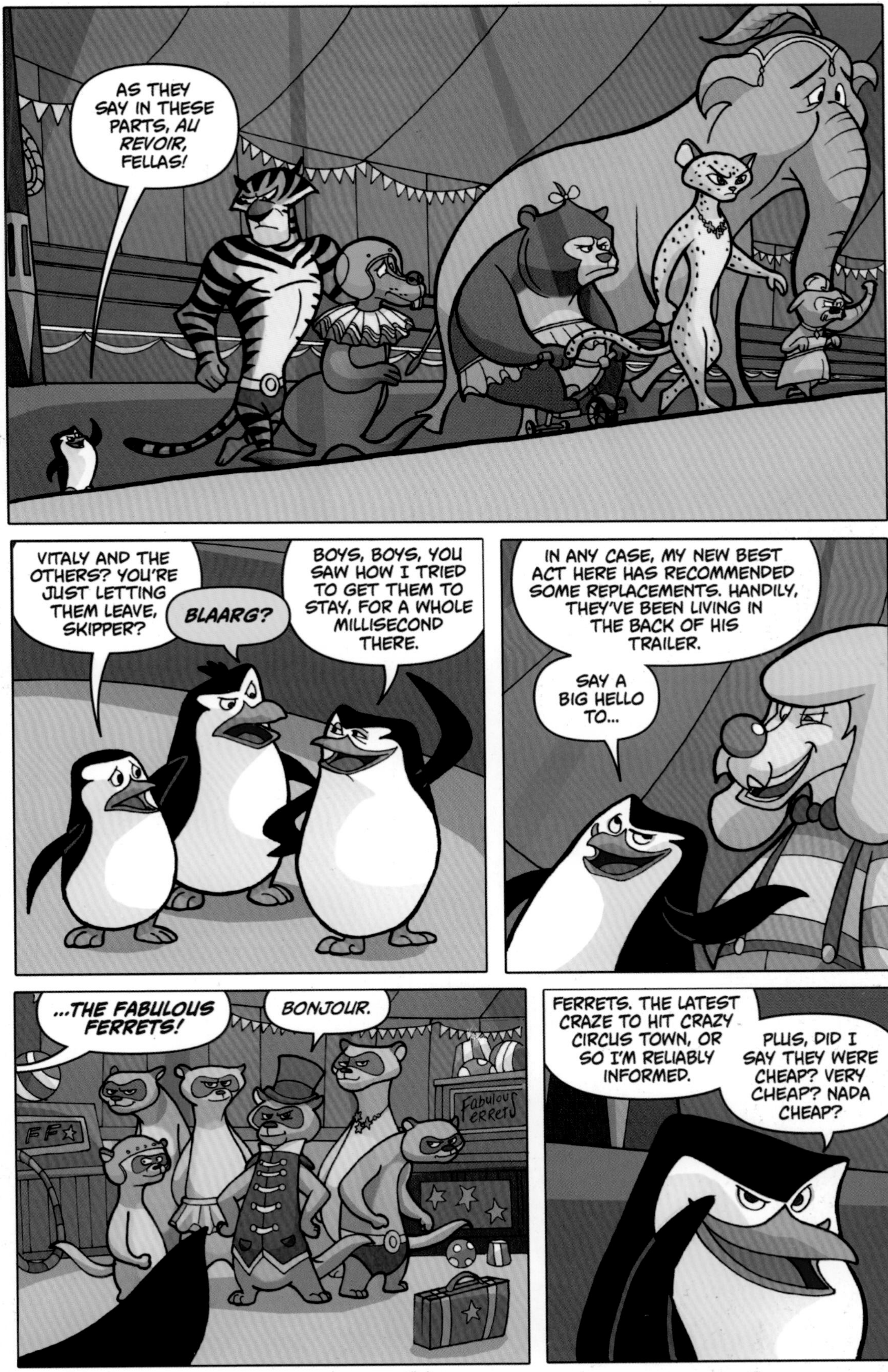
AS THEY SAY IN THESE PARTS, *AU REVOIR*, FELLAS!
VITALY AND THE OTHERS? YOU'RE JUST LETTING THEM LEAVE, SKIPPER?
BLAARG?
BOYS, BOYS, YOU SAW HOW I TRIED TO GET THEM TO STAY, FOR A WHOLE MILLISECOND THERE.
IN ANY CASE, MY NEW BEST ACT HERE HAS RECOMMENDED SOME REPLACEMENTS. HANDILY, THEY'VE BEEN LIVING IN THE BACK OF HIS TRAILER.
SAY A BIG HELLO TO...
...THE FABULOUS FERRETS!
BONJOUR.
FF
Fabulous Ferrets
FERRETS. THE LATEST CRAZE TO HIT CRAZY CIRCUS TOWN, OR SO I'M RELIABLY INFORMED.
PLUS, DID I SAY THEY WERE CHEAP? VERY CHEAP? NADA CHEAP?

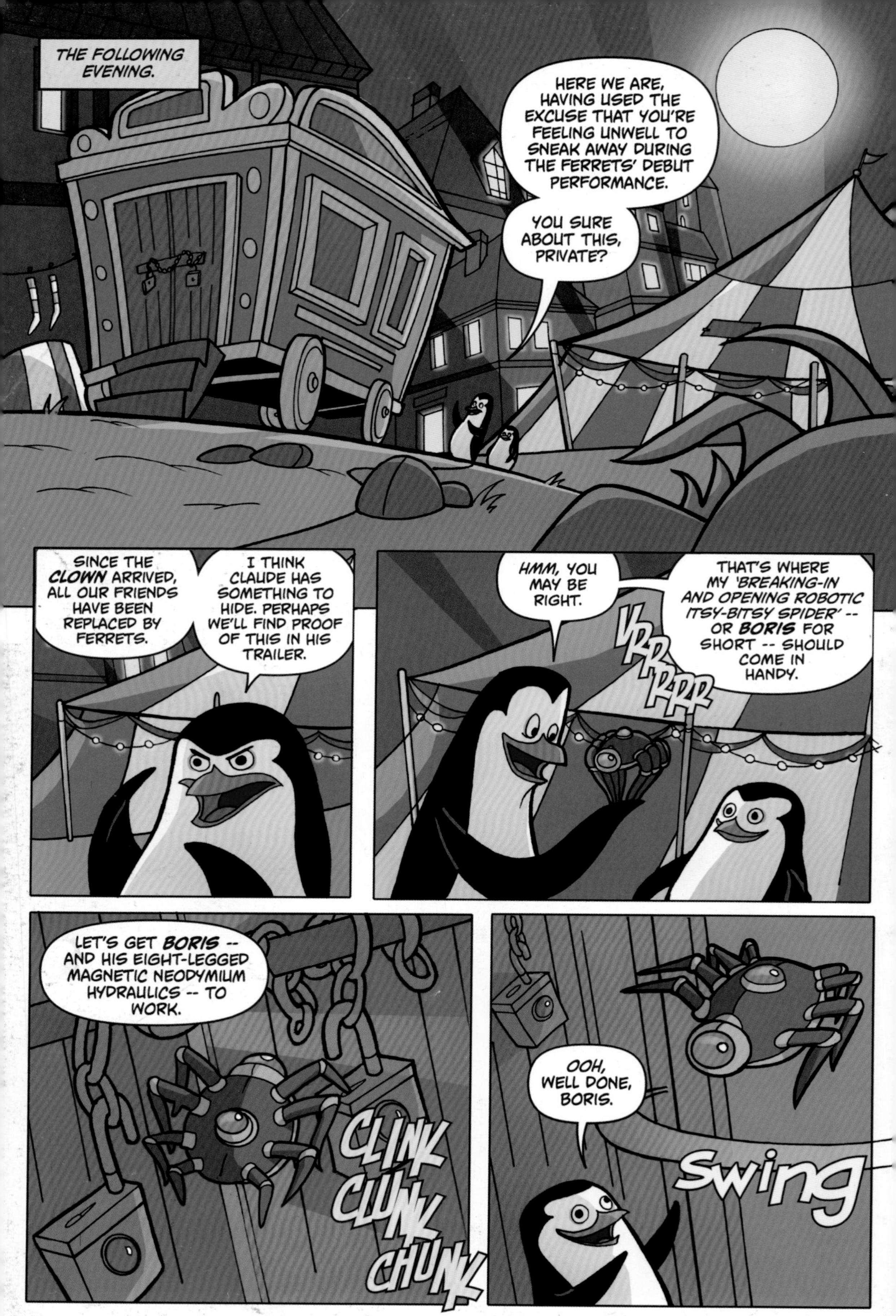

THE FOLLOWING EVENING.
HERE WE ARE, HAVING USED THE EXCUSE THAT YOU'RE FEELING UNWELL TO SNEAK AWAY DURING THE FERRETS' DEBUT PERFORMANCE.
YOU SURE ABOUT THIS, PRIVATE?
SINCE THE *CLOWN* ARRIVED, ALL OUR FRIENDS HAVE BEEN REPLACED BY FERRETS.
I THINK CLAUDE HAS SOMETHING TO HIDE. PERHAPS WE'LL FIND PROOF OF THIS IN HIS TRAILER.
HMM, YOU MAY BE RIGHT.
THAT'S WHERE MY *'BREAKING-IN AND OPENING ROBOTIC ITSY-BITSY SPIDER'* -- OR ***BORIS*** FOR SHORT -- SHOULD COME IN HANDY.
VRRRRRR
LET'S GET ***BORIS*** -- AND HIS EIGHT-LEGGED MAGNETIC NEODYMIUM HYDRAULICS -- TO WORK.
CLINK
CLUNK
CHUNK
OOH, WELL DONE, BORIS.
swing

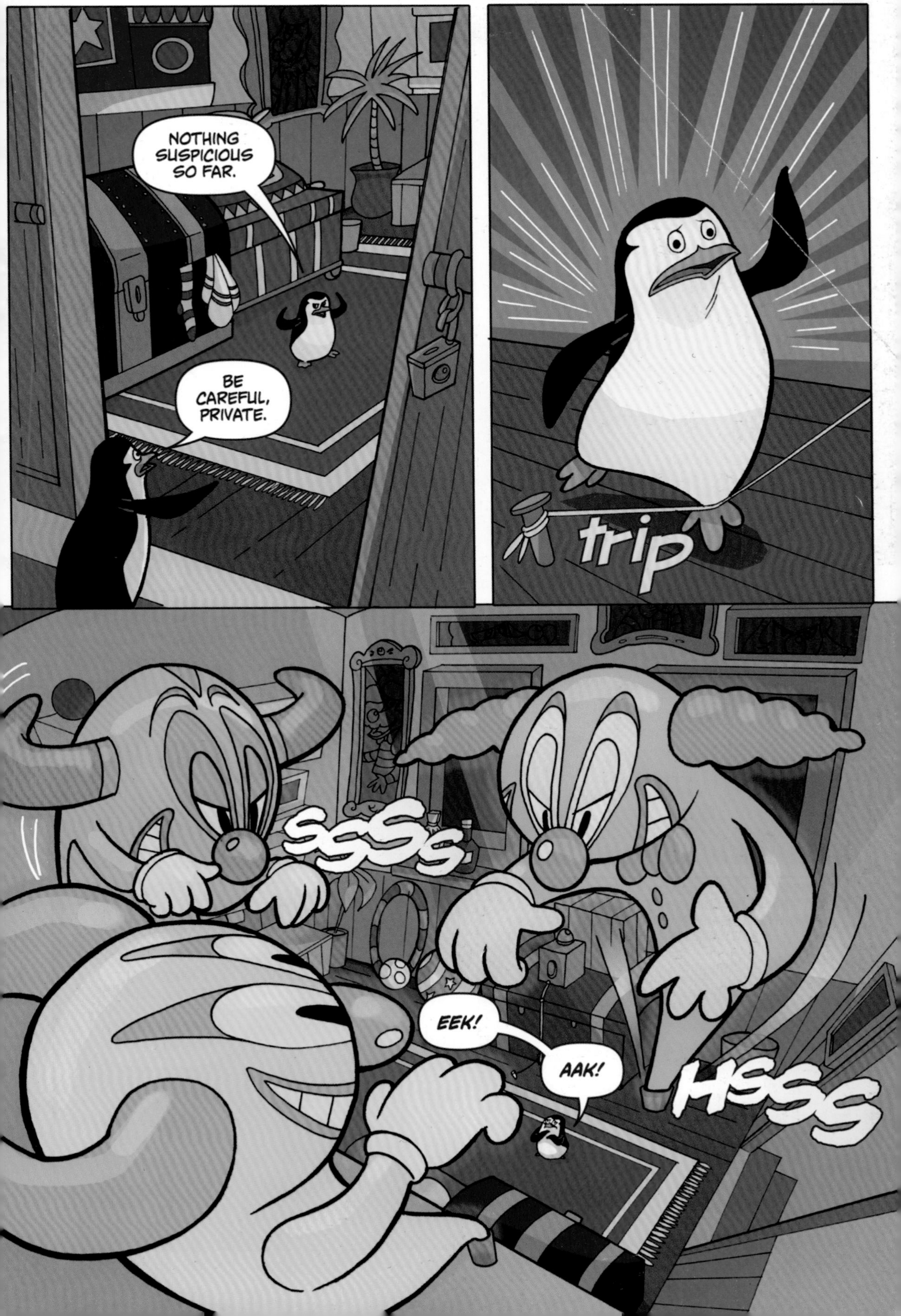

NOTHING SUSPICIOUS SO FAR.
BE CAREFUL, PRIVATE.
trip
SSSS
EEK!
AAK!
HSSS

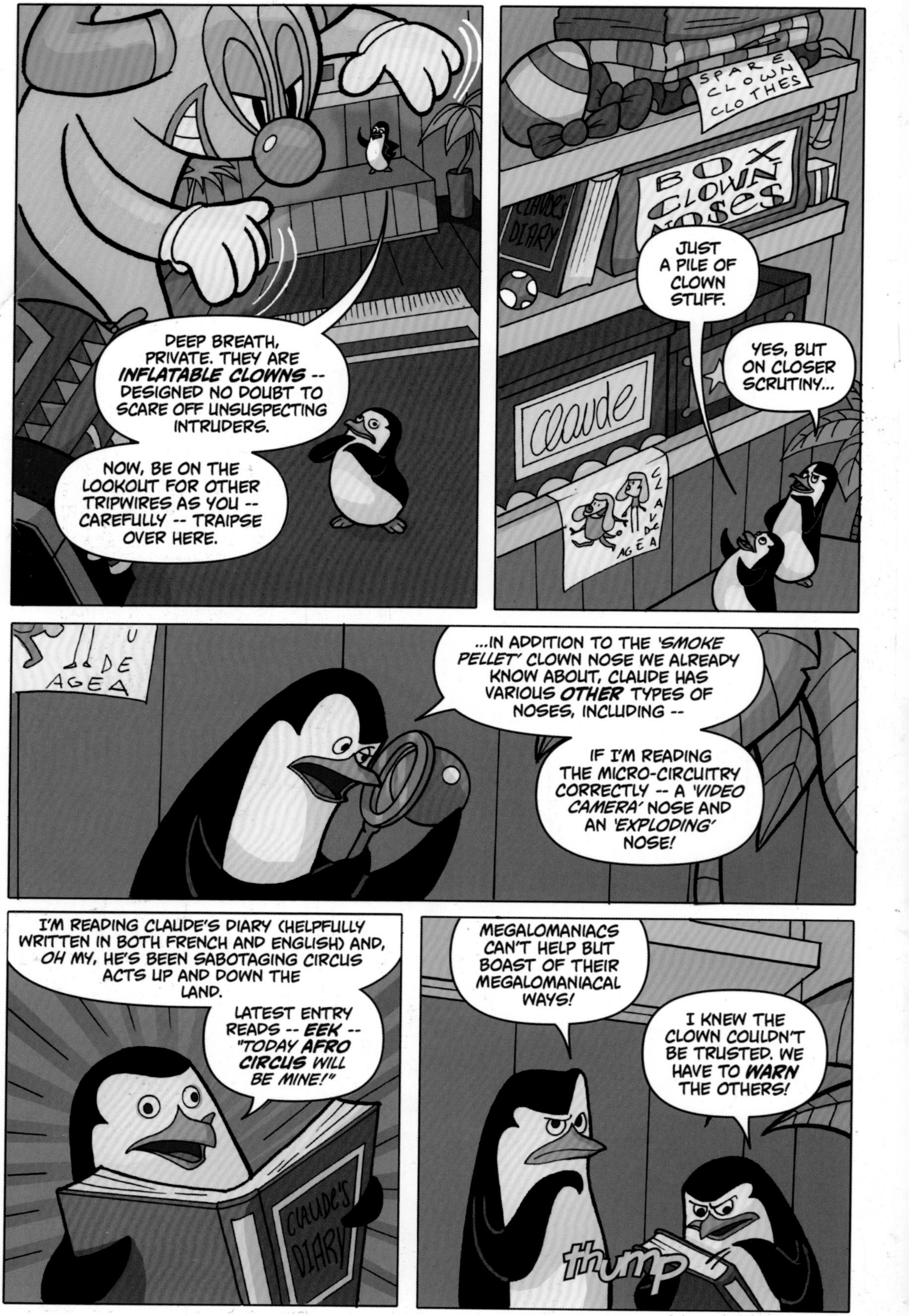
DEEP BREATH, PRIVATE. THEY ARE INFLATABLE CLOWNS -- DESIGNED NO DOUBT TO SCARE OFF UNSUSPECTING INTRUDERS.
NOW, BE ON THE LOOKOUT FOR OTHER TRIPWIRES AS YOU -- CAREFULLY -- TRAIPSE OVER HERE.
SPARE CLOWN CLOTHES
BOX CLOWN NOSES
CLAUDE'S DIARY
JUST A PILE OF CLOWN STUFF.
YES, BUT ON CLOSER SCRUTINY...
Claude
...IN ADDITION TO THE 'SMOKE PELLET' CLOWN NOSE WE ALREADY KNOW ABOUT, CLAUDE HAS VARIOUS OTHER TYPES OF NOSES, INCLUDING --
IF I'M READING THE MICRO-CIRCUITRY CORRECTLY -- A 'VIDEO CAMERA' NOSE AND AN 'EXPLODING' NOSE!
I'M READING CLAUDE'S DIARY (HELPFULLY WRITTEN IN BOTH FRENCH AND ENGLISH) AND, OH MY, HE'S BEEN SABOTAGING CIRCUS ACTS UP AND DOWN THE LAND.
LATEST ENTRY READS -- EEK -- "TODAY AFRO CIRCUS WILL BE MINE!"
CLAUDE'S DIARY
MEGALOMANIACS CAN'T HELP BUT BOAST OF THEIR MEGALOMANIACAL WAYS!
I KNEW THE CLOWN COULDN'T BE TRUSTED. WE HAVE TO WARN THE OTHERS!
thump

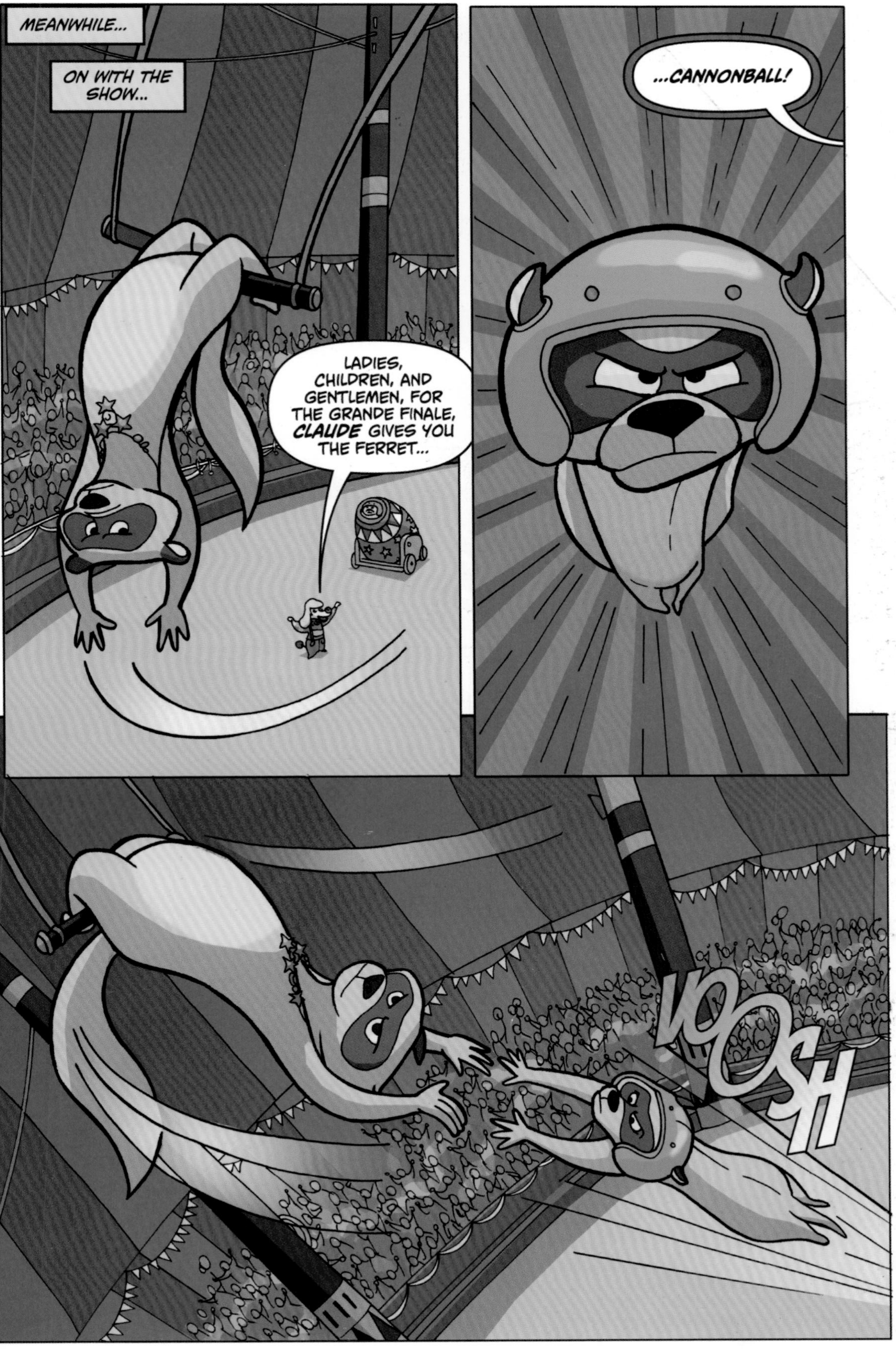
MEANWHILE...
ON WITH THE SHOW...
LADIES, CHILDREN, AND GENTLEMEN, FOR THE GRANDE FINALE, CLAUDE GIVES YOU THE FERRET...
...CANNONBALL!
WOOSH

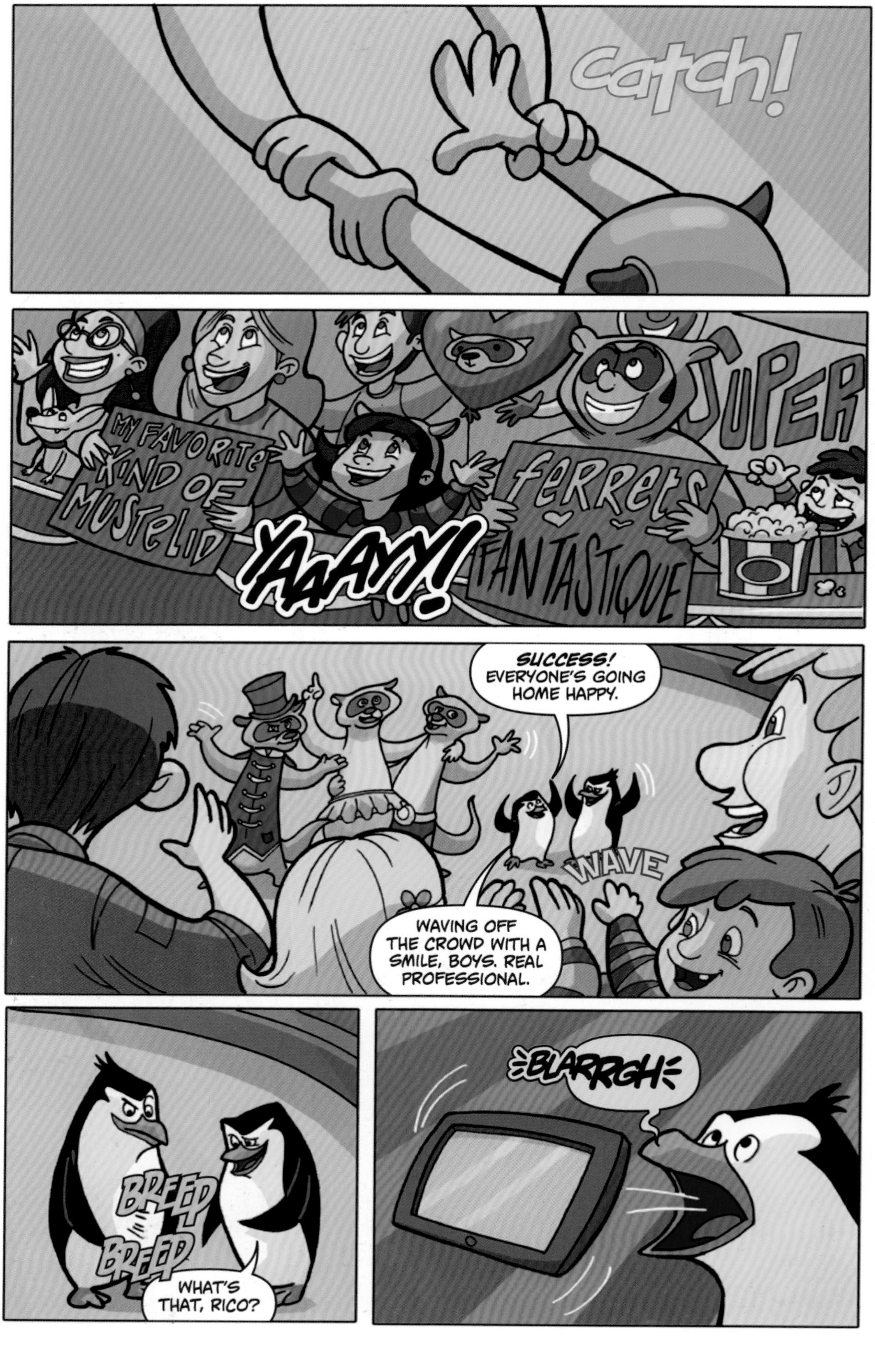
CATCH!
MY FAVORITE KIND OF MUSTELID
FERRETS FANTASTIQUE
SUPER
YAAAYY!
SUCCESS! EVERYONE'S GOING HOME HAPPY.
WAVE
WAVING OFF THE CROWD WITH A SMILE, BOYS. REAL PROFESSIONAL.
BREEP BREEP
WHAT'S THAT, RICO?
BLARRGH

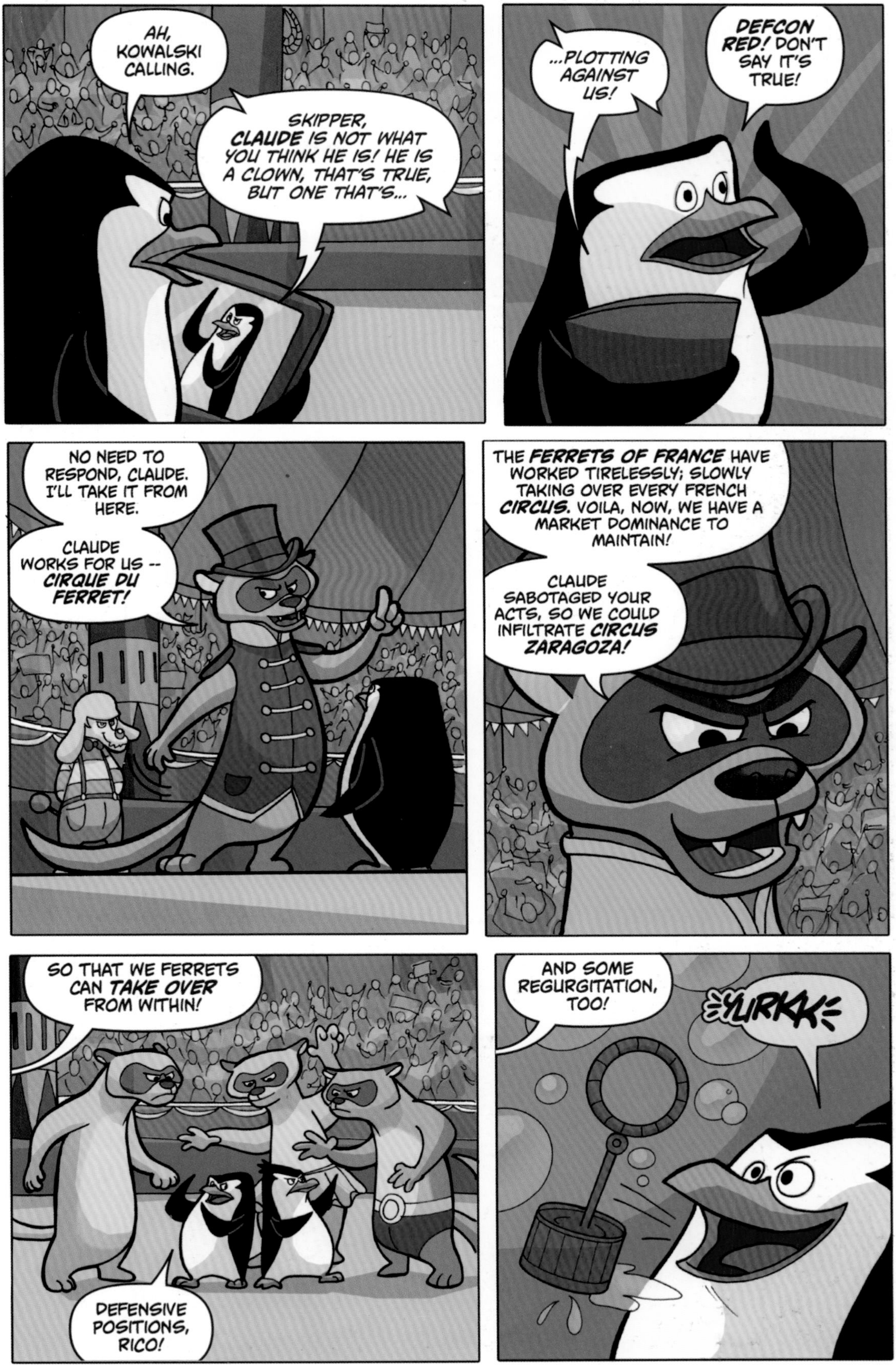

AH, KOWALSKI CALLING.
SKIPPER, CLAUDE IS NOT WHAT YOU THINK HE IS! HE IS A CLOWN, THAT'S TRUE, BUT ONE THAT'S...
...PLOTTING AGAINST US!
DEFCON RED! DON'T SAY IT'S TRUE!
NO NEED TO RESPOND, CLAUDE. I'LL TAKE IT FROM HERE.
CLAUDE WORKS FOR US -- CIRQUE DU FERRET!
THE FERRETS OF FRANCE HAVE WORKED TIRELESSLY; SLOWLY TAKING OVER EVERY FRENCH CIRCUS. VOILA, NOW, WE HAVE A MARKET DOMINANCE TO MAINTAIN!
CLAUDE SABOTAGED YOUR ACTS, SO WE COULD INFILTRATE CIRCUS ZARAGOZA!
SO THAT WE FERRETS CAN TAKE OVER FROM WITHIN!
DEFENSIVE POSITIONS, RICO!
AND SOME REGURGITATION, TOO!
YURKK

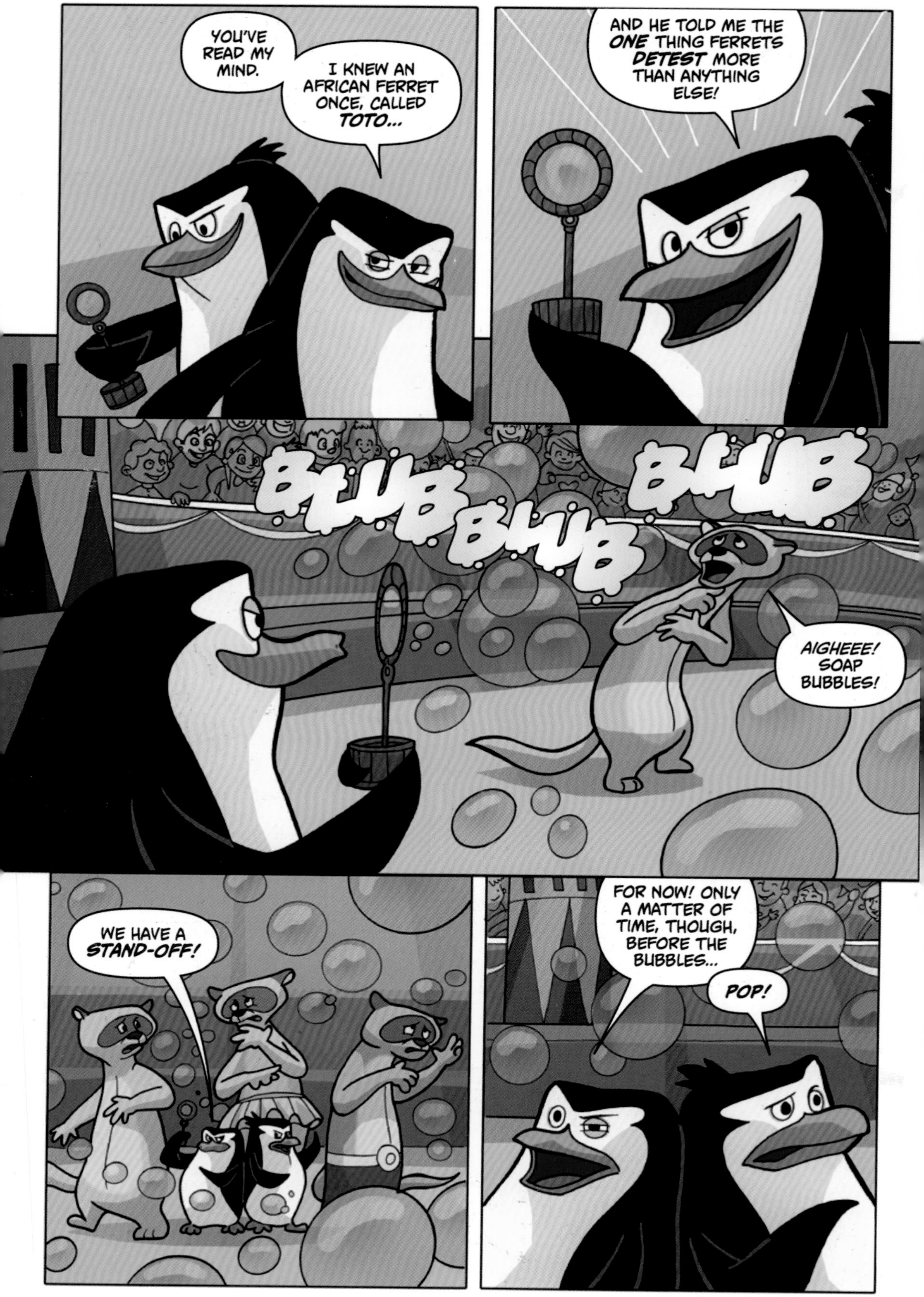
YOU'VE READ MY MIND.
I KNEW AN AFRICAN FERRET ONCE, CALLED TOTO...
AND HE TOLD ME THE ONE THING FERRETS DETEST MORE THAN ANYTHING ELSE!
BLUB BLUB BLUB
AIGHEEE! SOAP BUBBLES!
WE HAVE A STAND-OFF!
FOR NOW! ONLY A MATTER OF TIME, THOUGH, BEFORE THE BUBBLES...
POP!

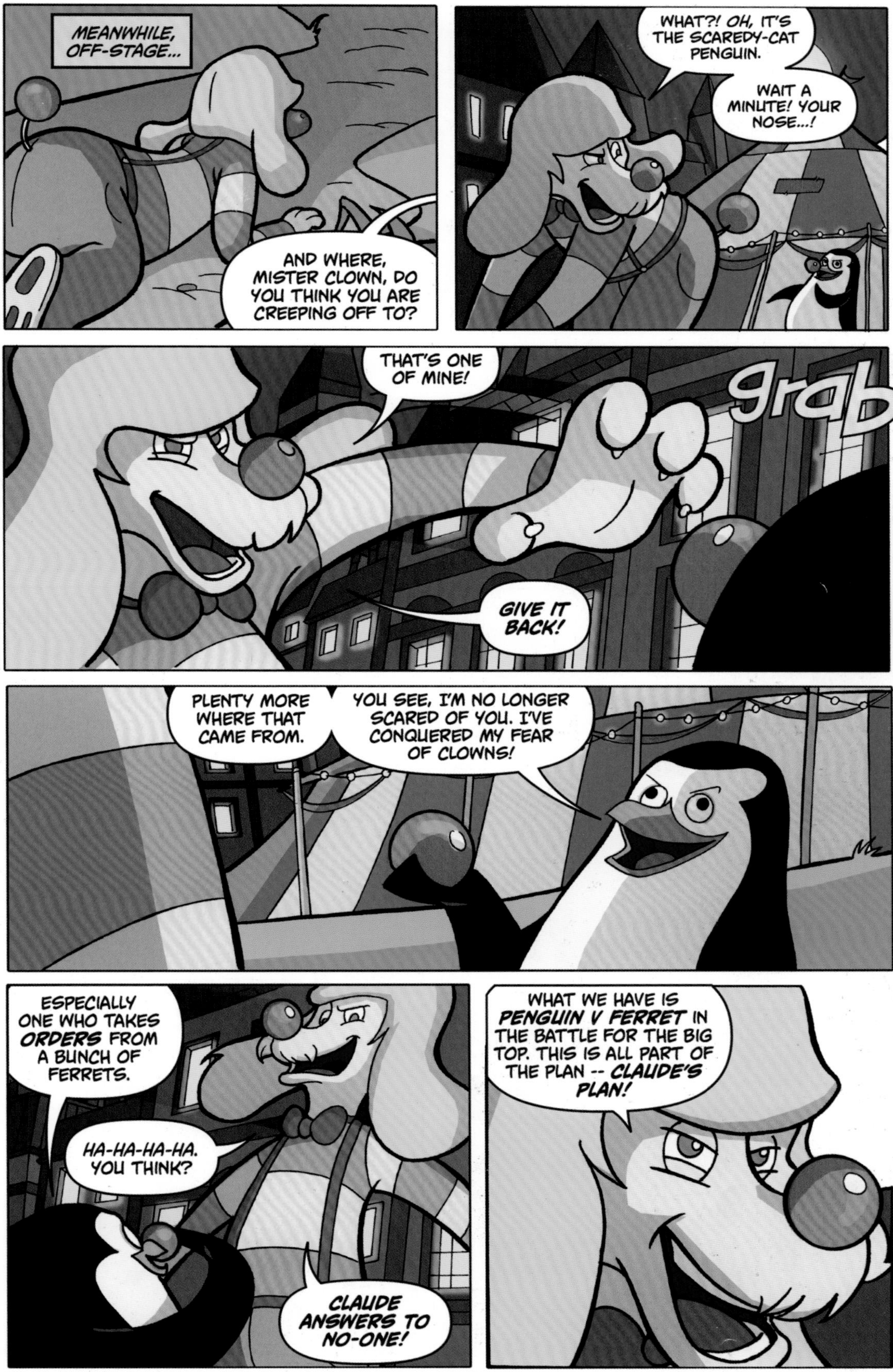
MEANWHILE, OFF-STAGE...
AND WHERE, MISTER CLOWN, DO YOU THINK YOU ARE CREEPING OFF TO?
WHAT?! OH, IT'S THE SCAREDY-CAT PENGUIN.
WAIT A MINUTE! YOUR NOSE...!
THAT'S ONE OF MINE!
grab
GIVE IT BACK!
PLENTY MORE WHERE THAT CAME FROM.
YOU SEE, I'M NO LONGER SCARED OF YOU. I'VE CONQUERED MY FEAR OF CLOWNS!
ESPECIALLY ONE WHO TAKES ORDERS FROM A BUNCH OF FERRETS.
HA-HA-HA-HA. YOU THINK?
CLAUDE ANSWERS TO NO-ONE!
WHAT WE HAVE IS PENGUIN V FERRET IN THE BATTLE FOR THE BIG TOP. THIS IS ALL PART OF THE PLAN -- CLAUDE'S PLAN!

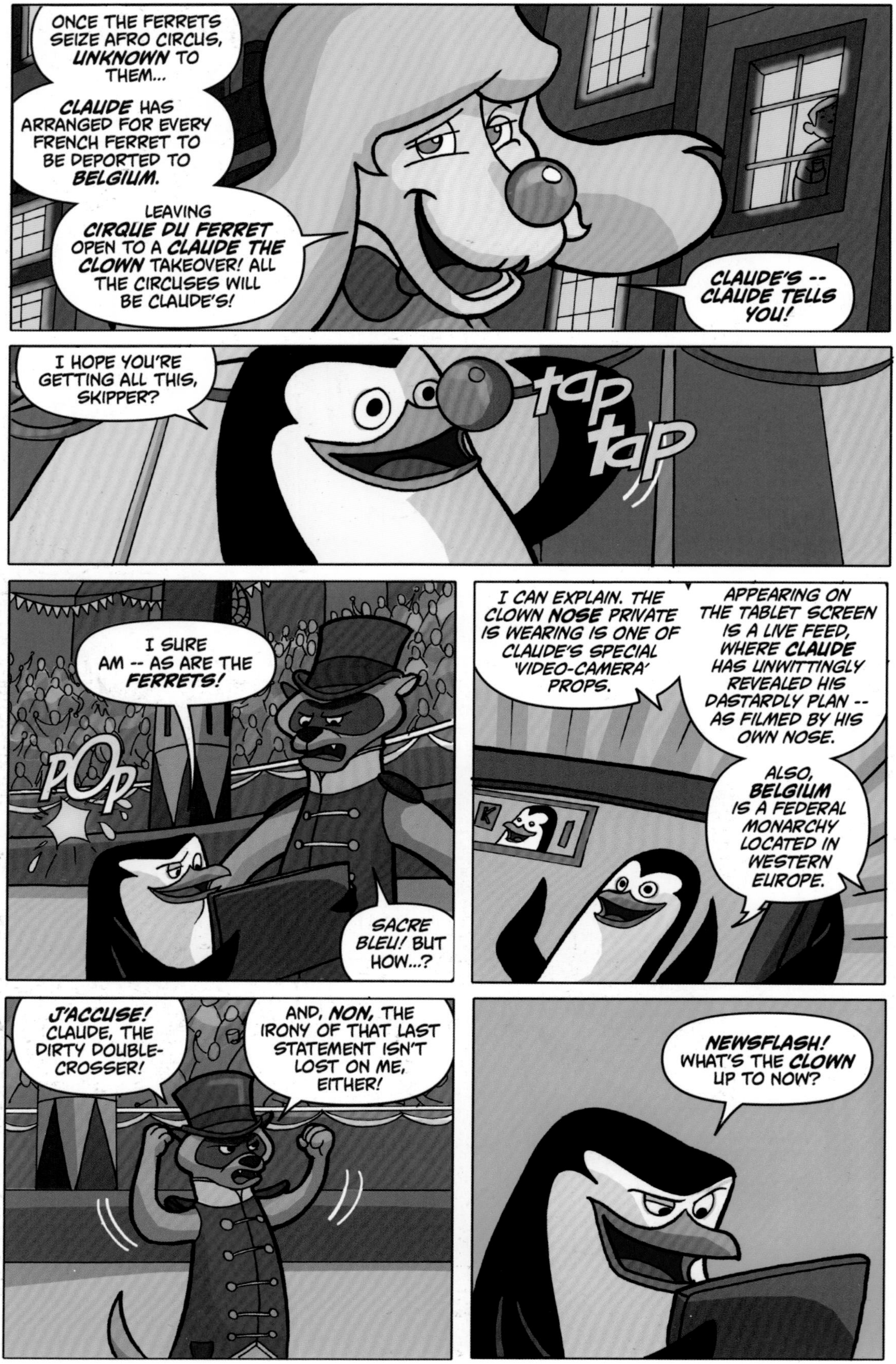
ONCE THE FERRETS SEIZE AFRO CIRCUS, UNKNOWN TO THEM...
CLAUDE HAS ARRANGED FOR EVERY FRENCH FERRET TO BE DEPORTED TO BELGIUM.
LEAVING CIRQUE DU FERRET OPEN TO A CLAUDE THE CLOWN TAKEOVER! ALL THE CIRCUSES WILL BE CLAUDE'S!
CLAUDE'S -- CLAUDE TELLS YOU!
I HOPE YOU'RE GETTING ALL THIS, SKIPPER?
tap tap
I SURE AM -- AS ARE THE FERRETS!
POP
SACRE BLEU! BUT HOW...?
I CAN EXPLAIN. THE CLOWN NOSE PRIVATE IS WEARING IS ONE OF CLAUDE'S SPECIAL 'VIDEO-CAMERA' PROPS.
APPEARING ON THE TABLET SCREEN IS A LIVE FEED, WHERE CLAUDE HAS UNWITTINGLY REVEALED HIS DASTARDLY PLAN -- AS FILMED BY HIS OWN NOSE.
ALSO, BELGIUM IS A FEDERAL MONARCHY LOCATED IN WESTERN EUROPE.
J'ACCUSE! CLAUDE, THE DIRTY DOUBLE-CROSSER!
AND, NON, THE IRONY OF THAT LAST STATEMENT ISN'T LOST ON ME, EITHER!
NEWSFLASH! WHAT'S THE CLOWN UP TO NOW?

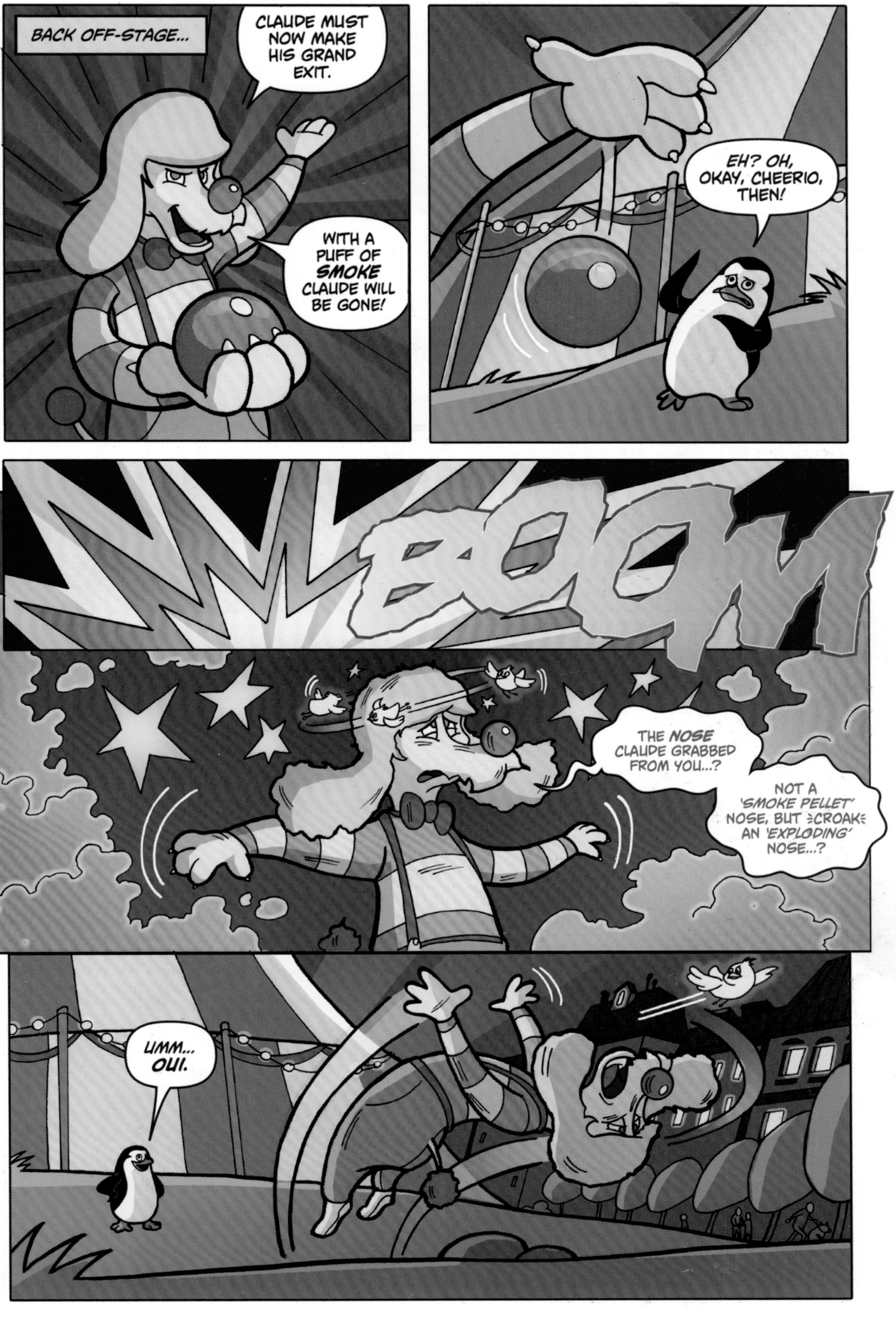
BACK OFF-STAGE...
CLAUDE MUST NOW MAKE HIS GRAND EXIT.
WITH A PUFF OF SMOKE CLAUDE WILL BE GONE!
EH? OH, OKAY, CHEERIO, THEN!
BOOM
THE NOSE CLAUDE GRABBED FROM YOU...?
NOT A 'SMOKE PELLET' NOSE, BUT CROAK AN 'EXPLODING' NOSE...?
UMM... OUI.

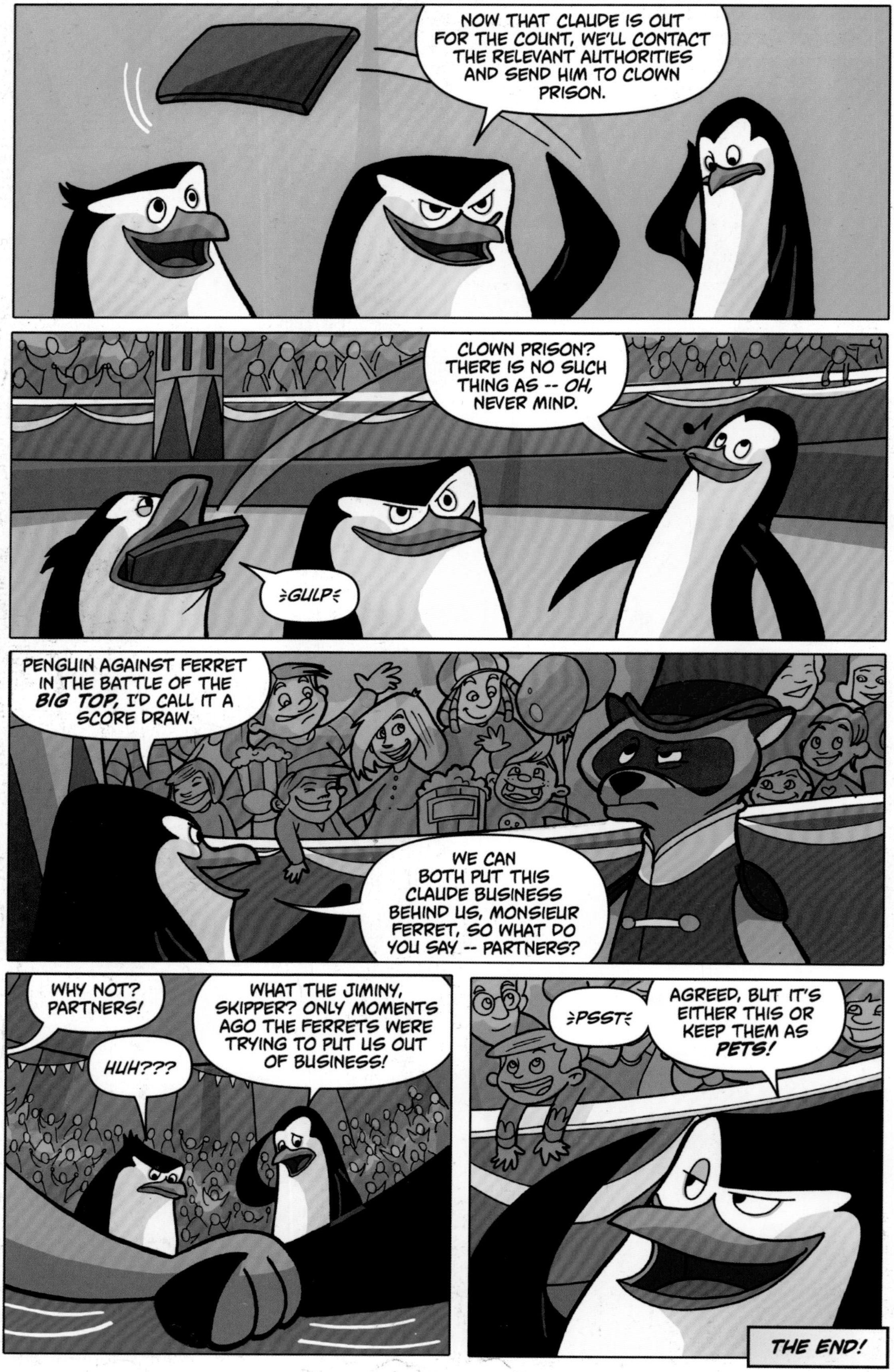
NOW THAT CLAUDE IS OUT FOR THE COUNT, WE'LL CONTACT THE RELEVANT AUTHORITIES AND SEND HIM TO CLOWN PRISON.
CLOWN PRISON? THERE IS NO SUCH THING AS -- OH, NEVER MIND.
GULP
PENGUIN AGAINST FERRET IN THE BATTLE OF THE BIG TOP, I'D CALL IT A SCORE DRAW.
WE CAN BOTH PUT THIS CLAUDE BUSINESS BEHIND US, MONSIEUR FERRET, SO WHAT DO YOU SAY -- PARTNERS?
WHY NOT? PARTNERS!
HUH???
WHAT THE JIMINY, SKIPPER? ONLY MOMENTS AGO THE FERRETS WERE TRYING TO PUT US OUT OF BUSINESS!
PSST
AGREED, BUT IT'S EITHER THIS OR KEEP THEM AS PETS!
THE END!

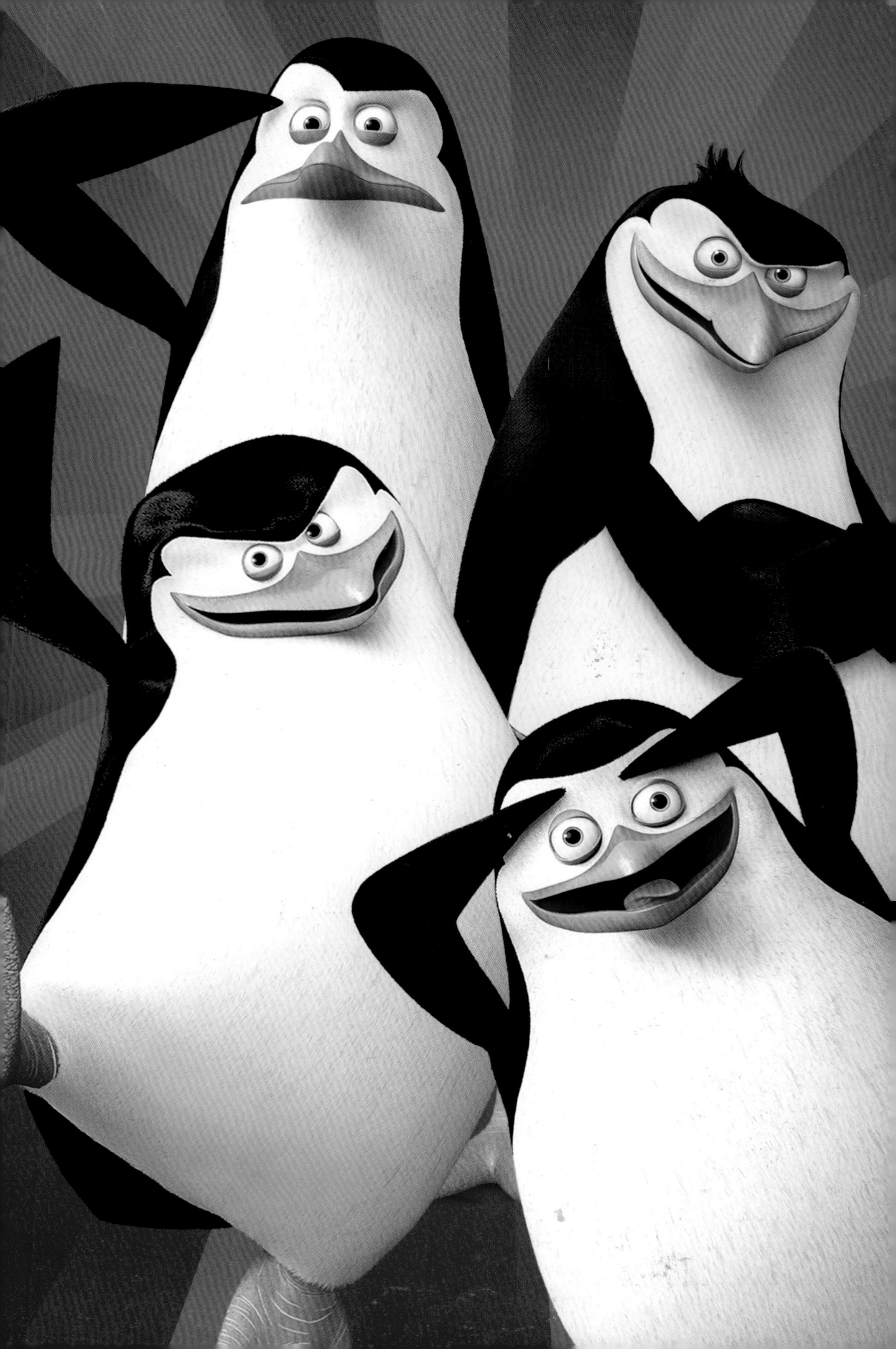

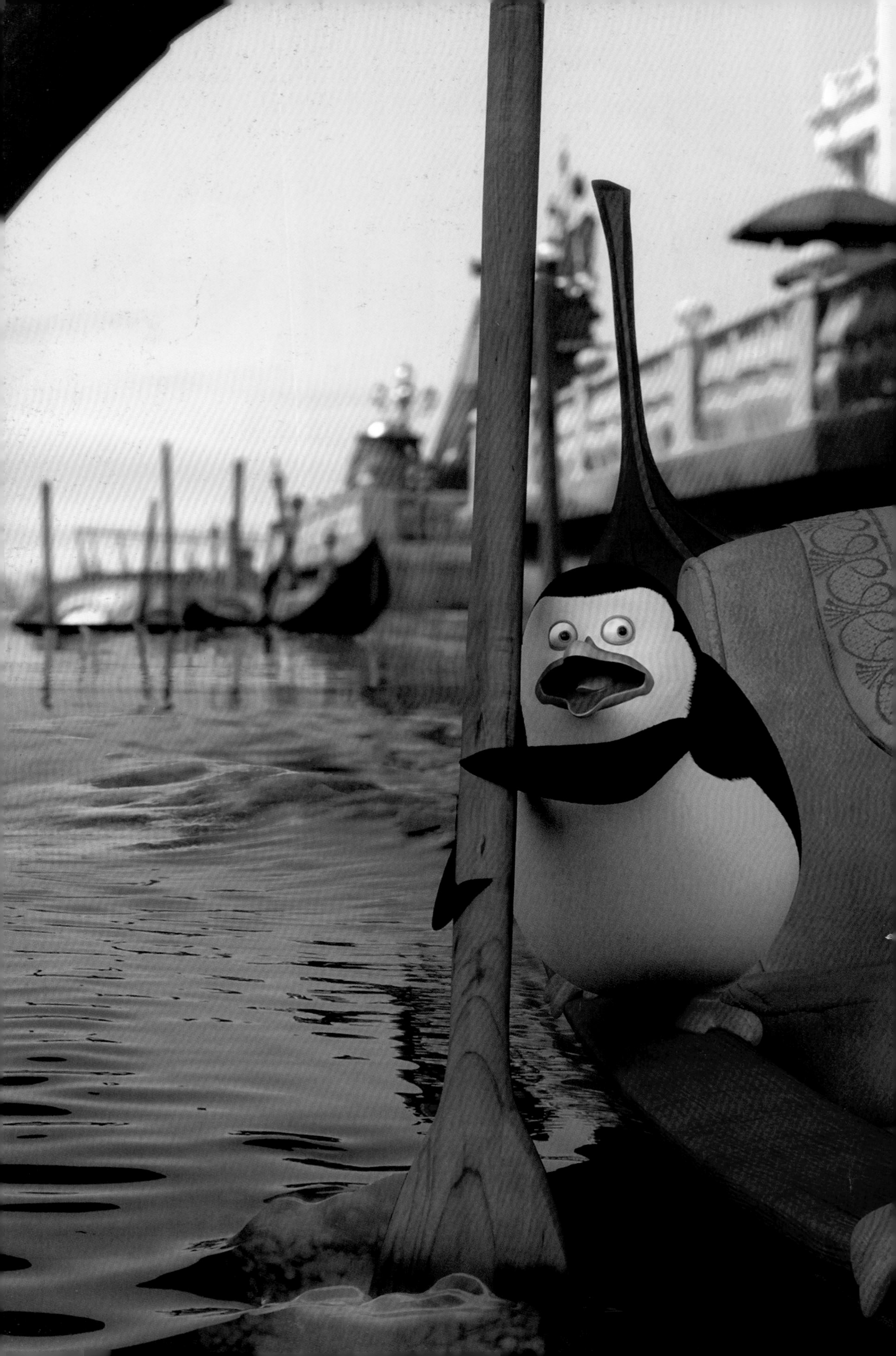

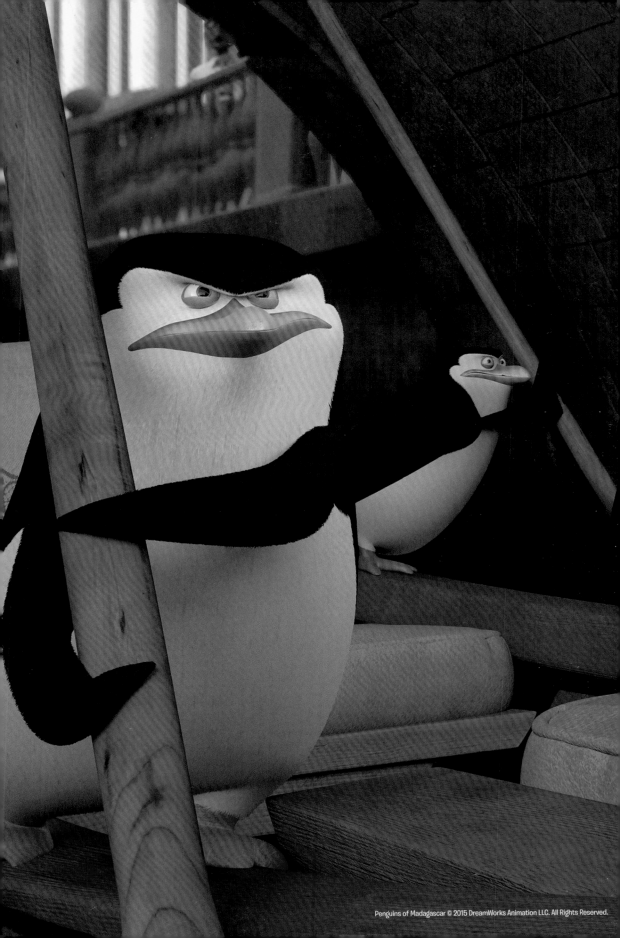

NIGHT OUT

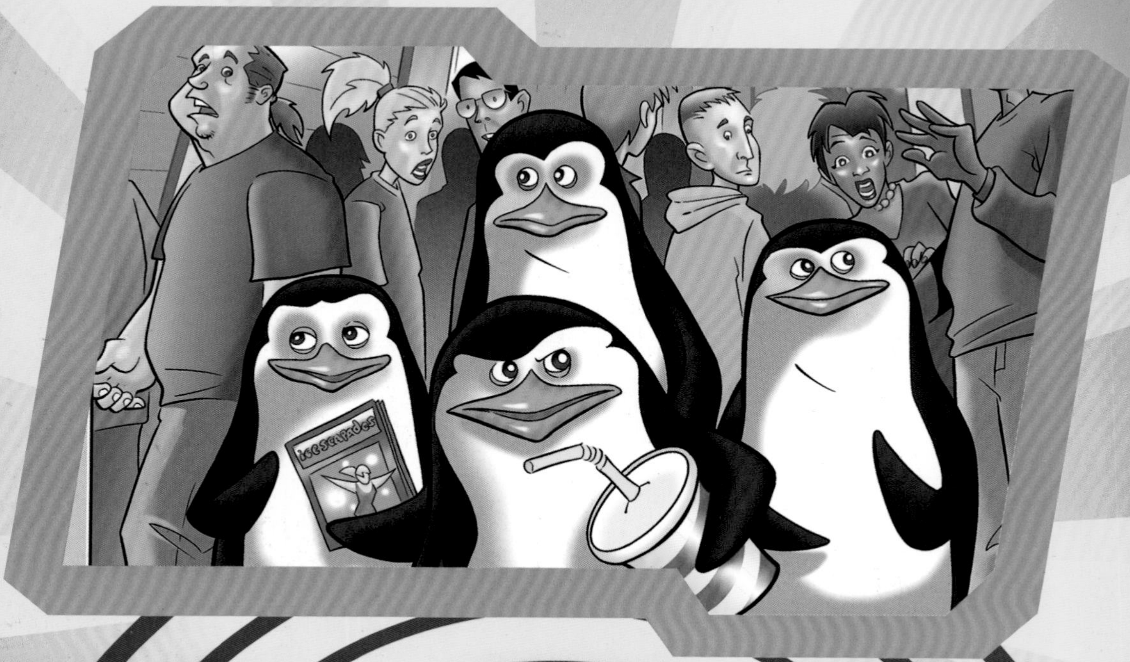
icescapades

SCRIPT
Dan Abnett & Andy Lanning

PENCILS
Anthony Williams

INKS
Dan Davis

COLORS
Robin Smith

LETTERING
Jimmy Betancourt/
Comicraft

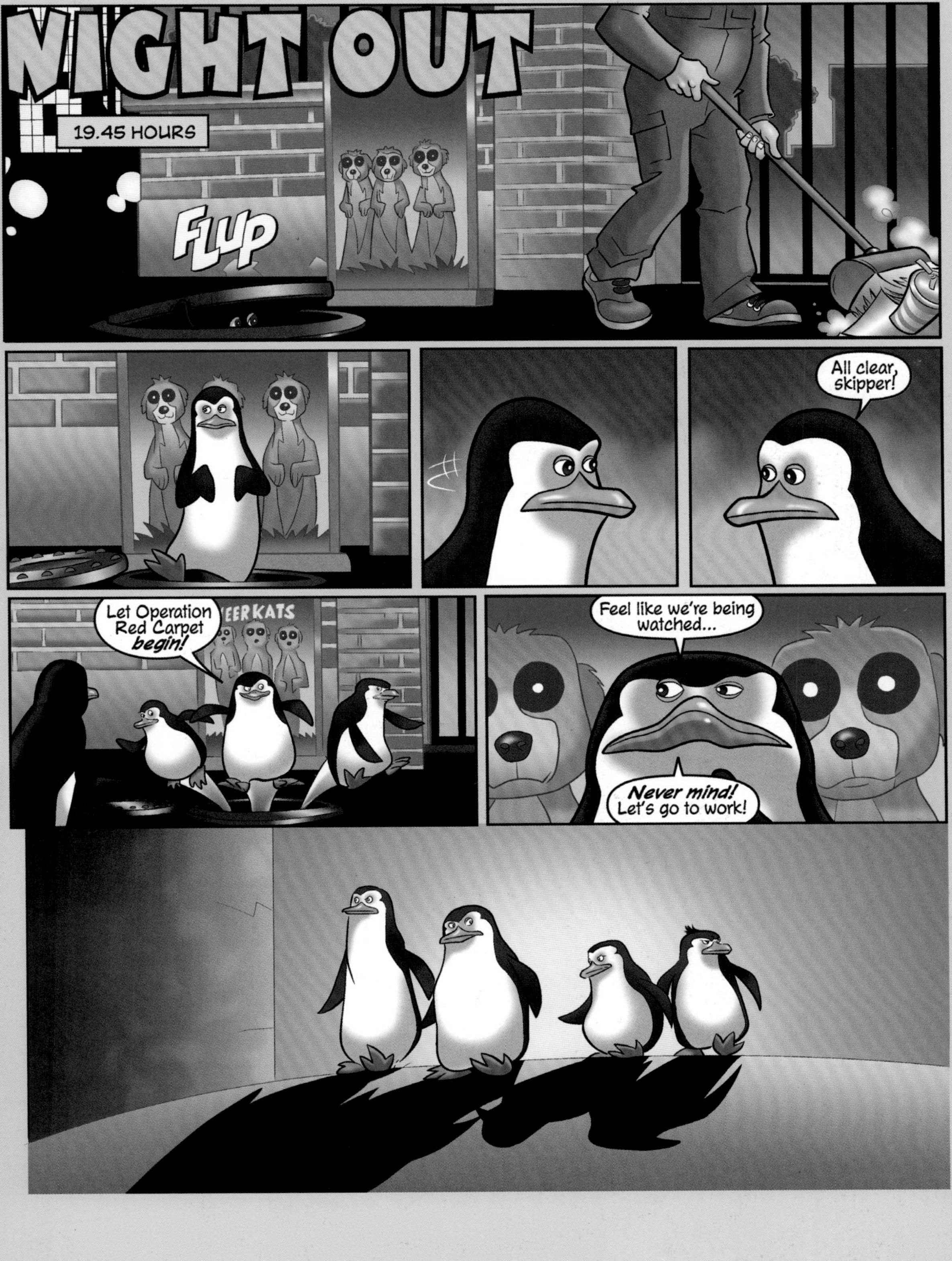
NIGHT OUT
19.45 HOURS
FLUP
All clear, skipper!
Let Operation Red Carpet begin!
EERKATS
Feel like we're being watched...
Never mind! Let's go to work!

Okay, boys... We need to be in position and locked down in the next five minutes!

Kowalski! Sit-rep!

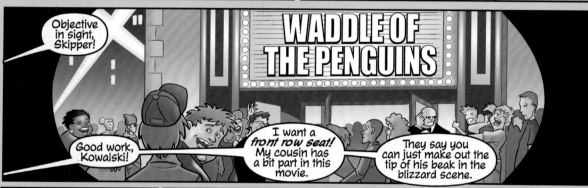

Objective in sight, Skipper!

WADDLE OF THE PENGUINS

Good work, Kowalski!

I want a *front row seat!* My cousin has a bit part in this movie.

They say you can just make out the tip of his beak in the blizzard scene.

Easy does it, boys...

Hey, dudes. Dig the costumes.

Just smile and wave, boys, smile and wave.

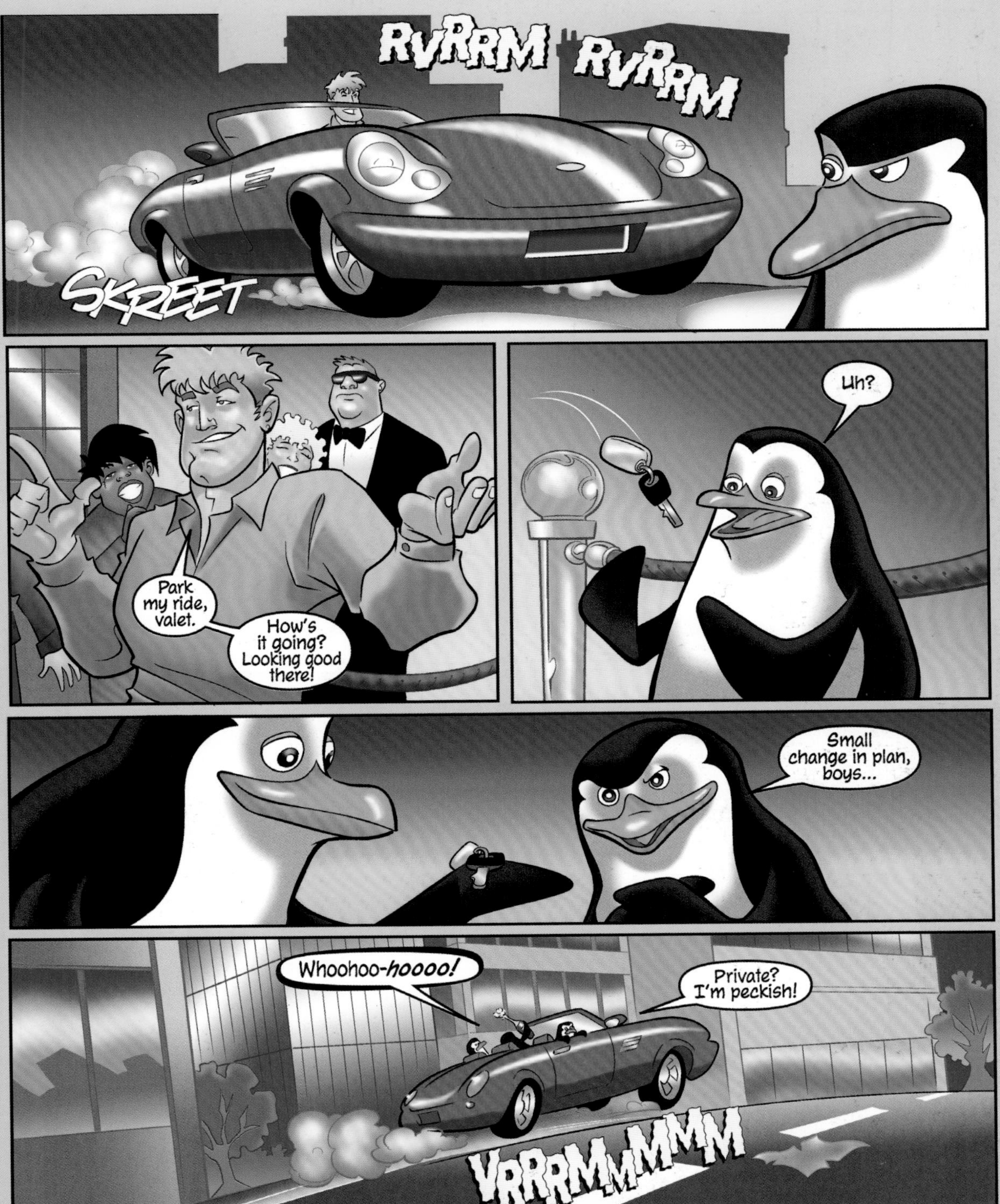
RVRRM RVRRM
SKREEET
Park my ride, valet.
How's it going? Looking good there!
Uh?
Small change in plan, boys...
Whoohoo-hoooo!
Private? I'm peckish!
VRRRMMMMM

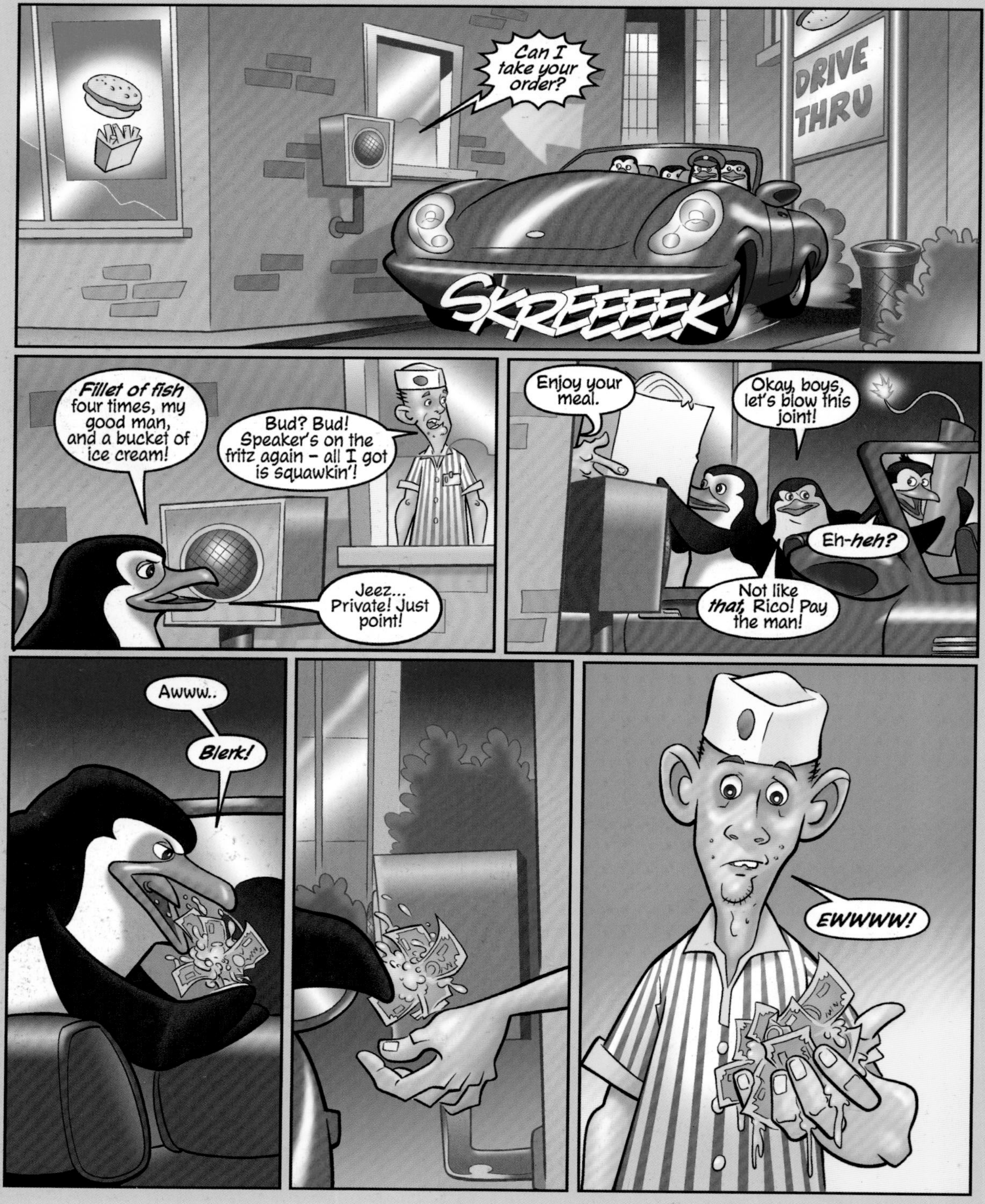
Can I take your order?
SKREEEEK
Fillet of fish four times, my good man, and a bucket of ice cream!
Bud? Bud! Speaker's on the fritz again – all I got is squawkin'!
Jeez... Private! Just point!
Enjoy your meal.
Okay, boys, let's blow this joint!
Eh-*heh?*
Not like *that,* Rico! Pay the man!
Awww..
Blerk!
EWWWW!

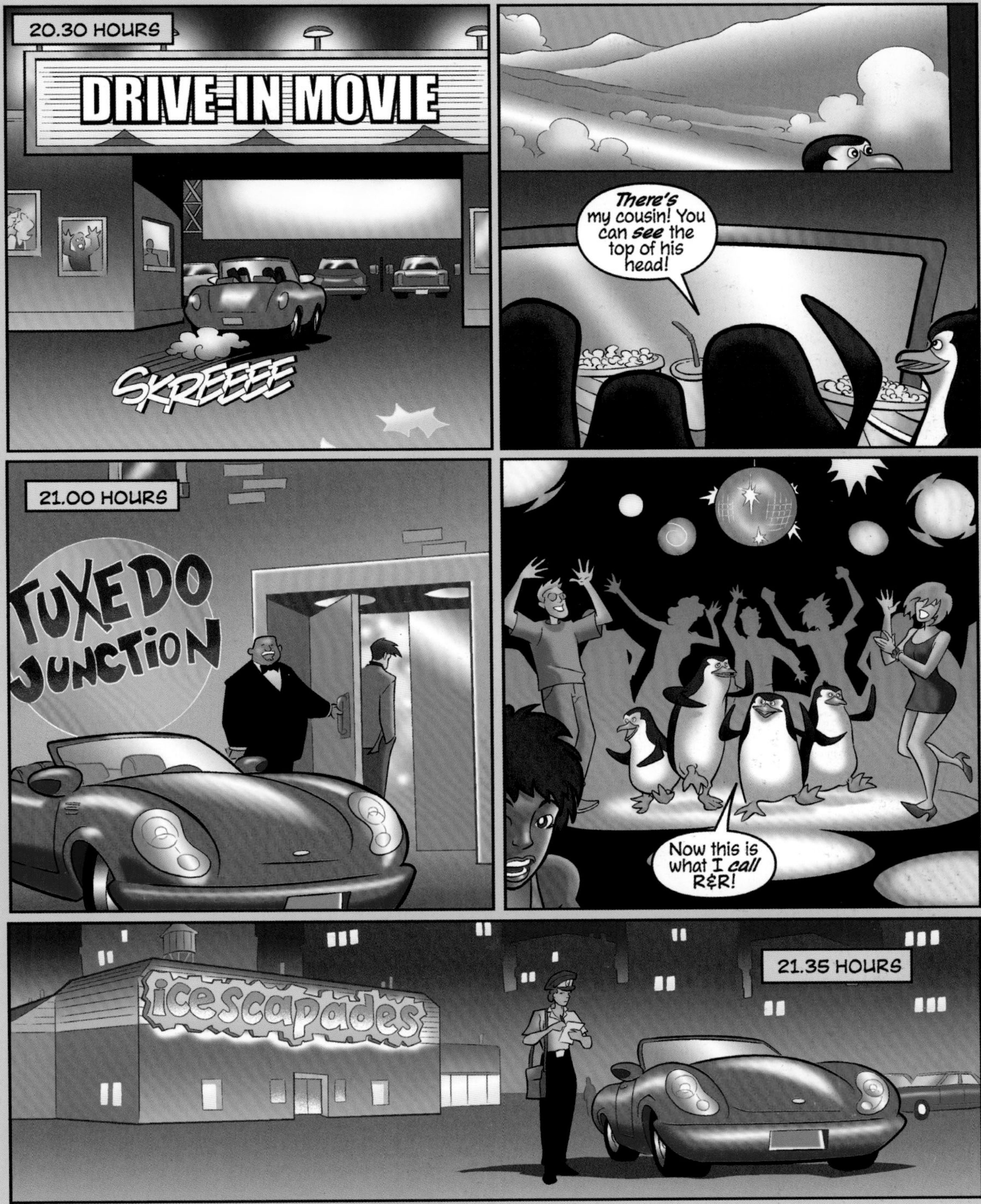
20.30 HOURS
DRIVE-IN MOVIE
SKREEEEE
There's my cousin! You can see the top of his head!
21.00 HOURS
TUXEDO JUNCTION
Now this is what I call R&R!
21.35 HOURS
icescapades

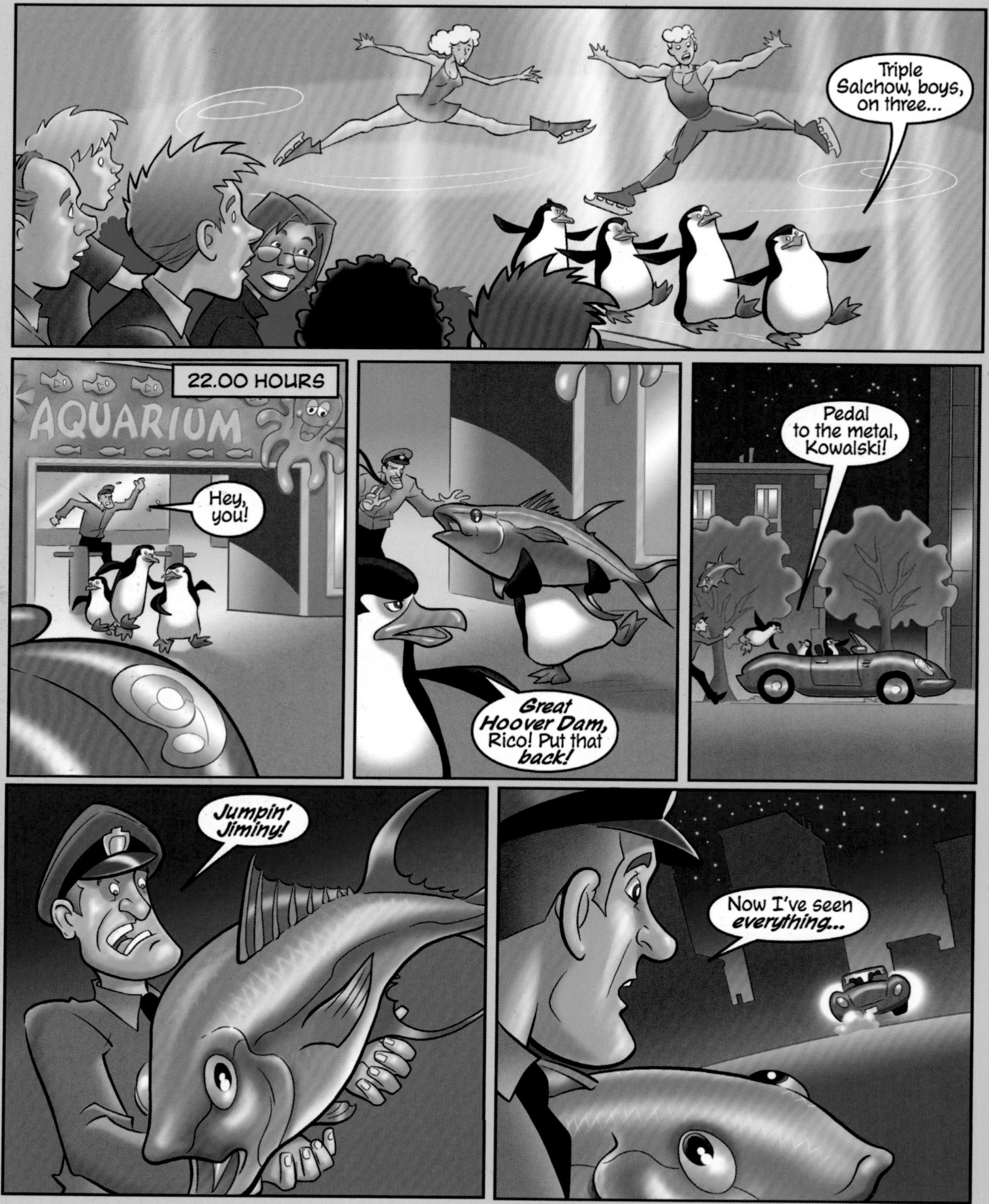
Triple Salchow, boys, on three...
22.00 HOURS
AQUARIUM
Hey, you!
Great Hoover Dam, Rico! Put that back!
Pedal to the metal, Kowalski!
Jumpin' Jiminy!
Now I've seen everything...

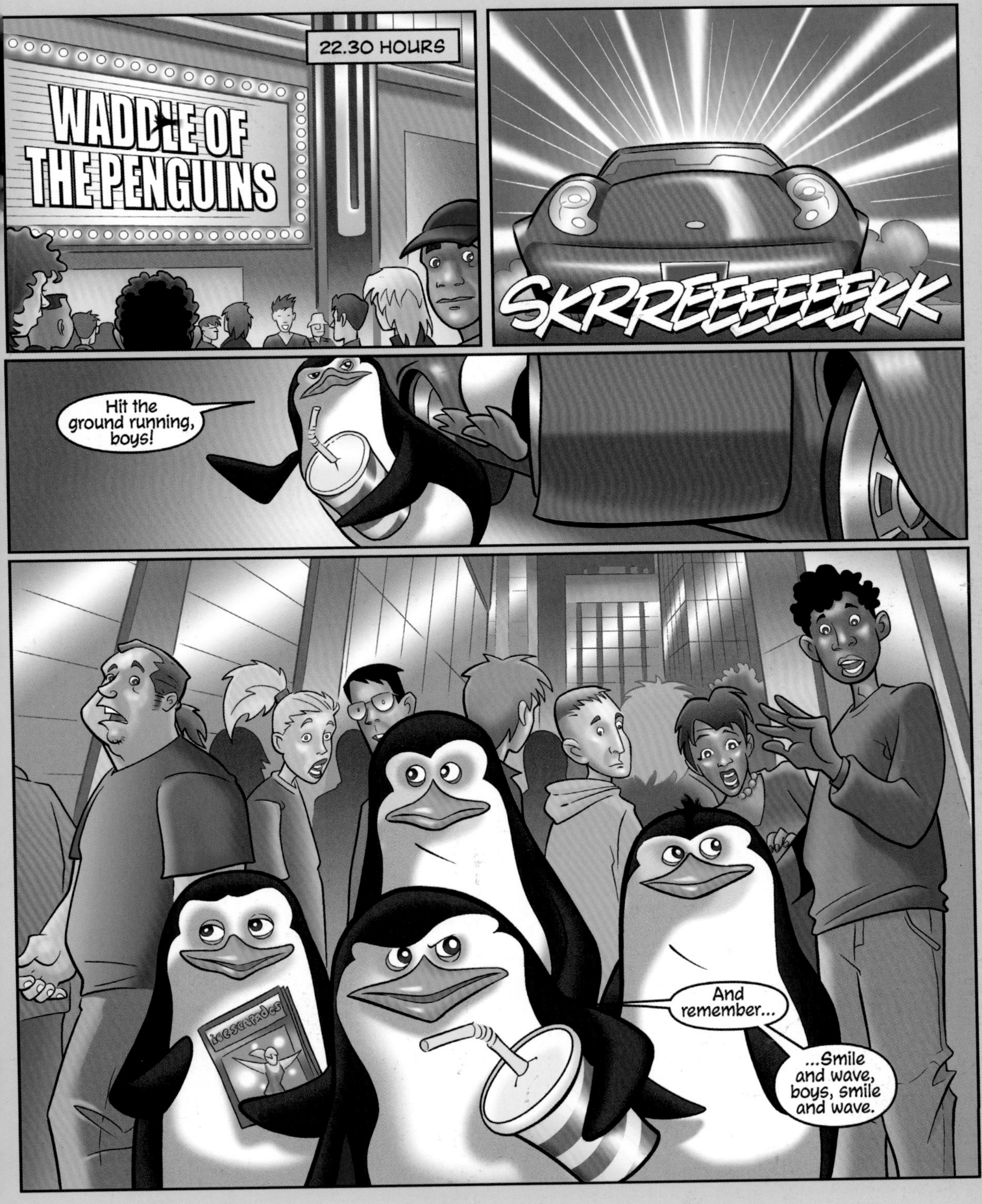

22.30 HOURS
WADDLE OF THE PENGUINS
SKRREEEEEEEKK
Hit the ground running, boys!
And remember...
...Smile and wave, boys, smile and wave.
ice scapades

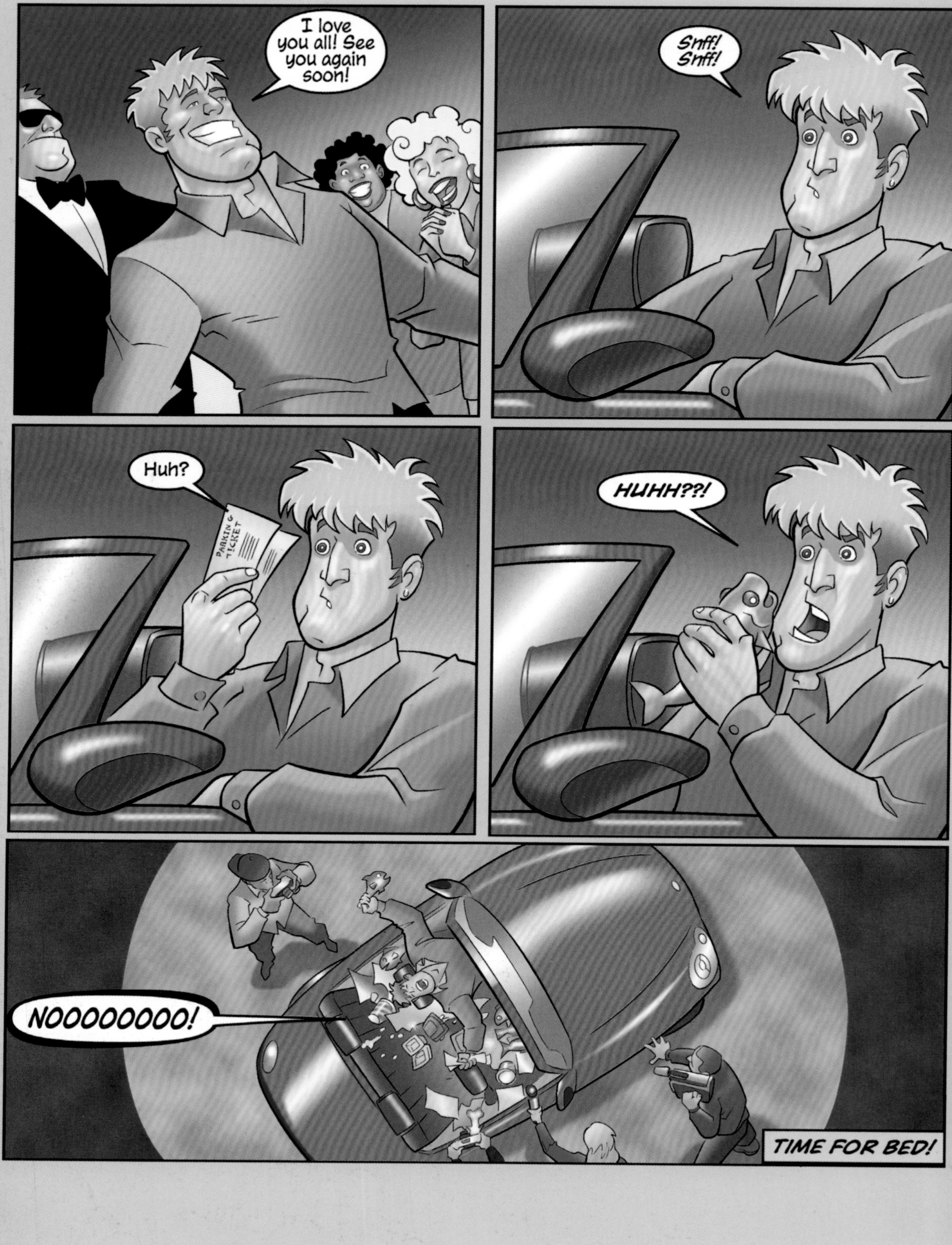

I love you all! See you again soon!
Snff! Snff!
Huh?
PARKING TICKET
HUHH??!
NOOOOOOOO!
TIME FOR BED!

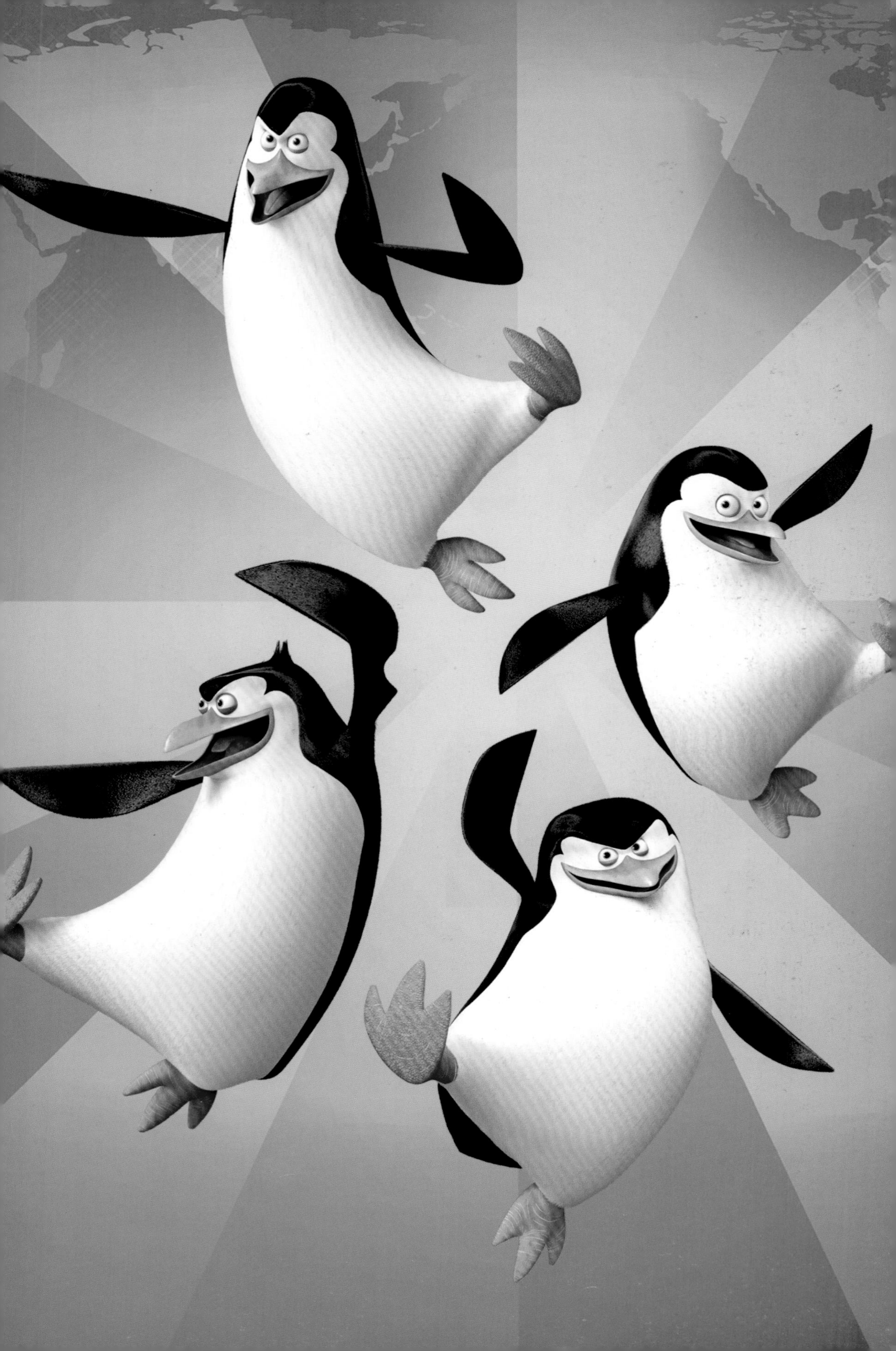

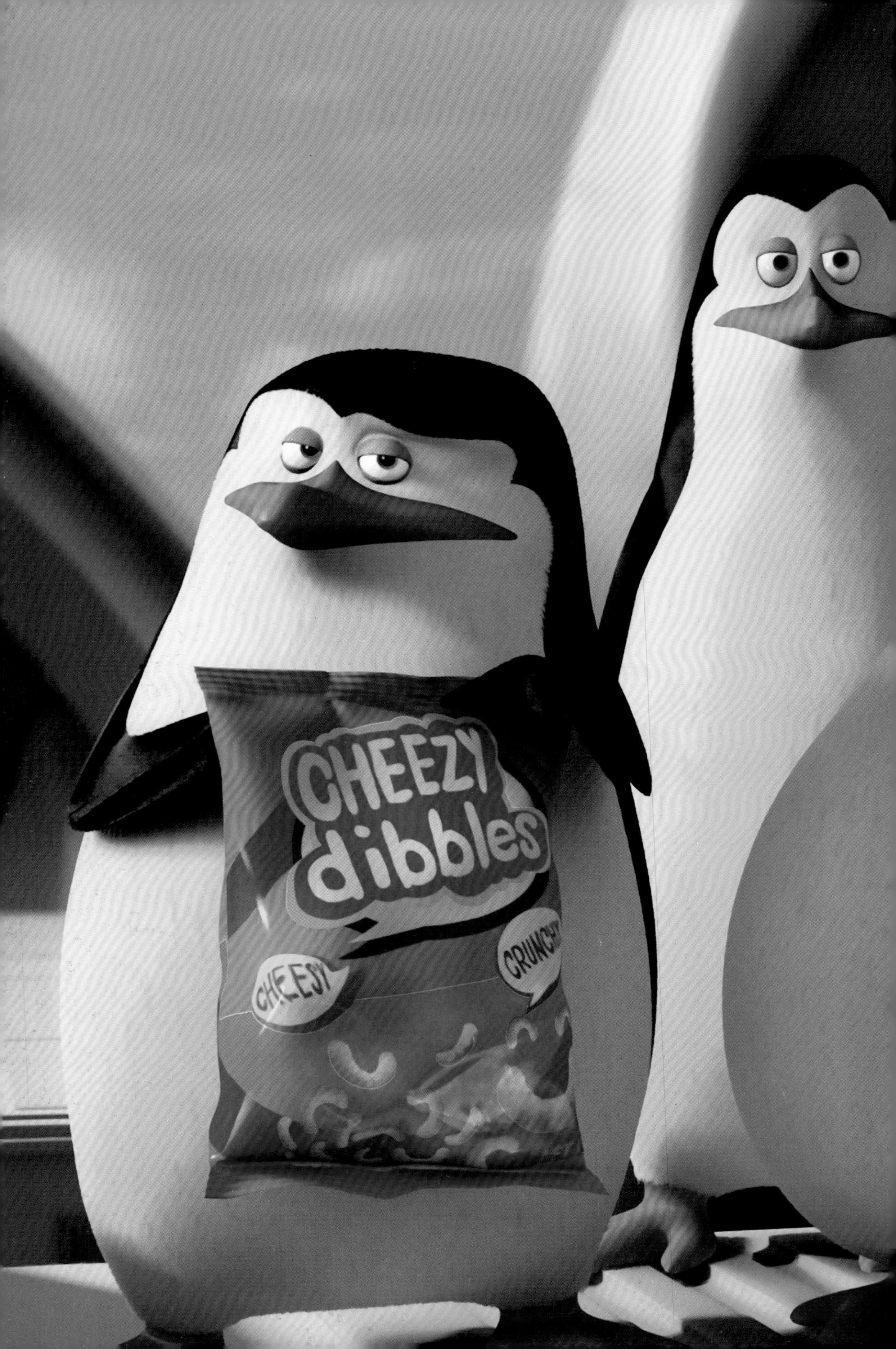
CHEEZY
dibbles
CHEESY
CRUNCHY

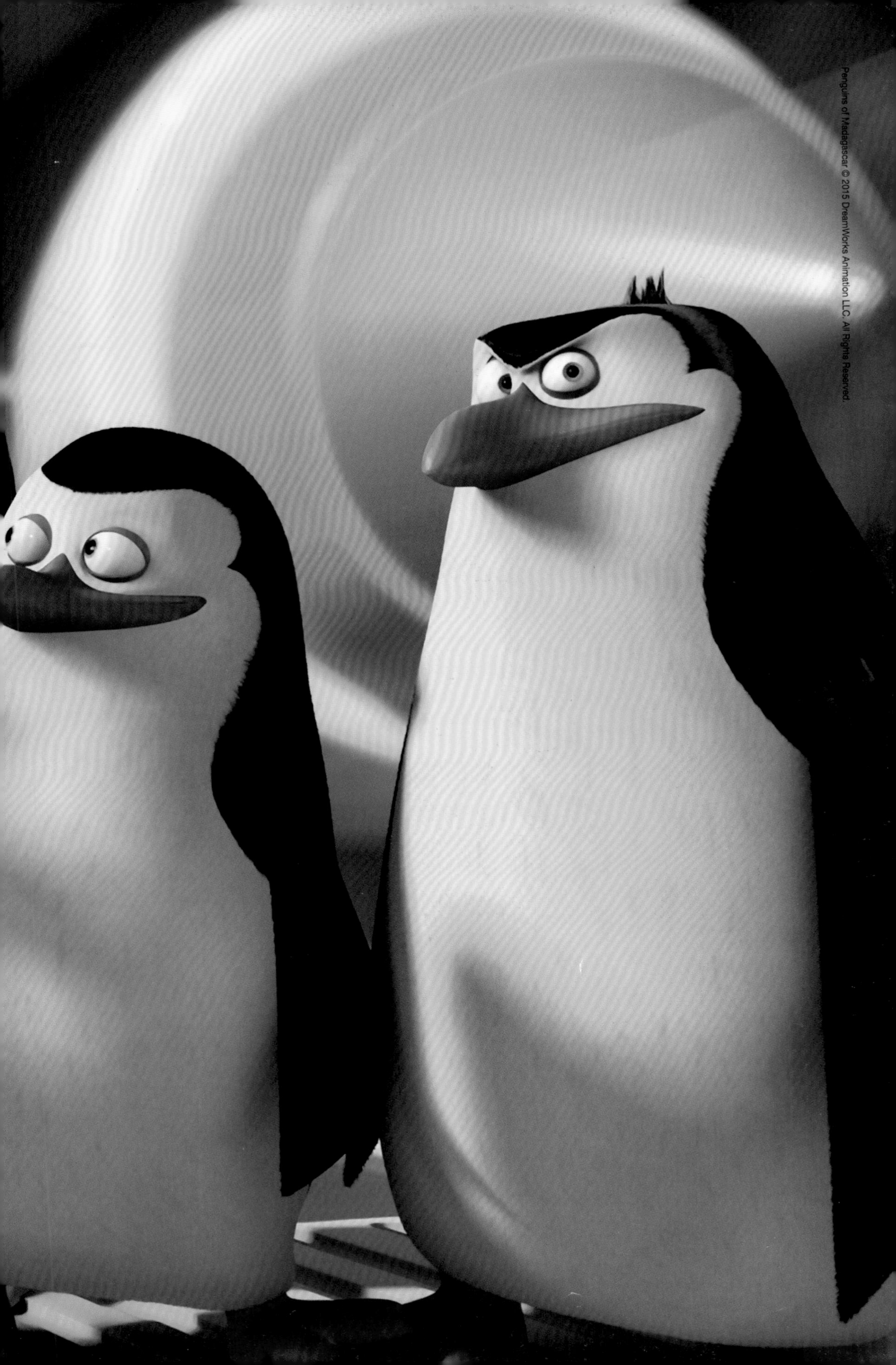

WHEN IN ROME

SCRIPT
Alex Matthews

PENCILS
Grant Perkins

INKS
**Steve Musgrave, Bambos Georgiou
& Robert Wells**

COLORS
John Burns and Tanya Roberts

LETTERING
Jim Campbell

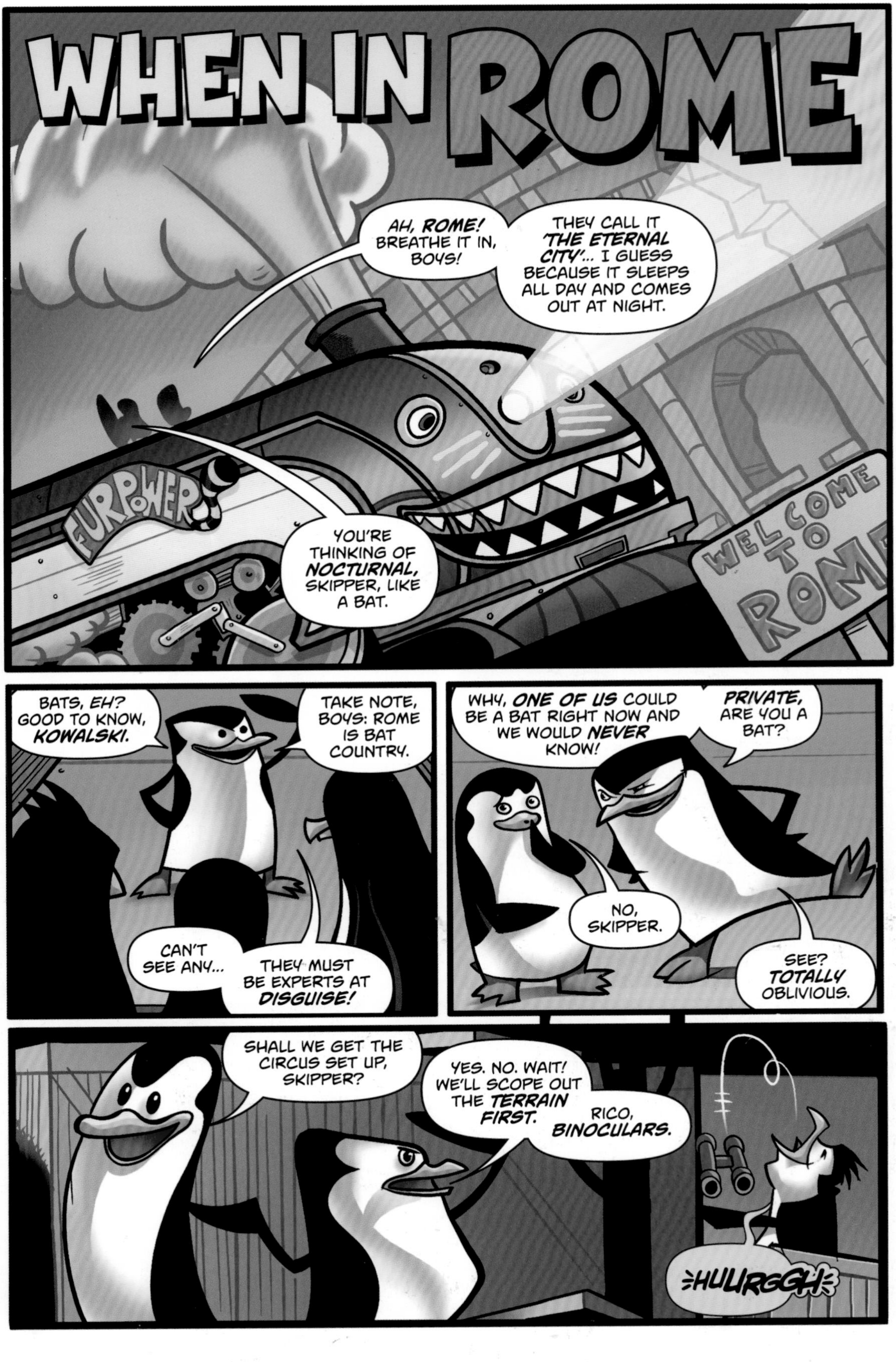
WHEN IN ROME
AH, ROME! BREATHE IT IN, BOYS!
THEY CALL IT 'THE ETERNAL CITY'... I GUESS BECAUSE IT SLEEPS ALL DAY AND COMES OUT AT NIGHT.
FURPOWER
YOU'RE THINKING OF NOCTURNAL, SKIPPER, LIKE A BAT.
WELCOME TO ROME
BATS, EH? GOOD TO KNOW, KOWALSKI.
TAKE NOTE, BOYS: ROME IS BAT COUNTRY.
CAN'T SEE ANY...
THEY MUST BE EXPERTS AT DISGUISE!
WHY, ONE OF US COULD BE A BAT RIGHT NOW AND WE WOULD NEVER KNOW!
PRIVATE, ARE YOU A BAT?
NO, SKIPPER.
SEE? TOTALLY OBLIVIOUS.
SHALL WE GET THE CIRCUS SET UP, SKIPPER?
YES. NO. WAIT! WE'LL SCOPE OUT THE TERRAIN FIRST.
RICO, BINOCULARS.
HUURGGH

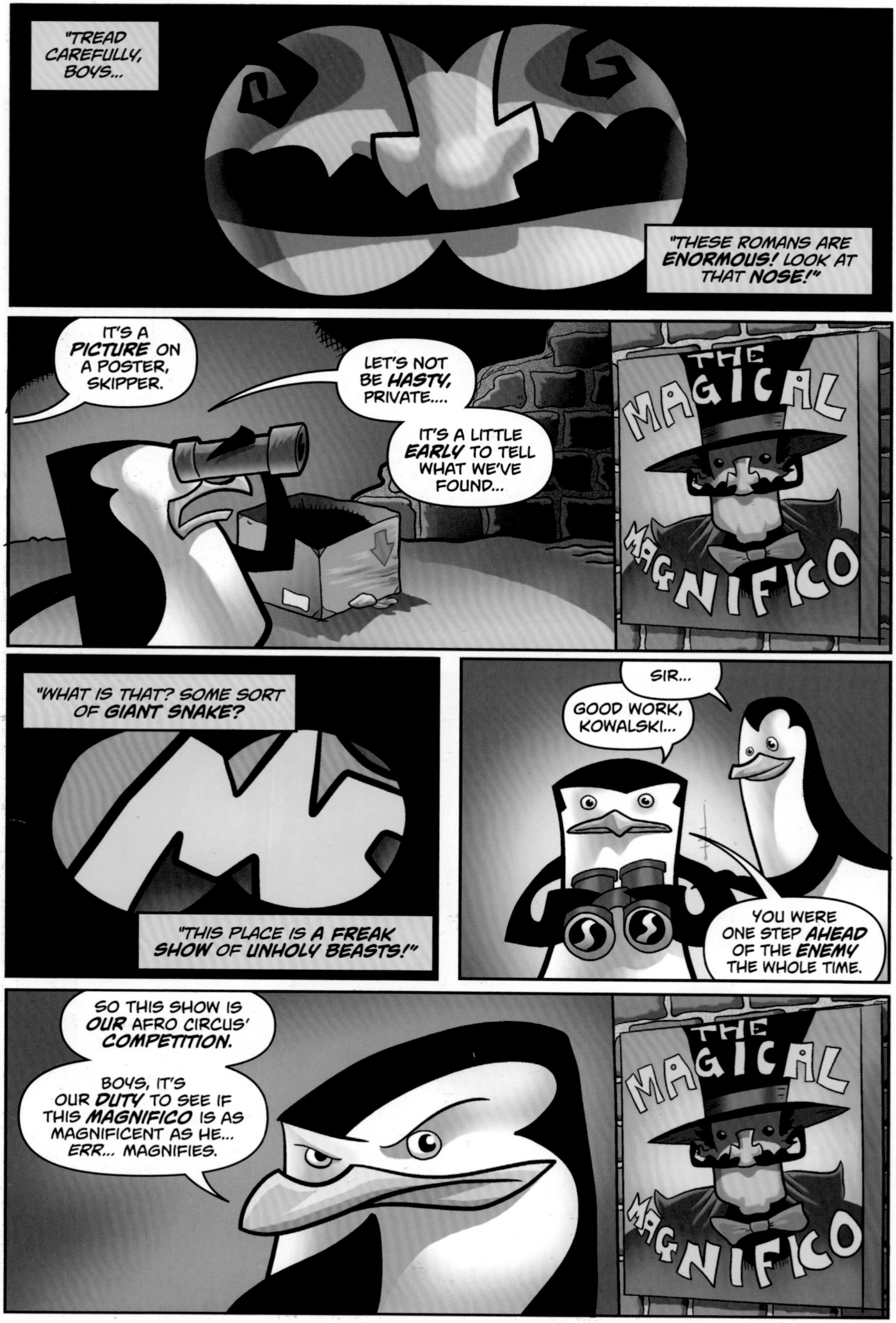
"TREAD CAREFULLY, BOYS...
"THESE ROMANS ARE ENORMOUS! LOOK AT THAT NOSE!"
IT'S A PICTURE ON A POSTER, SKIPPER.
LET'S NOT BE HASTY, PRIVATE....
IT'S A LITTLE EARLY TO TELL WHAT WE'VE FOUND...
THE MAGICAL MAGNIFICO
"WHAT IS THAT? SOME SORT OF GIANT SNAKE?
"THIS PLACE IS A FREAK SHOW OF UNHOLY BEASTS!"
SIR...
GOOD WORK, KOWALSKI...
YOU WERE ONE STEP AHEAD OF THE ENEMY THE WHOLE TIME.
SO THIS SHOW IS OUR AFRO CIRCUS' COMPETITION.
BOYS, IT'S OUR DUTY TO SEE IF THIS MAGNIFICO IS AS MAGNIFICENT AS HE... ERR... MAGNIFIES.
THE MAGICAL MAGNIFICO

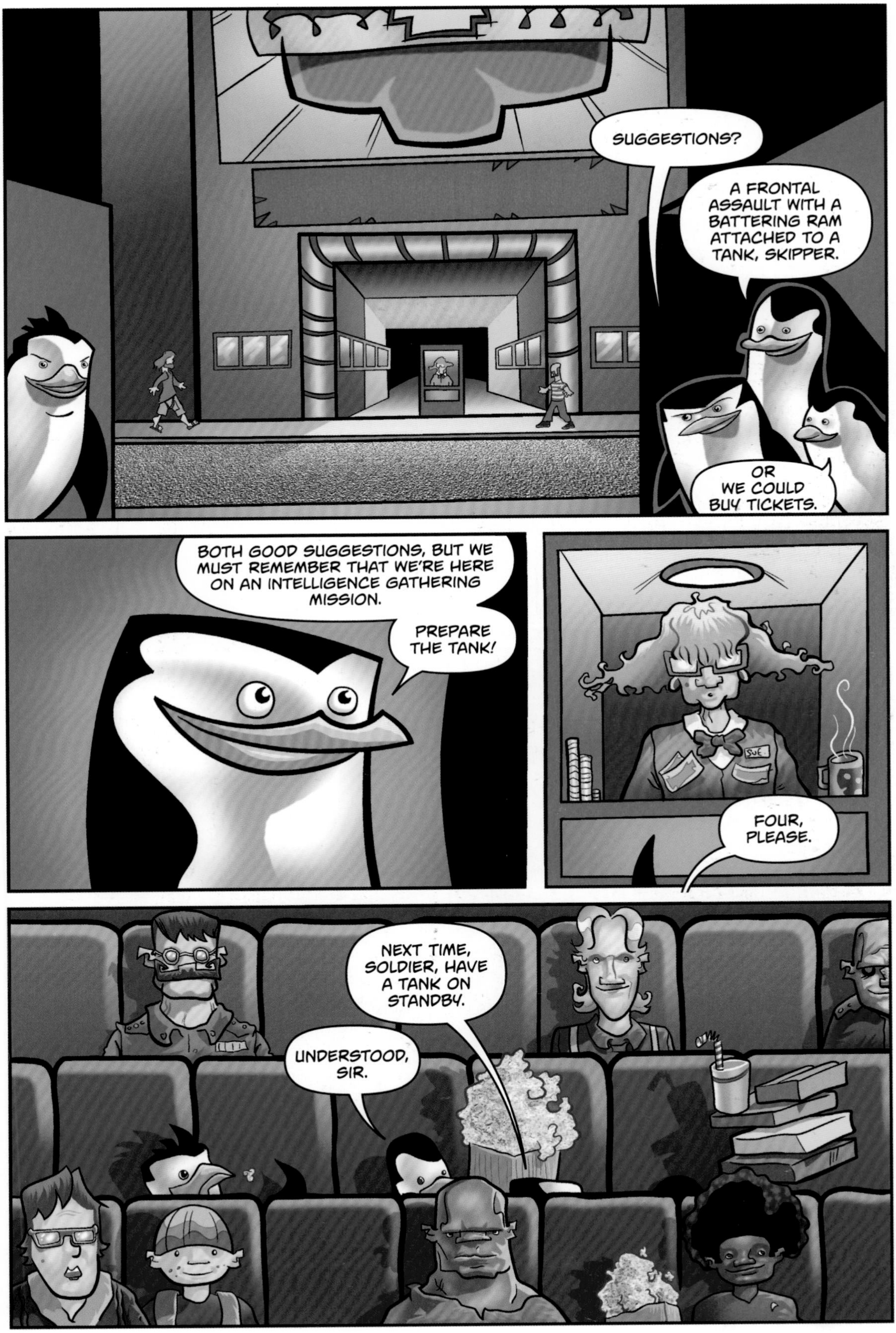
SUGGESTIONS?
A FRONTAL ASSAULT WITH A BATTERING RAM ATTACHED TO A TANK, SKIPPER.
OR WE COULD BUY TICKETS.
BOTH GOOD SUGGESTIONS, BUT WE MUST REMEMBER THAT WE'RE HERE ON AN INTELLIGENCE GATHERING MISSION.
PREPARE THE TANK!
SUE
FOUR, PLEASE.
NEXT TIME, SOLDIER, HAVE A TANK ON STANDBY.
UNDERSTOOD, SIR.

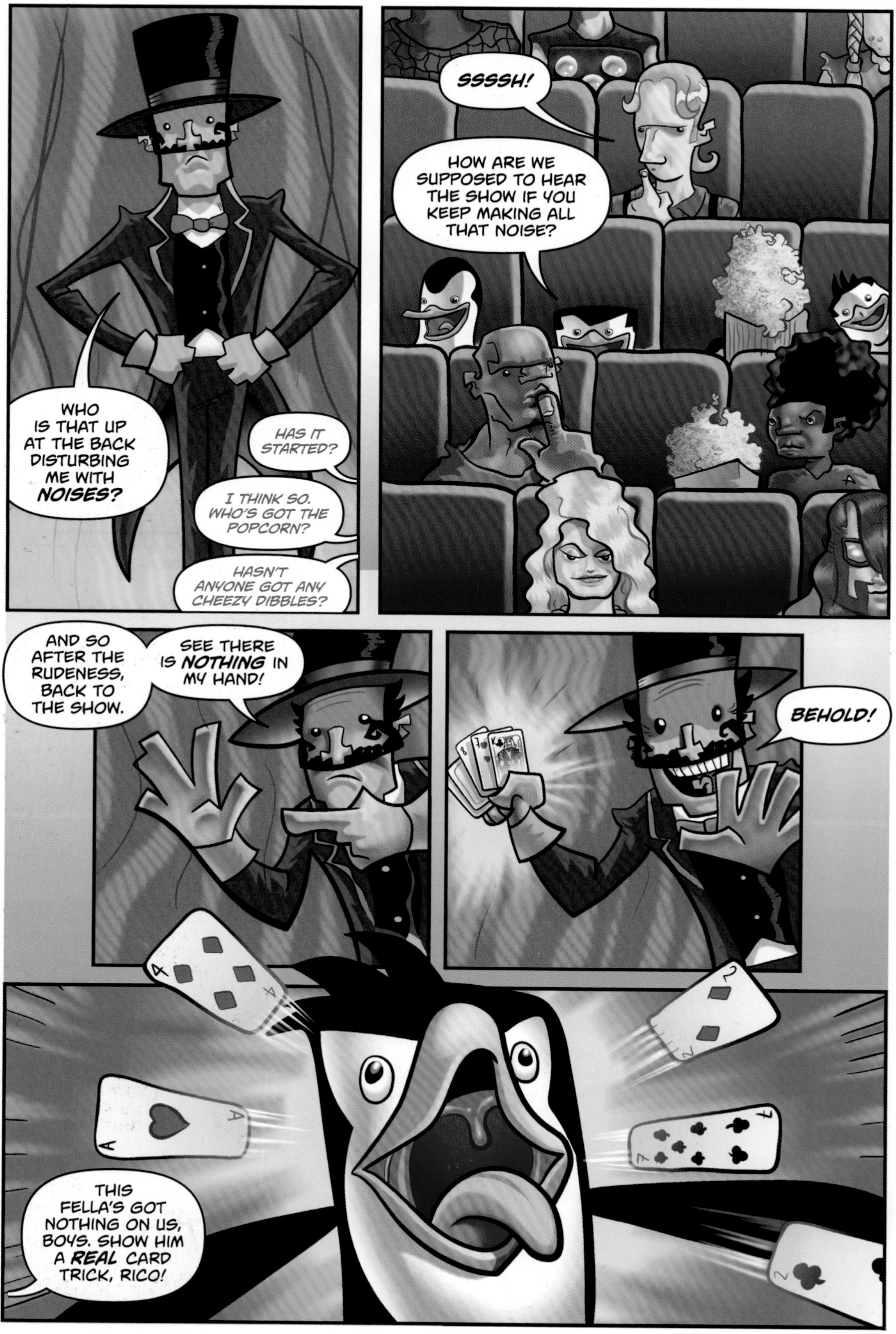
WHO IS THAT UP AT THE BACK DISTURBING ME WITH NOISES?
HAS IT STARTED?
I THINK SO. WHO'S GOT THE POPCORN?
HASN'T ANYONE GOT ANY CHEEZY DIBBLES?
SSSSH!
HOW ARE WE SUPPOSED TO HEAR THE SHOW IF YOU KEEP MAKING ALL THAT NOISE?
AND SO AFTER THE RUDENESS, BACK TO THE SHOW.
SEE THERE IS NOTHING IN MY HAND!
BEHOLD!
THIS FELLA'S GOT NOTHING ON US, BOYS. SHOW HIM A REAL CARD TRICK, RICO!

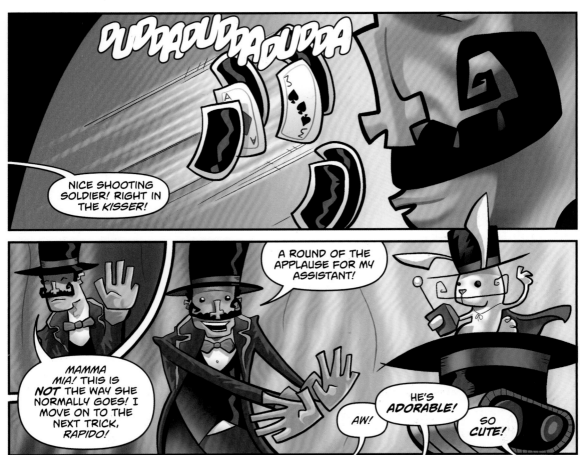

DUDDADUDDADUDDA

NICE SHOOTING SOLDIER! RIGHT IN THE *KISSER!*

A ROUND OF THE APPLAUSE FOR MY ASSISTANT!

MAMMA *MIA!* THIS IS *NOT* THE WAY SHE NORMALLY GOES! I MOVE ON TO THE NEXT TRICK, RAPIDO!

AW!

HE'S *ADORABLE!*

SO *CUTE!*

A *BAT!*

IT'S A *RABBIT,* SKIPPER.

APPEARANCES CAN BE *DECEPTIVE,* KOWALSKI. REMEMBER THE TALE OF THE *DOLPHIN* IN *CAMEL'S CLOTHING?*

I MUST HAVE MISSED THAT ONE.

REMIND ME HOW YOU GOT INTO THIS UNIT, SOLDIER.

SI, HE IS CUTE, BUT HE IS ALSO THE *MISCHIEF MAKER!* WHERE WILL HE APPEAR NEXT?

CLAPCLAPCLAP

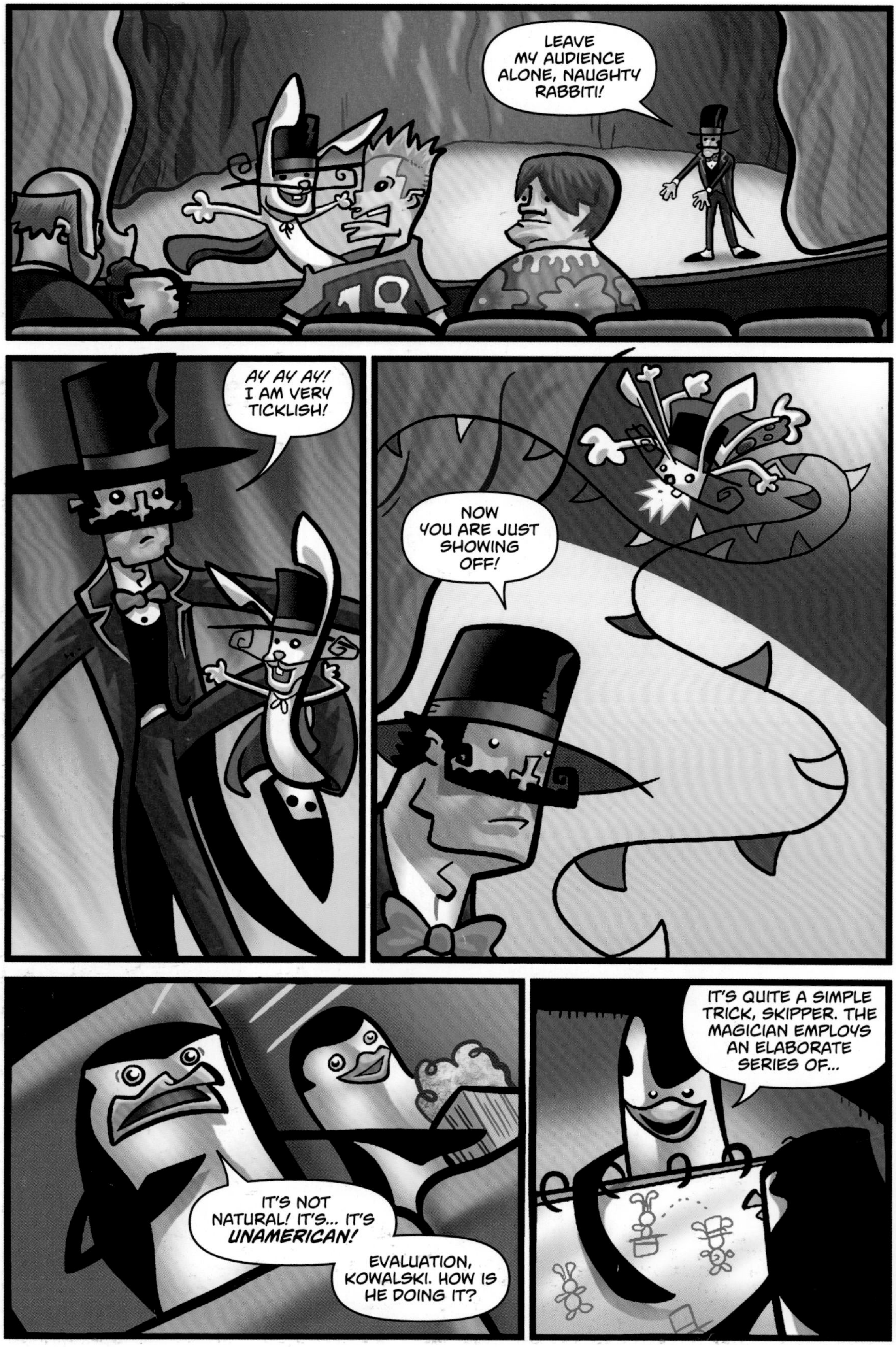

LEAVE MY AUDIENCE ALONE, NAUGHTY RABBITI!
AY AY AY! I AM VERY TICKLISH!
NOW YOU ARE JUST SHOWING OFF!
IT'S NOT NATURAL! IT'S... IT'S UNAMERICAN!
EVALUATION, KOWALSKI. HOW IS HE DOING IT?
IT'S QUITE A SIMPLE TRICK, SKIPPER. THE MAGICIAN EMPLOYS AN ELABORATE SERIES OF...

PRIVATE, I'M GOING TO NEED YOUR EYES ON THE SHOW WHILE I LISTEN INTENTLY TO EVERY WORD KOWALSKI SAYS.

YOU GOT IT, MR PENGUIN!

CODE RED! WE'VE BEEN *INFILTRATED!*

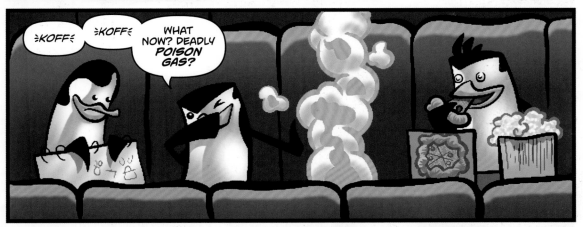

≷KOFF≷ ≷KOFF≷

WHAT NOW? DEADLY *POISON GAS?*

WHAT'S THAT, SKIPPER?

YOU'VE GOT TO HAND IT TO HIM, KOWALSKI, HE KNOWS A THING OR TWO ABOUT THE MAGICAL ARTS!

GRAZIE! THAT'S A VERY NICE THING TO SAY!

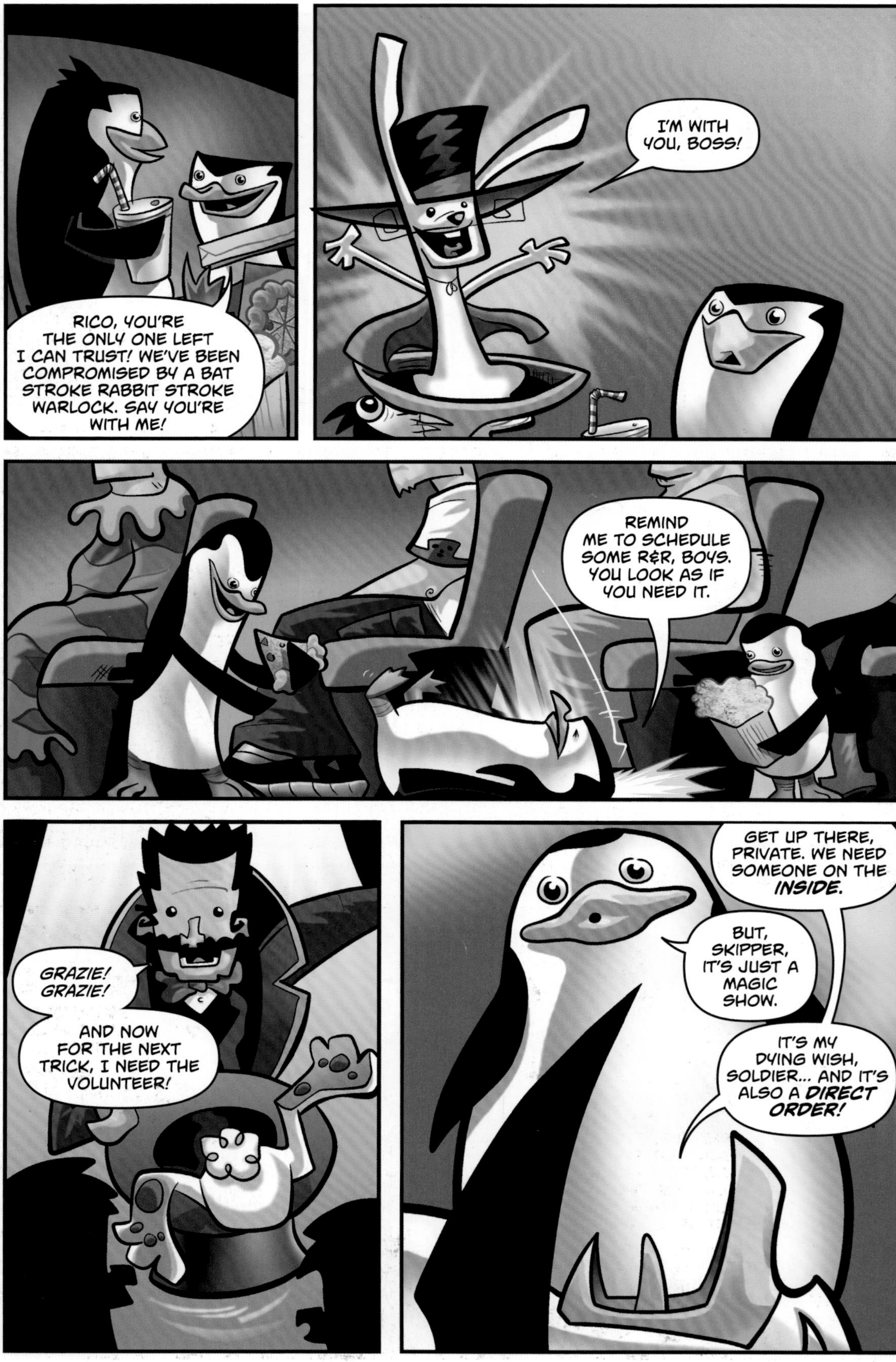
RICO, YOU'RE THE ONLY ONE LEFT I CAN TRUST! WE'VE BEEN COMPROMISED BY A BAT STROKE RABBIT STROKE WARLOCK. SAY YOU'RE WITH ME!
I'M WITH YOU, BOSS!
REMIND ME TO SCHEDULE SOME R&R, BOYS. YOU LOOK AS IF YOU NEED IT.
GRAZIE! GRAZIE!
AND NOW FOR THE NEXT TRICK, I NEED THE VOLUNTEER!
GET UP THERE, PRIVATE. WE NEED SOMEONE ON THE *INSIDE*.
BUT, SKIPPER, IT'S JUST A MAGIC SHOW.
IT'S MY DYING WISH, SOLDIER... AND IT'S ALSO A *DIRECT ORDER!*

WELCOME TO THE STAGE, THE BRAVE VOLUNTEER... UM... PENGUIN!

HELLO!

THE SAWING OF THE PENGUIN IN HALF IS THE CLASSIC TRICK, BUT MAGNIFICO HAS PUT HIS OWN MAGNIFICO TWIST ON IT!

SKIPPER, LOOK, I'M IN SHOW BUSINESS!

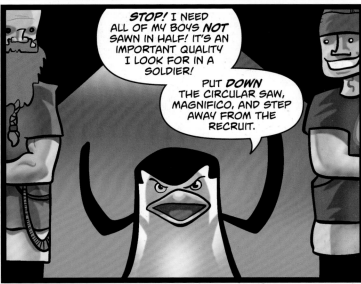

STOP! I NEED ALL OF MY BOYS NOT SAWN IN HALF! IT'S AN IMPORTANT QUALITY I LOOK FOR IN A SOLDIER!

PUT DOWN THE CIRCULAR SAW, MAGNIFICO, AND STEP AWAY FROM THE RECRUIT.

SKIPPER, IT'S ALL JUST AN ILLUSION. TO MAKE IT LOOK REAL THE MAGICIAN HAS SET UP A...

THE TIME FOR TALK IS OVER, KOWALSKI. NOW IT'S TIME FOR...

SECURITY!

SHOUTING! SEE, THIS GUY GETS IT.

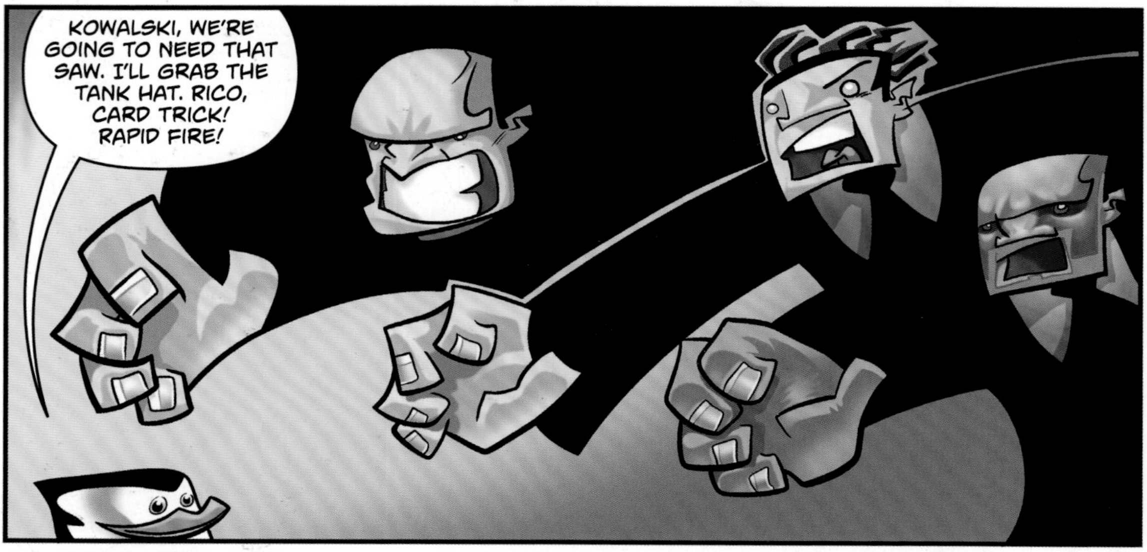
KOWALSKI, WE'RE GOING TO NEED THAT SAW. I'LL GRAB THE TANK HAT. RICO, CARD TRICK! RAPID FIRE!

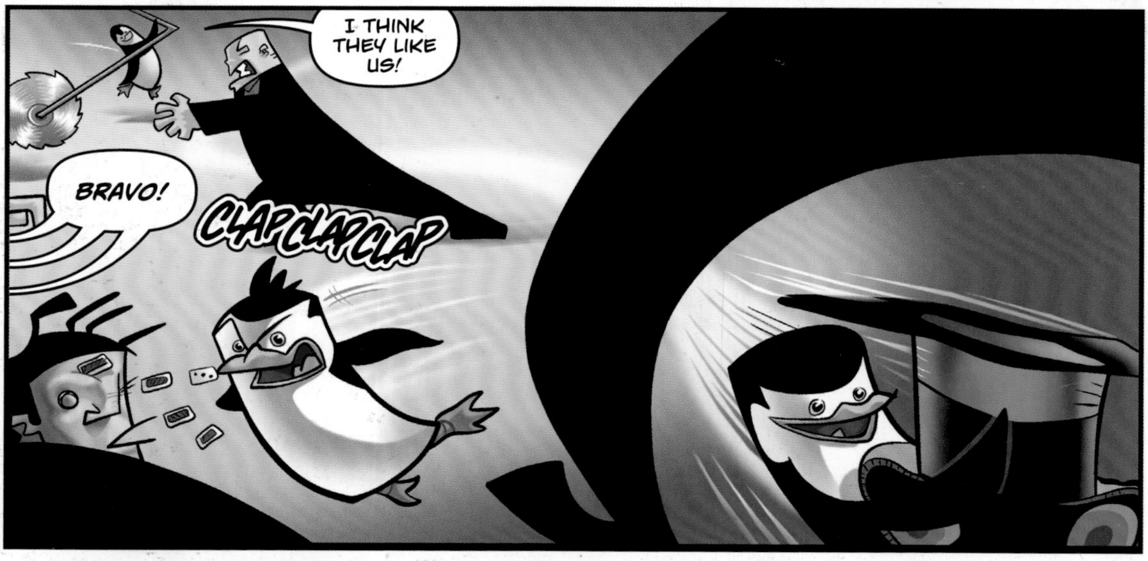
I THINK THEY LIKE US!
BRAVO!
CLAP CLAP CLAP

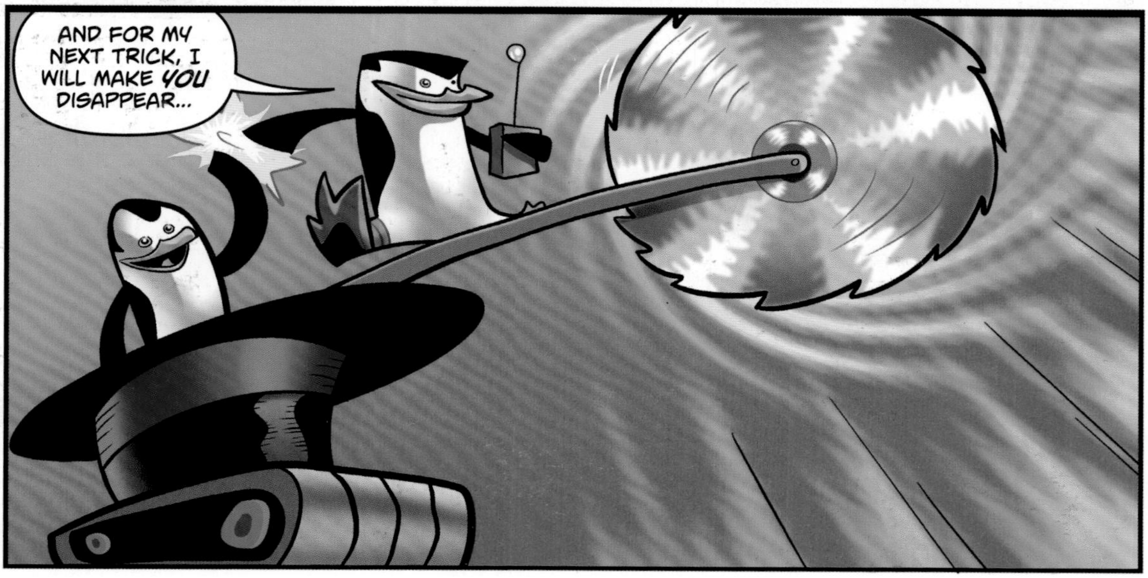
AND FOR MY NEXT TRICK, I WILL MAKE YOU DISAPPEAR...

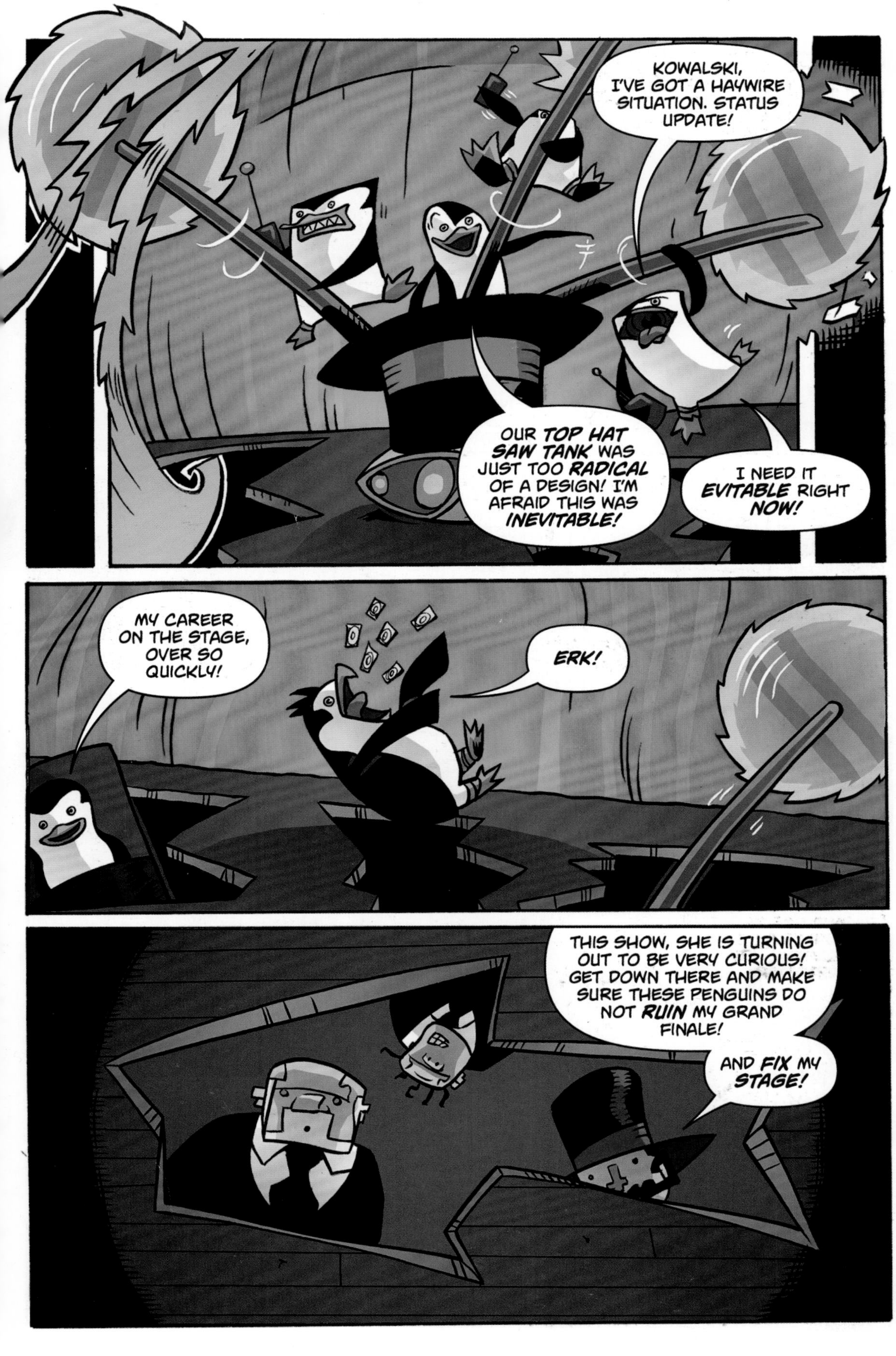
KOWALSKI, I'VE GOT A HAYWIRE SITUATION. STATUS UPDATE!
OUR TOP HAT SAW TANK WAS JUST TOO RADICAL OF A DESIGN! I'M AFRAID THIS WAS INEVITABLE!
I NEED IT EVITABLE RIGHT NOW!
MY CAREER ON THE STAGE, OVER SO QUICKLY!
ERK!
THIS SHOW, SHE IS TURNING OUT TO BE VERY CURIOUS! GET DOWN THERE AND MAKE SURE THESE PENGUINS DO NOT RUIN MY GRAND FINALE!
AND FIX MY STAGE!

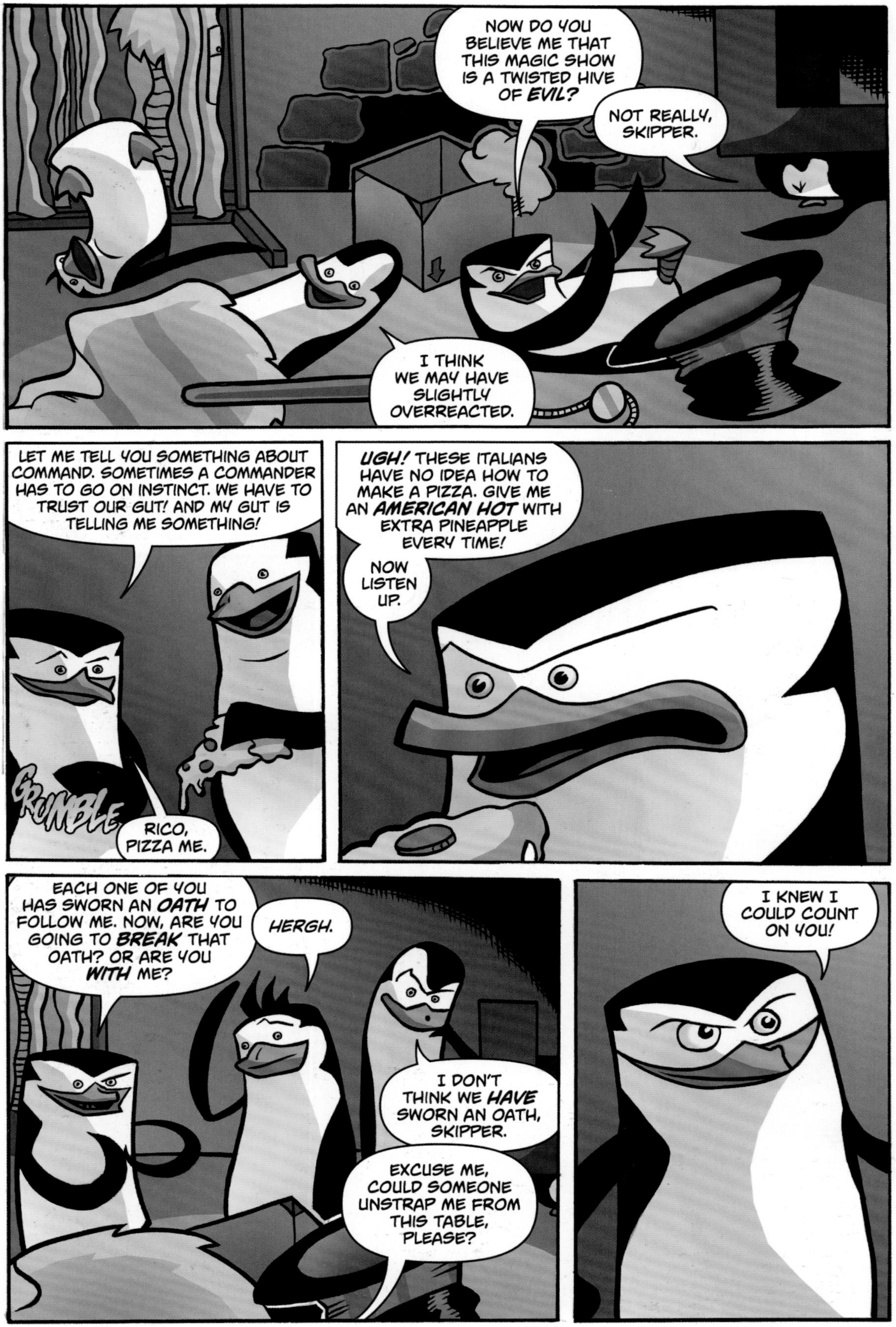
NOW DO YOU BELIEVE ME THAT THIS MAGIC SHOW IS A TWISTED HIVE OF EVIL?
NOT REALLY, SKIPPER.
I THINK WE MAY HAVE SLIGHTLY OVERREACTED.
LET ME TELL YOU SOMETHING ABOUT COMMAND. SOMETIMES A COMMANDER HAS TO GO ON INSTINCT. WE HAVE TO TRUST OUR GUT! AND MY GUT IS TELLING ME SOMETHING!
GRUMBLE
RICO, PIZZA ME.
UGH! THESE ITALIANS HAVE NO IDEA HOW TO MAKE A PIZZA. GIVE ME AN AMERICAN HOT WITH EXTRA PINEAPPLE EVERY TIME!
NOW LISTEN UP.
EACH ONE OF YOU HAS SWORN AN OATH TO FOLLOW ME. NOW, ARE YOU GOING TO BREAK THAT OATH? OR ARE YOU WITH ME?
HERGH.
I DON'T THINK WE HAVE SWORN AN OATH, SKIPPER.
EXCUSE ME, COULD SOMEONE UNSTRAP ME FROM THIS TABLE, PLEASE?
I KNEW I COULD COUNT ON YOU!

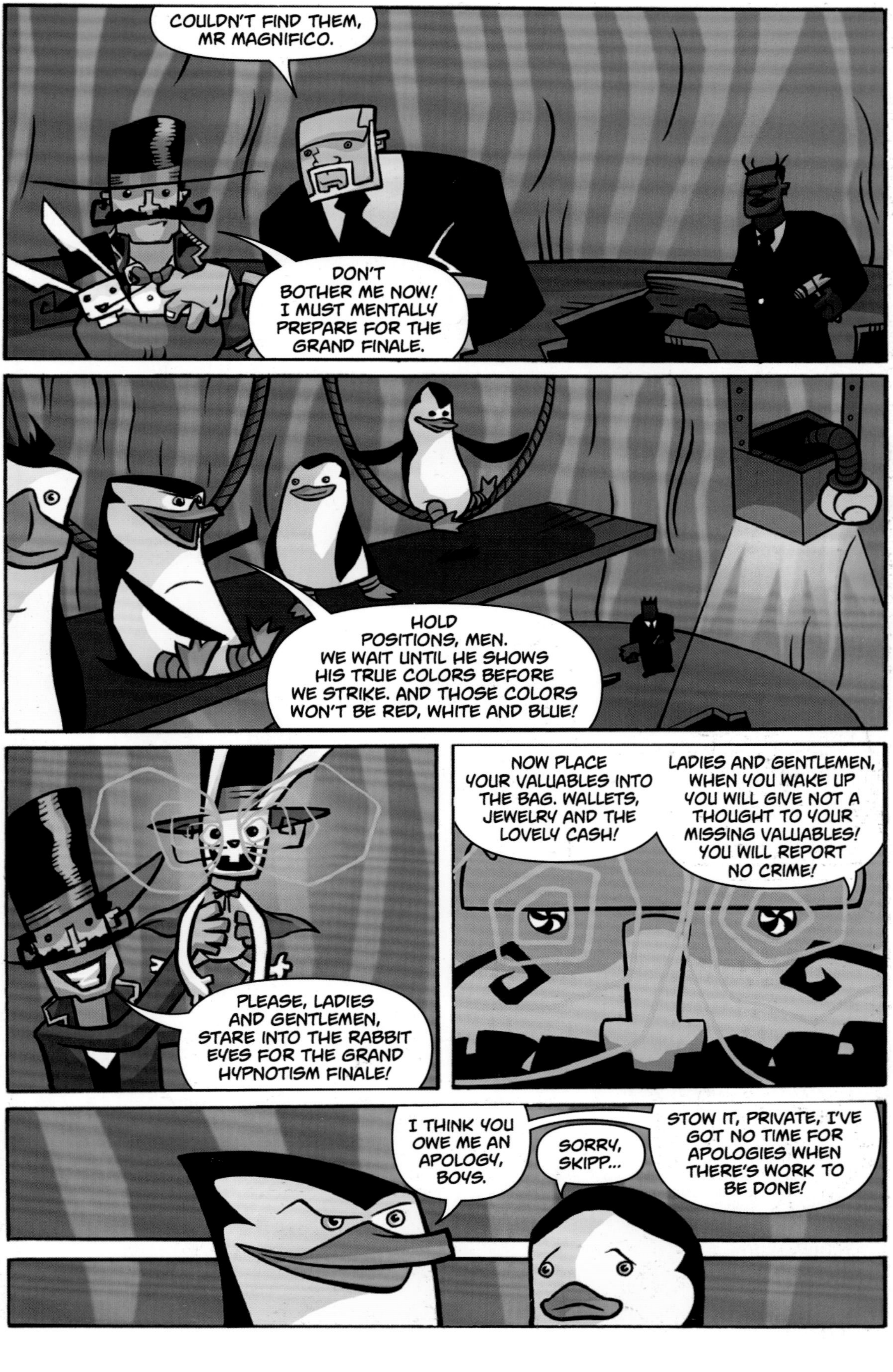
COULDN'T FIND THEM, MR MAGNIFICO.
DON'T BOTHER ME NOW! I MUST MENTALLY PREPARE FOR THE GRAND FINALE.
HOLD POSITIONS, MEN. WE WAIT UNTIL HE SHOWS HIS TRUE COLORS BEFORE WE STRIKE. AND THOSE COLORS WON'T BE RED, WHITE AND BLUE!
PLEASE, LADIES AND GENTLEMEN, STARE INTO THE RABBIT EYES FOR THE GRAND HYPNOTISM FINALE!
NOW PLACE YOUR VALUABLES INTO THE BAG. WALLETS, JEWELRY AND THE LOVELY CASH!
LADIES AND GENTLEMEN, WHEN YOU WAKE UP YOU WILL GIVE NOT A THOUGHT TO YOUR MISSING VALUABLES! YOU WILL REPORT NO CRIME!
I THINK YOU OWE ME AN APOLOGY, BOYS.
SORRY, SKIPP...
STOW IT, PRIVATE, I'VE GOT NO TIME FOR APOLOGIES WHEN THERE'S WORK TO BE DONE!

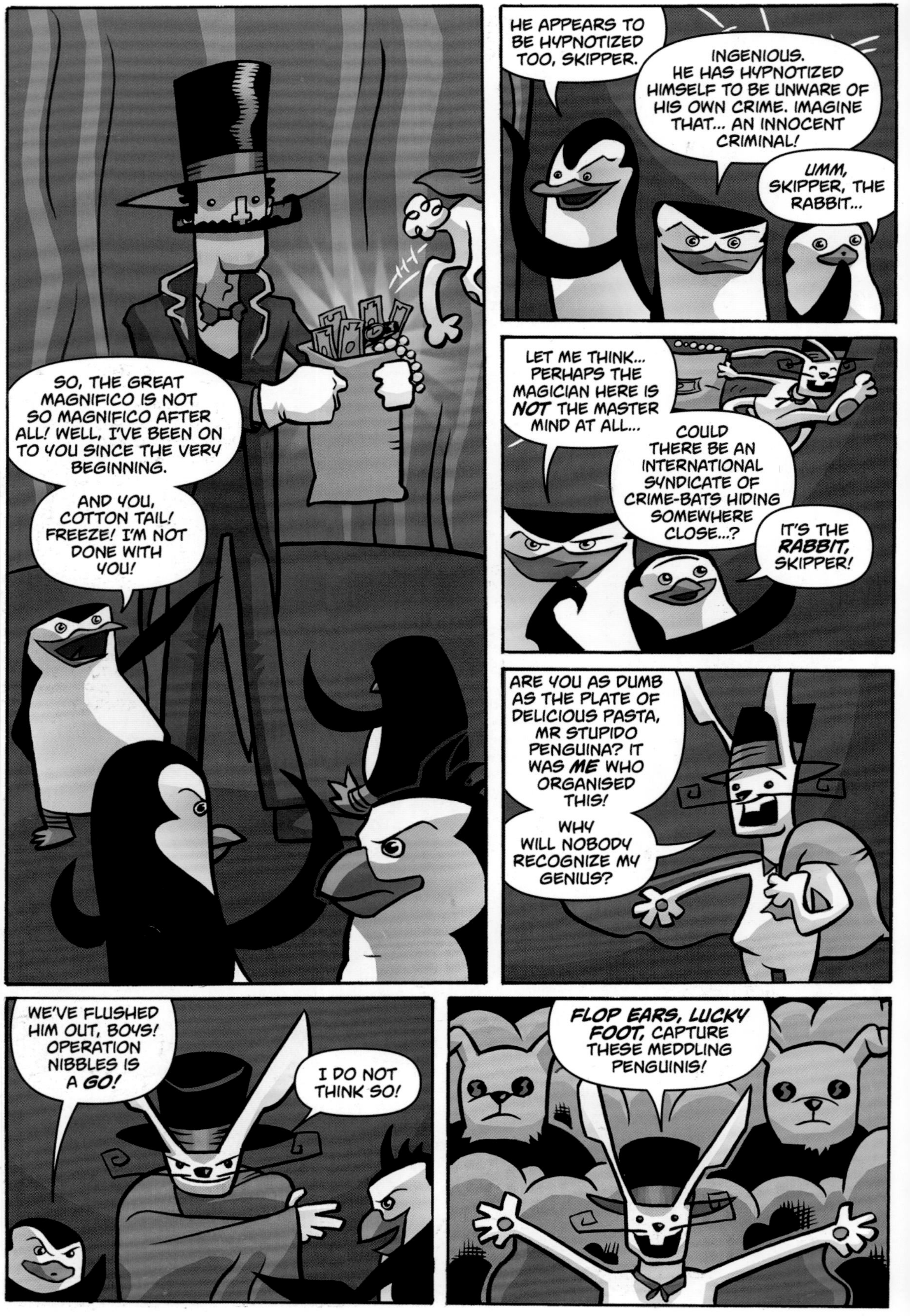
SO, THE GREAT MAGNIFICO IS NOT SO MAGNIFICO AFTER ALL! WELL, I'VE BEEN ON TO YOU SINCE THE VERY BEGINNING.
AND YOU, COTTON TAIL! FREEZE! I'M NOT DONE WITH YOU!
HE APPEARS TO BE HYPNOTIZED TOO, SKIPPER.
INGENIOUS. HE HAS HYPNOTIZED HIMSELF TO BE UNWARE OF HIS OWN CRIME. IMAGINE THAT... AN INNOCENT CRIMINAL!
UMM, SKIPPER, THE RABBIT...
LET ME THINK... PERHAPS THE MAGICIAN HERE IS ***NOT*** THE MASTER MIND AT ALL...
COULD THERE BE AN INTERNATIONAL SYNDICATE OF CRIME-BATS HIDING SOMEWHERE CLOSE...?
IT'S THE ***RABBIT,*** SKIPPER!
ARE YOU AS DUMB AS THE PLATE OF DELICIOUS PASTA, MR STUPIDO PENGUINA? IT WAS ***ME*** WHO ORGANISED THIS!
WHY WILL NOBODY RECOGNIZE MY GENIUS?
WE'VE FLUSHED HIM OUT, BOYS! OPERATION NIBBLES IS A ***GO!***
I DO NOT THINK SO!
FLOP EARS, LUCKY FOOT, CAPTURE THESE MEDDLING PENGUINIS!

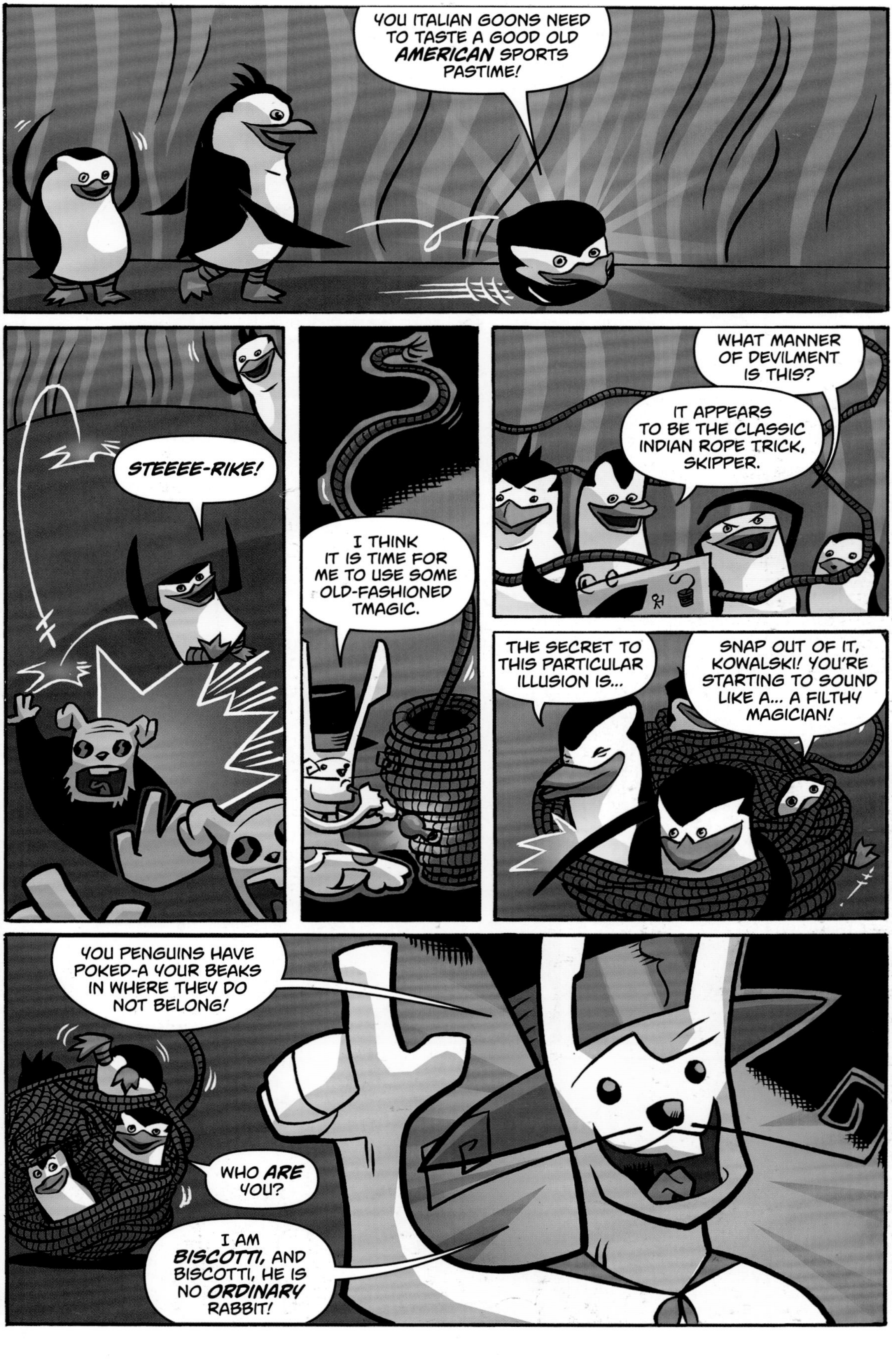
YOU ITALIAN GOONS NEED TO TASTE A GOOD OLD AMERICAN SPORTS PASTIME!
STEEEE-RIKE!
I THINK IT IS TIME FOR ME TO USE SOME OLD-FASHIONED TMAGIC.
WHAT MANNER OF DEVILMENT IS THIS?
IT APPEARS TO BE THE CLASSIC INDIAN ROPE TRICK, SKIPPER.
THE SECRET TO THIS PARTICULAR ILLUSION IS...
SNAP OUT OF IT, KOWALSKI! YOU'RE STARTING TO SOUND LIKE A... A FILTHY MAGICIAN!
YOU PENGUINS HAVE POKED-A YOUR BEAKS IN WHERE THEY DO NOT BELONG!
WHO ARE YOU?
I AM BISCOTTI, AND BISCOTTI, HE IS NO ORDINARY RABBIT!

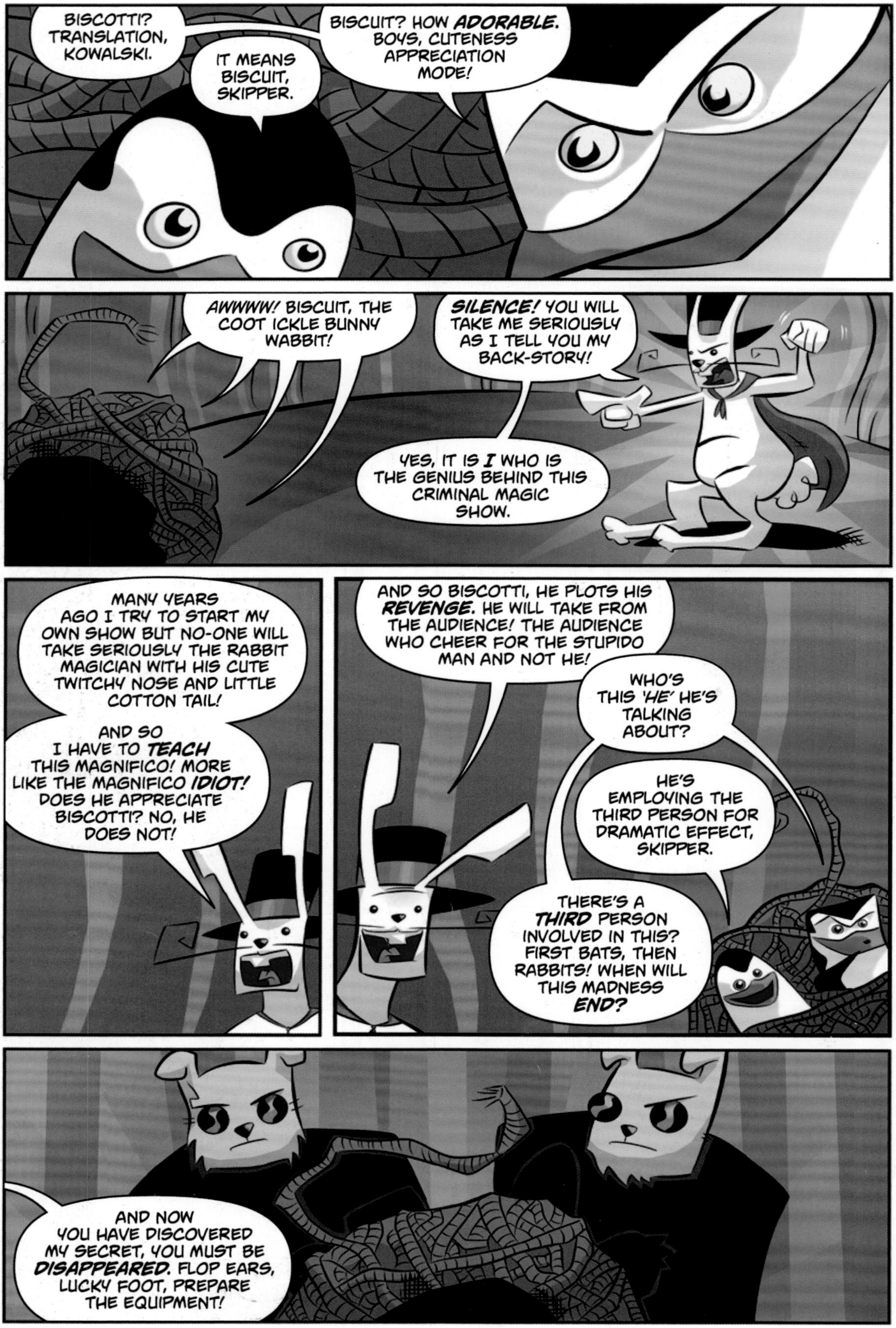
BISCOTTI? TRANSLATION, KOWALSKI.
IT MEANS BISCUIT, SKIPPER.
BISCUIT? HOW ADORABLE. BOYS, CUTENESS APPRECIATION MODE!
AWWWW! BISCUIT, THE COOT ICKLE BUNNY WABBIT!
SILENCE! YOU WILL TAKE ME SERIOUSLY AS I TELL YOU MY BACK-STORY!
YES, IT IS I WHO IS THE GENIUS BEHIND THIS CRIMINAL MAGIC SHOW.
MANY YEARS AGO I TRY TO START MY OWN SHOW BUT NO-ONE WILL TAKE SERIOUSLY THE RABBIT MAGICIAN WITH HIS CUTE TWITCHY NOSE AND LITTLE COTTON TAIL!
AND SO I HAVE TO TEACH THIS MAGNIFICO! MORE LIKE THE MAGNIFICO IDIOT! DOES HE APPRECIATE BISCOTTI? NO, HE DOES NOT!
AND SO BISCOTTI, HE PLOTS HIS REVENGE. HE WILL TAKE FROM THE AUDIENCE! THE AUDIENCE WHO CHEER FOR THE STUPIDO MAN AND NOT HE!
WHO'S THIS 'HE' HE'S TALKING ABOUT?
HE'S EMPLOYING THE THIRD PERSON FOR DRAMATIC EFFECT, SKIPPER.
THERE'S A THIRD PERSON INVOLVED IN THIS? FIRST BATS, THEN RABBITS! WHEN WILL THIS MADNESS END?
AND NOW YOU HAVE DISCOVERED MY SECRET, YOU MUST BE DISAPPEARED. FLOP EARS, LUCKY FOOT, PREPARE THE EQUIPMENT!

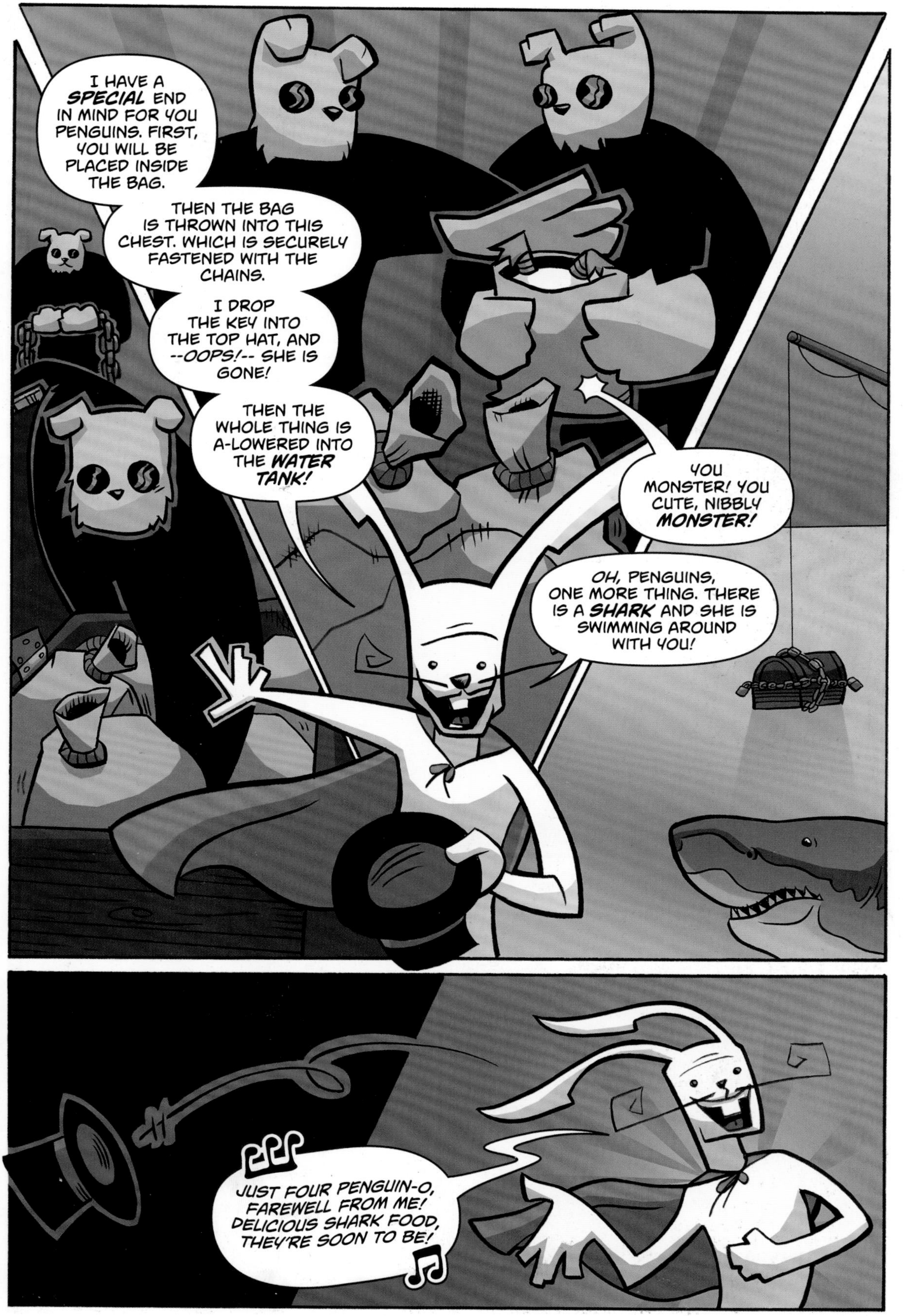
I HAVE A SPECIAL END IN MIND FOR YOU PENGUINS. FIRST, YOU WILL BE PLACED INSIDE THE BAG.
THEN THE BAG IS THROWN INTO THIS CHEST. WHICH IS SECURELY FASTENED WITH THE CHAINS.
I DROP THE KEY INTO THE TOP HAT, AND --OOPS!-- SHE IS GONE!
THEN THE WHOLE THING IS A-LOWERED INTO THE WATER TANK!
YOU MONSTER! YOU CUTE, NIBBLY MONSTER!
OH, PENGUINS, ONE MORE THING. THERE IS A SHARK AND SHE IS SWIMMING AROUND WITH YOU!
JUST FOUR PENGUIN-O, FAREWELL FROM ME! DELICIOUS SHARK FOOD, THEY'RE SOON TO BE!

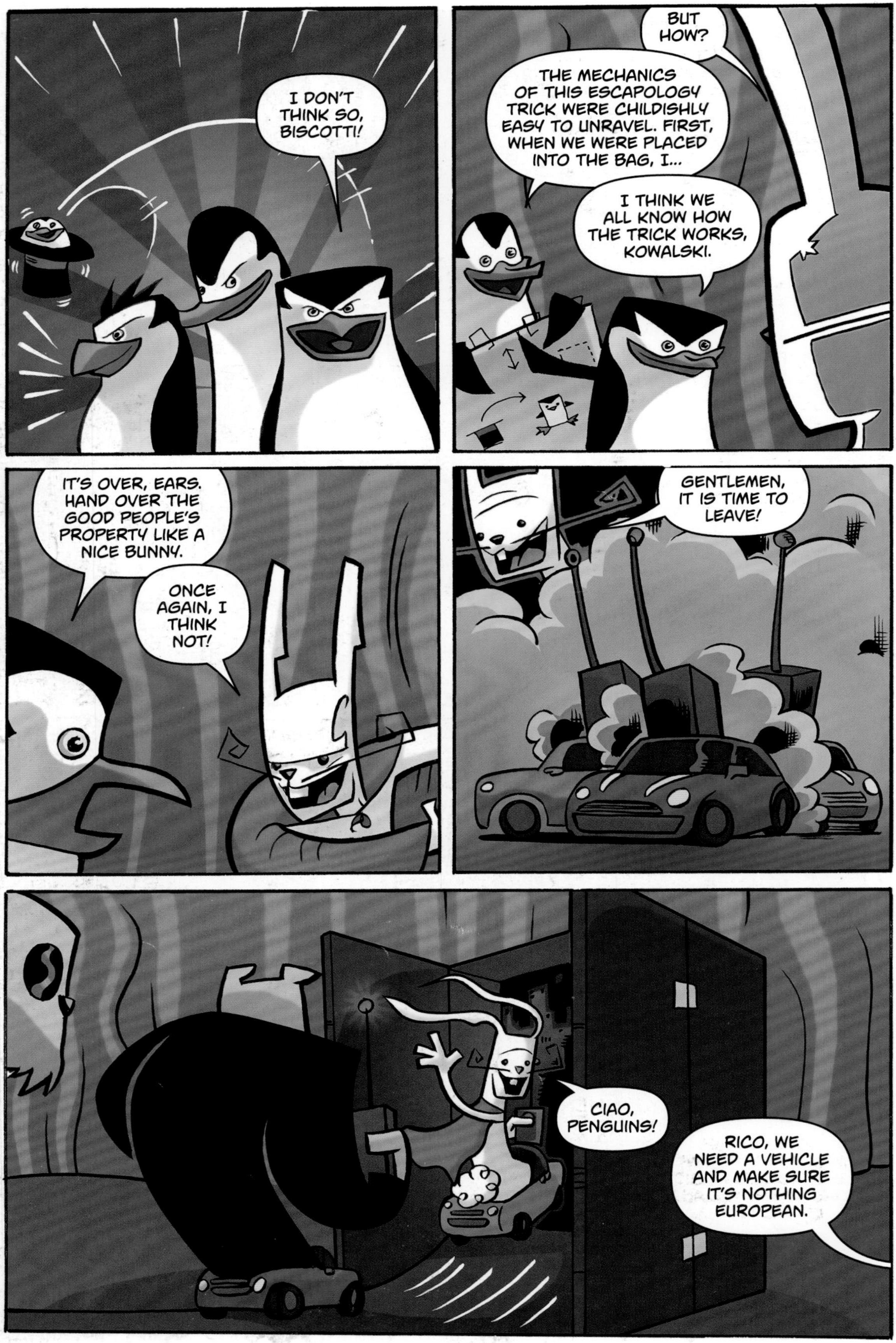
I DON'T THINK SO, BISCOTTI!
BUT HOW?
THE MECHANICS OF THIS ESCAPOLOGY TRICK WERE CHILDISHLY EASY TO UNRAVEL. FIRST, WHEN WE WERE PLACED INTO THE BAG, I...
I THINK WE ALL KNOW HOW THE TRICK WORKS, KOWALSKI.
IT'S OVER, EARS. HAND OVER THE GOOD PEOPLE'S PROPERTY LIKE A NICE BUNNY.
ONCE AGAIN, I THINK NOT!
GENTLEMEN, IT IS TIME TO LEAVE!
CIAO, PENGUINS!
RICO, WE NEED A VEHICLE AND MAKE SURE IT'S NOTHING EUROPEAN.

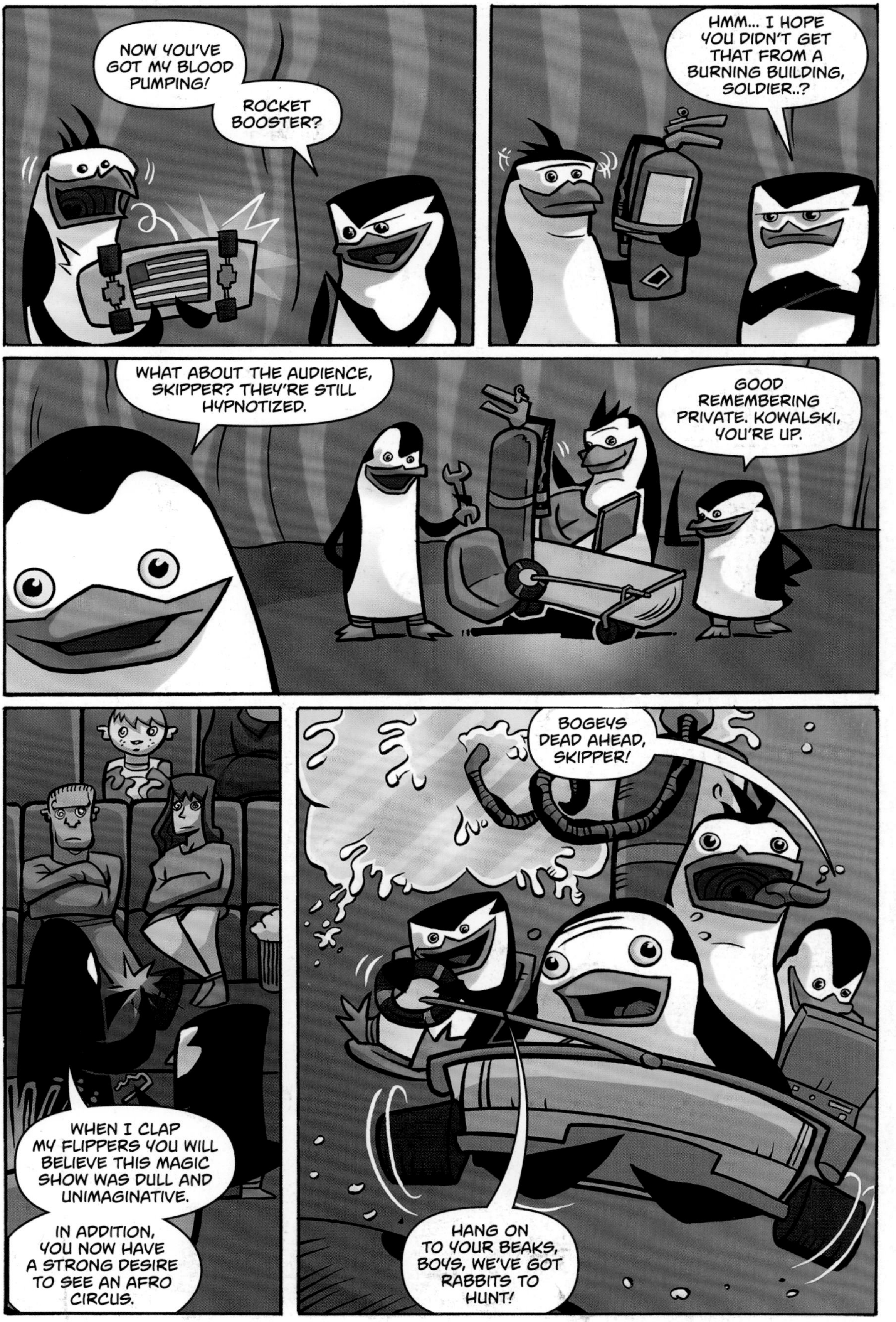
NOW YOU'VE GOT MY BLOOD PUMPING!
ROCKET BOOSTER?
HMM... I HOPE YOU DIDN'T GET THAT FROM A BURNING BUILDING, SOLDIER..?
WHAT ABOUT THE AUDIENCE, SKIPPER? THEY'RE STILL HYPNOTIZED.
GOOD REMEMBERING PRIVATE. KOWALSKI, YOU'RE UP.
WHEN I CLAP MY FLIPPERS YOU WILL BELIEVE THIS MAGIC SHOW WAS DULL AND UNIMAGINATIVE.
IN ADDITION, YOU NOW HAVE A STRONG DESIRE TO SEE AN AFRO CIRCUS.
BOGEYS DEAD AHEAD, SKIPPER!
HANG ON TO YOUR BEAKS, BOYS, WE'VE GOT RABBITS TO HUNT!

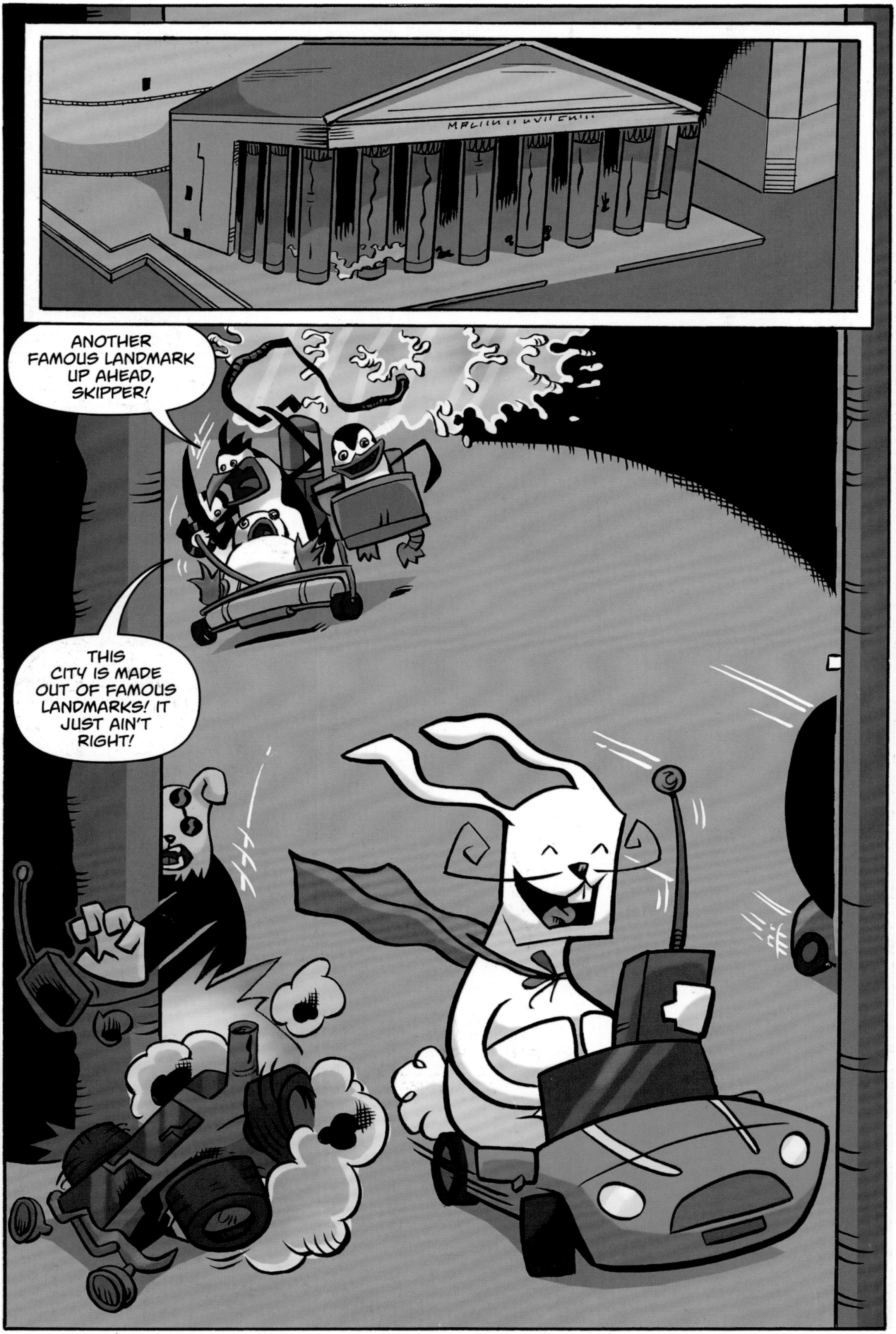
ANOTHER FAMOUS LANDMARK UP AHEAD, SKIPPER!
THIS CITY IS MADE OUT OF FAMOUS LANDMARKS! IT JUST AIN'T RIGHT!

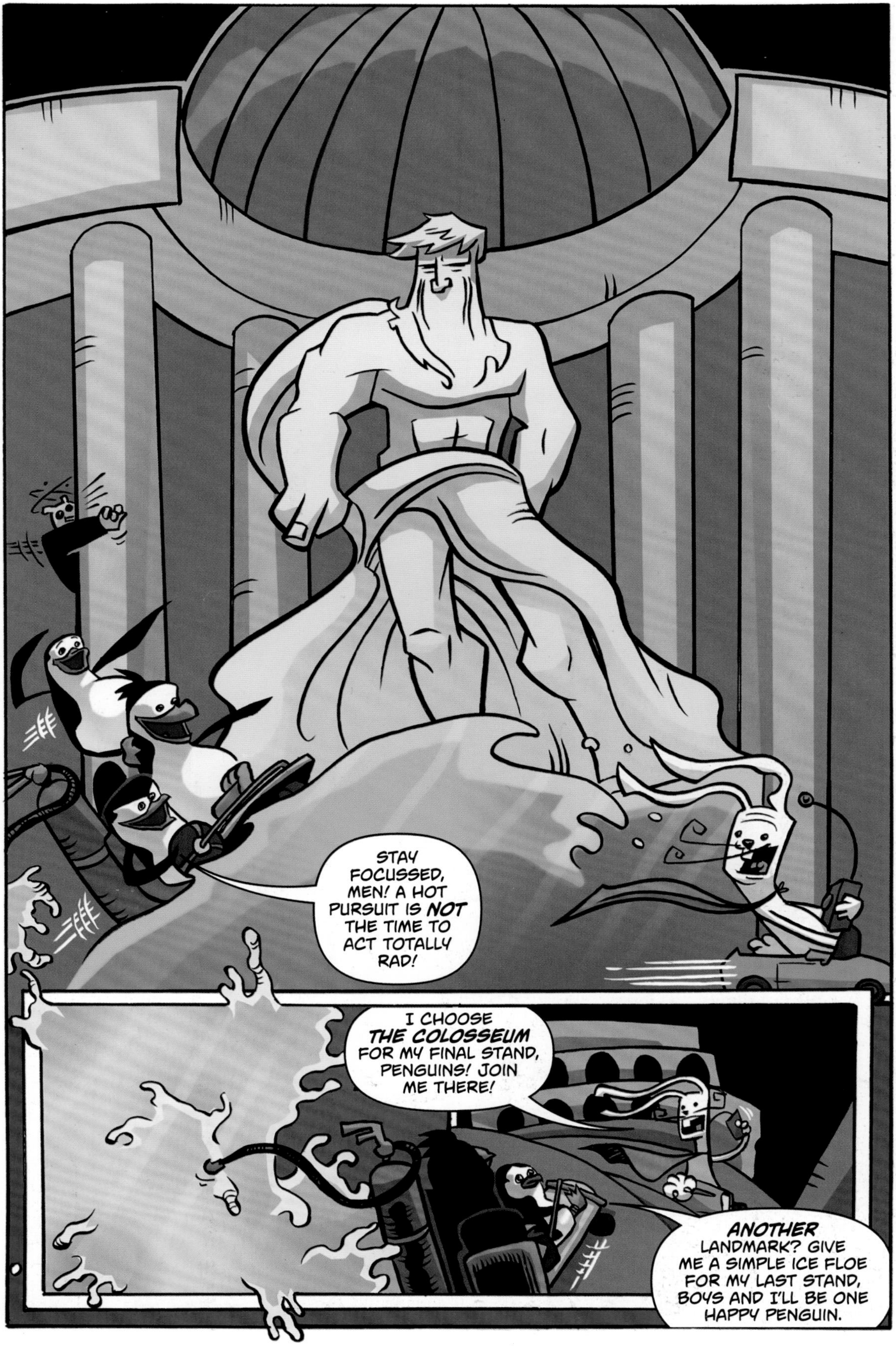
STAY FOCUSSED, MEN! A HOT PURSUIT IS **NOT** THE TIME TO ACT TOTALLY RAD!
I CHOOSE ***THE COLOSSEUM*** FOR MY FINAL STAND, PENGUINS! JOIN ME THERE!
ANOTHER LANDMARK? GIVE ME A SIMPLE ICE FLOE FOR MY LAST STAND, BOYS AND I'LL BE ONE HAPPY PENGUIN.

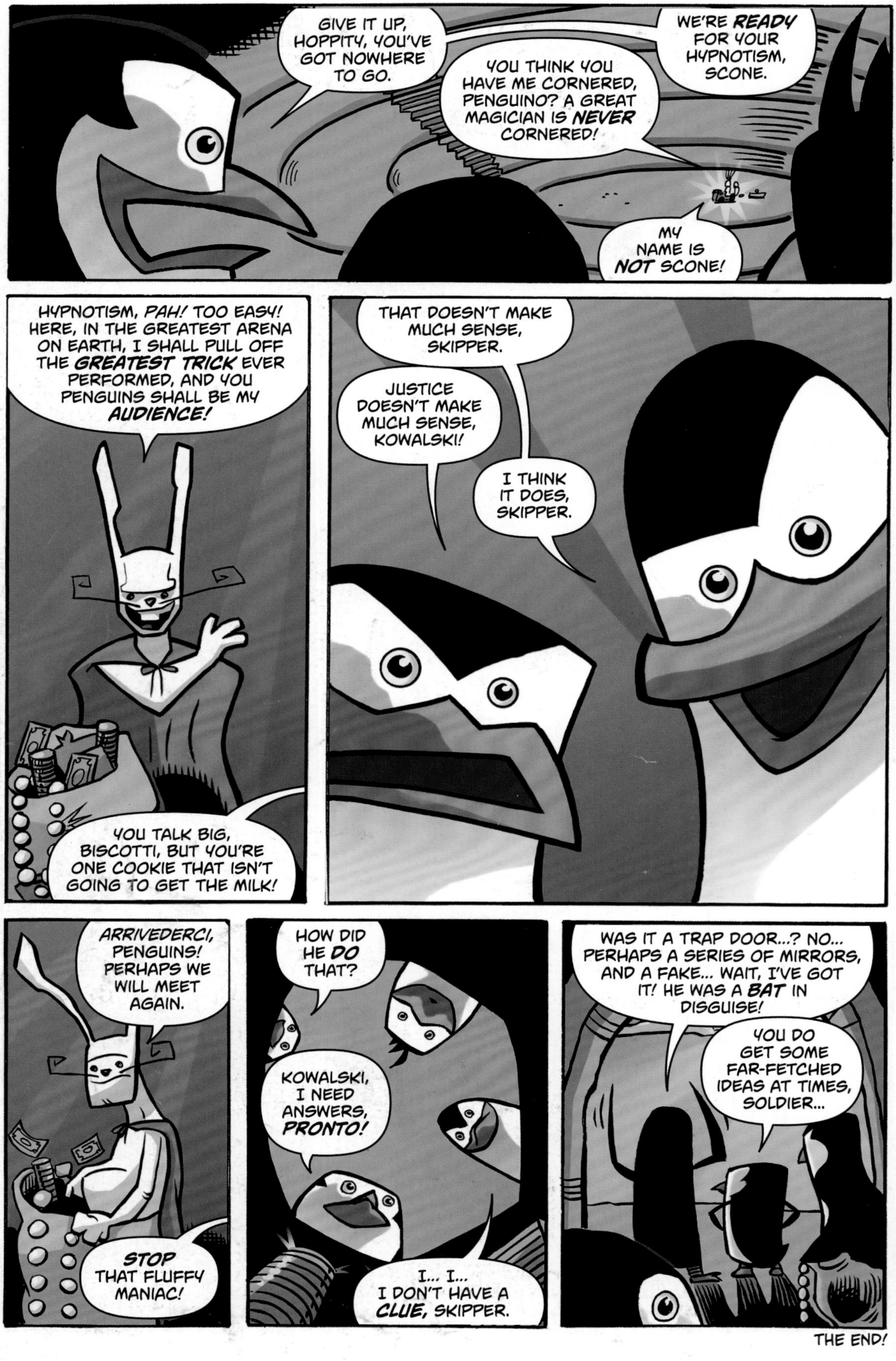
GIVE IT UP, HOPPITY, YOU'VE GOT NOWHERE TO GO.
WE'RE READY FOR YOUR HYPNOTISM, SCONE.
YOU THINK YOU HAVE ME CORNERED, PENGUINO? A GREAT MAGICIAN IS NEVER CORNERED!
MY NAME IS NOT SCONE!
HYPNOTISM, PAH! TOO EASY! HERE, IN THE GREATEST ARENA ON EARTH, I SHALL PULL OFF THE GREATEST TRICK EVER PERFORMED, AND YOU PENGUINS SHALL BE MY AUDIENCE!
YOU TALK BIG, BISCOTTI, BUT YOU'RE ONE COOKIE THAT ISN'T GOING TO GET THE MILK!
THAT DOESN'T MAKE MUCH SENSE, SKIPPER.
JUSTICE DOESN'T MAKE MUCH SENSE, KOWALSKI!
I THINK IT DOES, SKIPPER.
ARRIVEDERCI, PENGUINS! PERHAPS WE WILL MEET AGAIN.
STOP THAT FLUFFY MANIAC!
HOW DID HE DO THAT?
KOWALSKI, I NEED ANSWERS, PRONTO!
I... I... I DON'T HAVE A CLUE, SKIPPER.
WAS IT A TRAP DOOR...? NO... PERHAPS A SERIES OF MIRRORS, AND A FAKE... WAIT, I'VE GOT IT! HE WAS A BAT IN DISGUISE!
YOU DO GET SOME FAR-FETCHED IDEAS AT TIMES, SOLDIER...

THE END!

HOME VOL. 1

BRAND NEW STORIES FEATURING OH, TIP, PIG AND THE BOOV FROM DREAMWORKS ANIMATION'S HIT MOVIE, *HOME!*

Based on DreamWorks Animation's smash hit movie *Home*, Titan Comics bring you the all-new adventures of the friendliest, goofiest world dominators you've ever seen!

In these original stories, Tip and the Boov alien, Oh, attempt to play hide-and-seek – with inter-dimensional consequences! And Oh faces the perilous pitfalls of job-hunting! Plus, 'Pig in Space' and 'The Funny Pages'!

ON SALE NOW!

WWW.TITAN-COMICS.COM

Contents

A Christmas Carol

Dramatis Personæ

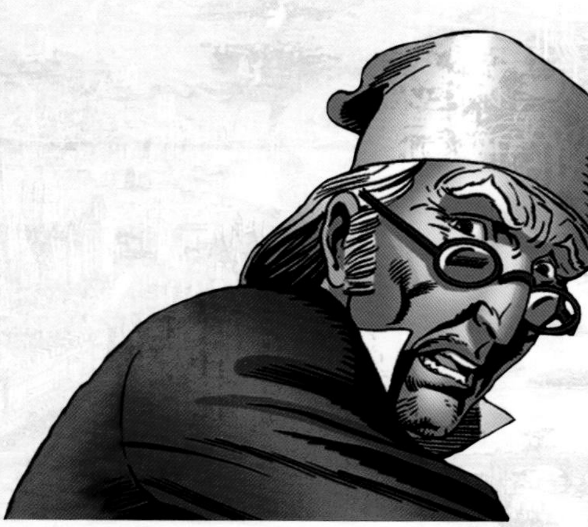

Ebenezer Scrooge

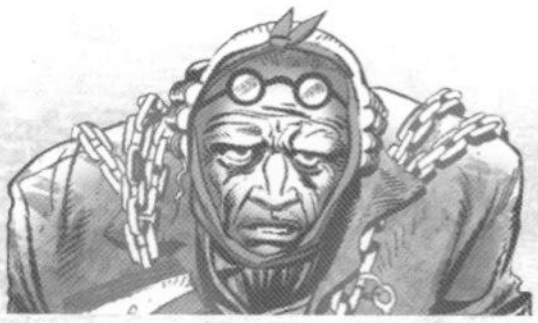

Ghost of Jacob Marley

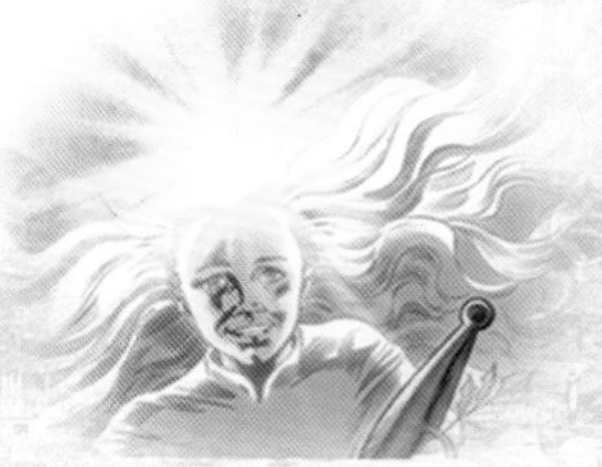

Ghost of Christmas Past

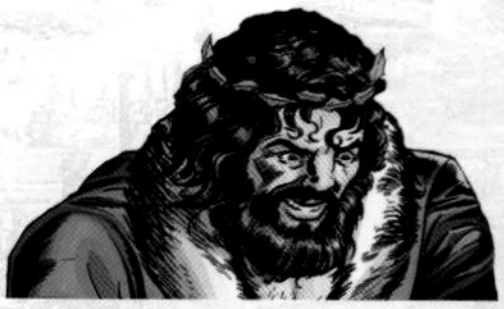

Ghost of Christmas Present

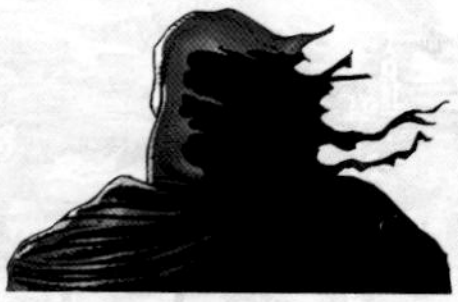

Ghost of Christmas Yet to Come

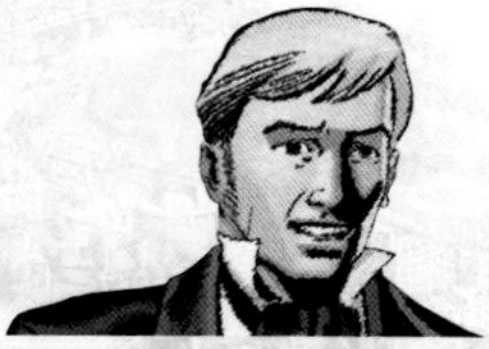

Bob Cratchit
Scrooge's clerk

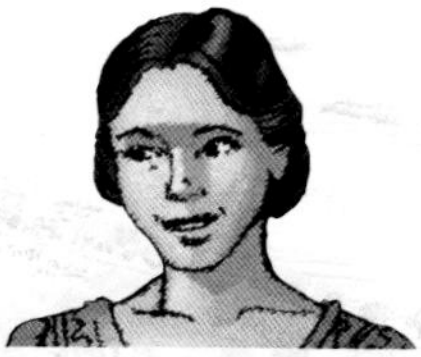

Mrs. Cratchit
Bob's wife

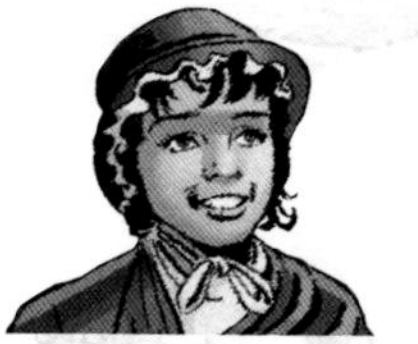

Martha Cratchit
Bob's eldest daughter

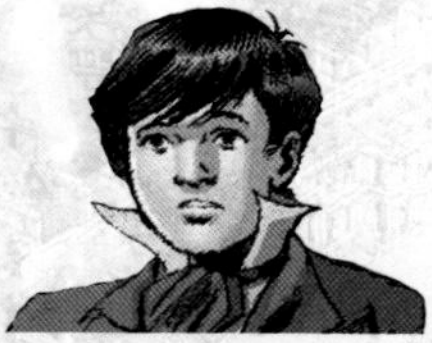

Peter Cratchit
Bob's eldest son

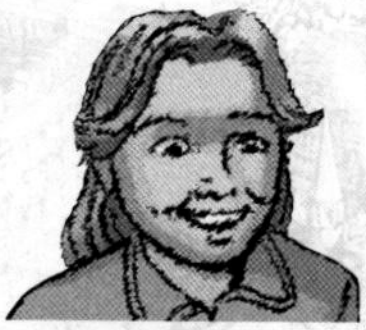

Belinda Cratchit
Bob's second daughter

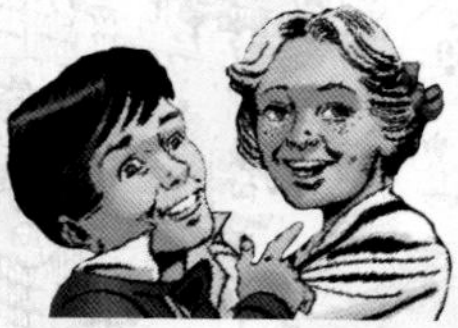

Cratchit children

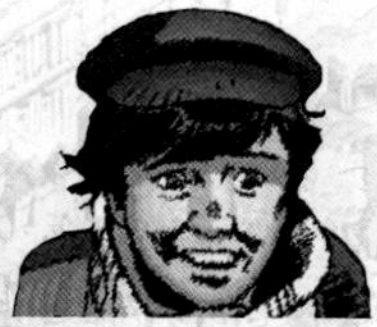

Tiny Tim Cratchit
Bob's youngest son

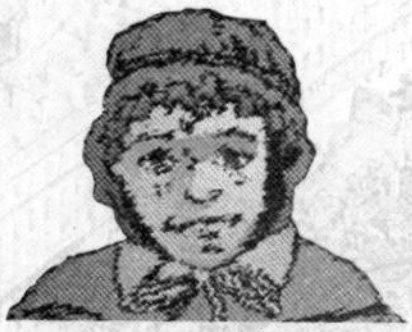

Fan
Scrooge's sister

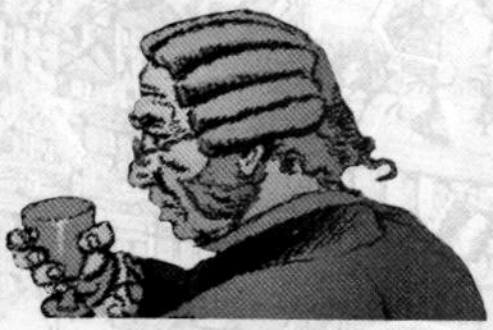

Schoolmaster